Bitches'
Brew

Bitches' Brew

Fred Khumalo

First published by Jacana Media (Pty) Ltd in 2006
Reprinted 2006, 2007, 2009

10 Orange Street
Sunnyside
Auckland Park 2092
South Africa
+2711 628 3200

ISBN 978-1-77009-190-0

Set in Bembo 12/15
Printed by CTP Book Printers
Job No. 000972

See a complete list of Jacana titles at www.jacana.co.za

Dedications

To my parents Bhanoyi and Thokozile for teaching me to fight and be a survivor.
To Mafika Pascal Gwala, my mentor, my brother and one of the country's most
brilliant poets, for opening my eyes and ears to the magic of John Coltrane and
Miles Davis whose heart-warming horns you will hear bellowing and screaming
through the pages of this book. To my other brothers Dudley Moloi and
Tiisetso Makube for reinforcing my love and respect for this sophisticated
art form called jazz.

To my children whose cryptic but sometimes exasperating chastisements
have taught me to be a more sensitive and, hopefully, better father.
To my lovely wife Nomvuzo who takes my bouts of madness within her stride.
As you will notice, this book is a jazz story, but also a love story,
and also the story of a nation's reawakening – all rolled in one.
So, to all the jazzophiles in the world – keep on jamming.
To all the lovers in this world –
keep on loving!

To all South Africans –
stand firm and fan the flames of hope.

One

I Got It Bad
(And that ain't Good)

Dear Zakes,

Some women say it's the feel, and not the size, of a man's penis that matters. But others say, no, doll, it's the balls behind the penis that matter, because the balls are the engine that drives the whole business down there. Yet others say, no way, honey, it's the man's heart that matters because it decides for him whether he should have a hard-on or not. But others say bollocks, the dick has got its own mind, anyway. It will get a hard-on even if its owner sees a one-breasted woman with no teeth, and squinty eyes, just as long as she holds promise of a nice behind, agreeable thighs – a succulent woman.

Yes, Zakes, you men actually use these words when talking about us: succulent, delectable, mouth-watering, chewy, juicy; just as if we were loose pieces of flesh to be devoured at will. If not quite juicy enough, just good enough to be chewed for a while and then spat out into the gutter.

(Zakes, I'm enjoying a neat whisky on the rocks in a crystal glass as I'm writing this missive to you; so do pardon me for the digressions and lapses…)

Anyway, in case you don't remember I am 59 years old now, have nine grown up children of my own. One of them is your own son. Most of my children are dead now. In fact, six of them have passed on, but in my mind I still have all nine of them. They all live within me. I have several grandchildren. I am a retired shebeen queen. I'm still beautiful. And I know it. That's me.

As a shebeen queen you learn a lot about the men who drink at your place. In fact you learn a lot about men in general. Their fears, their likes and dislikes, their aspirations, their outlook on life. You become a sister who gives them a shoulder to cry on when they find themselves teetering on the brink, over the valley of sadness. You become a marriage counsellor who tells them how to humble themselves before their spouses, and when to fight back if their kindness is being taken for granted. You become a doctor who tells them when to stop drinking, when to ease off on those cigarettes. You become a banker who takes care of their finances, their human resources manager who shouts at them when they stay away from work. In short, I've experienced and studied the world of men, and it's a funny world. Like the desert whose landscape changes with the blowing winds only to return to its original form later, the life of a man is whimsical and ever changing but somehow predictable. Like the desert, no matter how many times a man changes from kind-hearted to angry, from sweet to nasty and dangerous, trust a man to always go back to what he really, really is: a bastard. But we love these bastards. We give them our hearts knowing how they are bound to tear them to pieces.

That much I know about men. That having been said, however, I still haven't been able to arrive at my own independent conclusion about the importance of the size and shape of a man's penis for a woman.

But I have heard it said that the man who lives permanently in a woman's heart and mind is the one who deflowers her. The meaning of this, I suppose, is that the woman subliminally holds a grudge against him, for violating her chastity and purity, for robbing her of her innocence.

Perhaps it's not a grudge per se. Perhaps it's a sense of gratitude. The woman immortalises him in her mind and heart for the joy he brought her, for his gallant act of opening for her new vistas of self-knowledge and self-discovery.

My friend Esther feels indebted to the guy who deflowered her. Her eyes light up at the mention of his name. Words crowd her mouth, and she begins to stutter when she talks of him.

She even remembers the shape of her first man's thing: 'Oh, darling, it was so ugly and twisted like a wild banana I almost ran away in horror and disgust. It was shiny and angry, like a snake from a bygone era. A snake ready to strike with a vengeance. A viper dying to spit out its venom. But once it was inside me I screamed Glory Hallelujahs and Hail Marys with a gusto that would have impressed the Virgin herself. The gates of Heaven were wide open, ready for me to enter. I felt reborn. I experienced a spiritual high. Me, I don't blame Eve for having succumbed to the charms of that snake in that beautiful garden.'

But Zakes, you must be wondering why an old hag like me is going on about first sexual encounters and stuff.

Perhaps all I am trying to do is relive the past. That way, I suppose, I will be able to exorcise my demons, demons that have been skulking in the recesses of my mind. I am trying to remember in order to forget, trying to remember the good things I've had done to me in order to forget the bad ones.

But try as I might, I just can't agree with the notion that the first man you had sex with should be immortalised in your mind.

Maybe some women believe that. But in my case, it's the fourth guy to impregnate me who stands out by a mile in my mind. And it's his story I want to tell; it's his story I want to relive. I have him to thank for the woman that I am today. But to tell his story I have to start somewhere.

(I've just lit myself a cigarette, Zakes. Ah, these Craven As are good for my chest. A whisky and a Craven A! Shit, that's some combination! But, to go on...)

(Then)
Two

Prelude to a Kiss

WHEN I WAS GROWING UP, my mother was away from home most of the time. As a result I grew up not knowing what it meant to be a woman, how to handle my woman's body and how to relate to men. Indeed, how to relate to other women.

I guess my situation was true for many other girls who grew up away from their mothers. They found themselves in the territory of womanhood without knowing what it meant to be a woman. As a result, once they discovered what it meant, they didn't tell their girl children because nobody had told them. For a woman brought up this way, the only way of understanding what womanhood means is by going down the dangerous, dark back alley where demons of heartache lurk, where the ogre called regret reigns supreme, where the monster called self-blame lives.

This is the kind of woman who puts on make-up to hide the scars on her face, and lies about how wonderful her man is. Some even go to the grave without ever understanding the essence of their womanhood, so subservient and fearful of the opposite sex that they never come out of their cocoons of insecurity. As a result, they never discover who they really are. Understand?

Anyway, back to talking about the men I've had, or the men who've had me. All I remember about the first one was the violence he exuded the minute I said yes to his amorous entreaties. I suppose he didn't mean to be violent, but things just happened that way. Do I detect self-pity and self-blame in what I've just said? Anyway, I am finding it hard to think he, the first one, meant me any harm.

So unkind of me to call this man 'The First One' as if he had no name. His name was Thabiso.

Before I get down to dissecting Thabiso, let me hasten to add that I cannot for the life of me remember the other men who were to enter my life in later years in any intimate, loving detail. Altogether, I have lost count of the men who have known me in the biblical sense. I have given birth to nine children in my life, as I've said, from nine different men who entered my life at different stages.

In township parlance, my children are called Choice Assorteds. This is after the famous brand of miscellaneous biscuits including lemon creams, Scottish shortbread, flavoured wafers, coconut cakes and more – all in a single box! In other words, my children resided in the same womb even though they have different fathers. Choice Assorteds. Township people can be cruel.

Anyway, I love and cherish all the children these men gave me. But even looking deep into the faces and listening hard to the voices of the three remaining children, I can't conjure the essence of their fathers. They are just blurs of smell, touch, noise, and physical pain. That's all. The years have long mended the broken pieces of my heart. I can't feel any emotion for these men. I suppose that's because none of them spent long enough with me. Some of them spent only a night, a week, sometimes two, and then moved on, hardly realising they had given me a child. I don't know why they left me. Maybe I lacked the skill and the tenacity to keep them. Maybe I lived too much inside my heart, brooded too much and intimidated them. I don't know. Loving is a skill, I've been told. You have to work hard on it. You get better at it the harder you work on it. Just like a game of golf. You can never improve your handicap unless you work hard on your swing.

What I do know is that many times after a man left me, I kept feeding my heart with hope that the next one would be better, the next one would stay; the next one would understand me and the thoughts that lived within me. There is nothing as dangerous as hope because it doesn't tell you when to give up on it, as somebody once said.

Ah, Lettie, poor Lettie, I say to myself, you are getting carried away now! Let's start at the beginning. Let's start with Thabiso.

He was a boy from the village just next to mine. A fairly educated boy, from what I heard. He had been to the big cities and could speak the white man's language. Now that I make the association between him and the cities and the white man, I seem to recall that Thabiso had a funny smell about him, the sweet smell of a city girl. It was said he had acquired the smell from the small bottle that he carried in his pocket. Every now and then he could be seen rubbing his armpits with this funny bottle of his. Apart from this smell, which we associated with city women, Thabiso also had shiny, greasy hair like the girls from the cities. The smell that hung about him, I later learnt, was called perfume.

He also tried to speak the white man's language, 'Open up your heart, girl, and let me in', he once wrote in a letter to me when he was still trying to establish the girl-boy relationship. I could read a bit of English because I was a school-going girl. Even the pages of his letter smelled like perfume. Funny boy. Anyway, that's what I remember about him: his clothes, his funny smell, his words. But the face is just a blur. I can't even remember his voice.

'Don't be a fool, Lettie,' my friend Maki said when she heard that I wasn't interested in Thabiso. 'This is a civilised man from the cities. He's got all the money in the world. He's a walking bank. Say yes to him and you will be the richest and the best-dressed girl in all of Teya-Teyaneng.'

'What kind of a man stretches and greases his hair like a woman from the cities? You want people to laugh at my choice of man?'

'Grow up, Lettie. Go to the cities. You will soon see that the man is with it. He is a man amongst men in the cities. He speaks the street lingo. He walks the city walk – unlike the bumpkins from the villages who dawdle around like baboons, and carry about them the smell of urine and cow dung.'

'I can't even smell the dung you are talking about because it is a part of me. It is a part of us here. Look at what we are doing now: picking up dry cow dung so we can go home and make fire with it. Maki, don't try to be what you are not!'

We had a long laugh as we continued walking down the footpath, picking up blobs of dry cow dung. Cow dung was second nature to me. Because I was the eldest I was assigned the task of collecting dry cow dung for the home hearth. In addition to this, I also looked after my father's goats after school. I milked them so we could have milk for drinking, and for cheese.

I finally said yes to Thabiso's entreaties. He was clearly overjoyed. He started singing some funny songs in the white man's language. When I asked him what he was on about, he said that he was serenading me for opening my heart to him. Funny boy. Serenading was a word I had never heard before. So he had to explain in our language what it meant.

Anyway, the very afternoon I accepted him, he said he was taking me for a walk. This was another strange thing. In our culture you don't just go for a walk. You walk with the aim of getting somewhere.

He called himself a love poet. Where I come from we have all kinds of poets: praise poets who sing praises to our chiefs; war poets who inspire men to go to war; poets who sing to the gods to bring rain. But I had never heard of a love poet. Anyway, he continued reciting these things in the white man's language, saying they were poems of love. Lyrics, he called them. I was getting irritated with him saying these things in the white man's language. I told him to remember that I wasn't some white woman. 'Sing these things of yours in our language', I said.

He complained that our language was not ripe and advanced enough to convey emotions about matters of the heart. He said only the white man had developed his language to that level. I wanted to contradict him, but decided to let is pass.

'Let me fill your heart with the sweetness of honey,' he said. 'Let your heart sing in sweet harmony with mine. Allow our minds to talk the sweet language of love…'

We walked on under the big open sky. The sun was pouring its yellow liquid upon the land. Sunflower plantations on either side of the footpath accepted its generosity. The yellow sun and the yellow sunflowers combined to form a yellow river that flowed peacefully across the land. The cool breeze whispering in our ears sounded as if it was happy, as if it was smiling its approval.

There were birds twittering about, their long pointed beaks at war with the sunflower heads.

The sight of sunflowers always made me feel happy. They always brightened my mood no matter how many worries gnawed at my heart.

'Let me be part of your dreams,' he continued, 'let me be part of your thoughts.'

I found the music of nature more alluring than the drone of the love poet's voice.

'I want to go back home now,' I said.

He ignored my abrupt statement, and continued talking: 'You are so beautiful I suspect you bathe with milk, and towel your face with slices of polony...'

I began to giggle: 'Where did you hear such foolishness?'

With a serious expression on his face, he said: 'It's a Zulu saying, which means you're pure and priceless.'

'Humph!' I said, 'I don't care for Zulus. I am a proud Mosotho girl. Now, can I go home?'

'But you can't break such a happy mood.'

'You may like hearing your own voice, but I don't. Let's part ways now so you can continue saying your poems and enjoying the drone of your own voice.'

Not once did I look at him. On the past few occasions he had accosted me, begging for my love, I had never bothered to take a careful look at him. This, I suppose, is why I can't remember his face now.

'Can I love you now?' he said, touching my hand.

I looked very briefly into his face. But my eyes quickly went back to exploring the sand between my bare toes.

He lifted my chin with his hand. He brought his face closer to mine. I closed my eyes. Our lips met. He pushed his tongue into my mouth. I tried to pull back. He cupped his hand at the back of my neck and continued to probe my mouth with his tongue. I was tempted to bite the offending tongue. But I decided against it. There was no need to hurt him. My heart was not full of malice.

While the rest of him smelled like sweets, his mouth smelt like my father's Boxer tobacco. Pungent. I was gagging. The mouth tasted bitter, like my grandmother's herbs for fixing a bad tummy. I pulled away from him. I started to run down the path. He caught up with me. He started dragging me into the thickness of the sunflower field. I wanted to scream, to fight back. But he was my lover. Not so long ago I had told him I loved him – whatever that meant.

'Why are you refusing my love?' he asked in a hurt voice.

'I am not. I told you I love you. Now what more do you want? Why are you forcing your tongue into my mouth?'

'I'm only kissing you, angel of the mountain kingdom. But why are you running away from me?' He grabbed me and threw me onto the soft ground, moving fast to pin me down. He lifted my dress.

He laughed when he realised that I had no panties on under my dress that was made from a mielie meal sack. Girls my age didn't wear panties then. What for? All that discomfort, all the trouble of having to wash the smelly garments? Who needs panties?

'But why are you being like this?' I cried, 'I told you I love you but why are you being violent like this?'

'Shut up!' he slapped my face. His voice had lost all the sweetness of honey, the coolness of poetry.

He hit me again. My nose started dripping with blood. I had heard about things that took place between boys and girls, where boys put their things between the legs of girls. But I had never imagined that this game involved such violence and blood. He pushed his pants to his ankles.

Then I saw his boy thing. It was black. Swollen. Angry. I had in the past caught glimpses of drunken men's things as they peed by the roadside. Yes, just a glance at the drunk man's ugly black thing, then look away, only to look again, then look away. But I had never seen a man's thing so hard and angry.

20

He threw himself on top of me. He pushed his thing hard into my girlhood a number of times. I screamed. He slapped me again.

His voice was all sweet again, 'Don't cry baby girl, I am making love to you. I want us to be one person. Let's float together to the heavens…' Or something like that.

Then it was all over. I felt a stickiness around my girl area. He lay on top of me, panting. I heaved him off. I got up and ran home. Crying all the way, the yellowness of the sunflower plants forming a blur of colour as my feet gained speed.

Three

Grandma's Hands

As soon as I got home, I went to my bedroom and got under the blankets. I sobbed bitterly until late into the night. I heard my grandmother's voice from the adjoining room. The walls were paper-thin. Voices carried over easily from one room to the next. My grandmother was sniggering: 'Poor little Lettie doesn't know how to treat a man! Such a big woman doesn't know how to handle a man. When you are ready, come and speak to granny about what happened there in between the sunflowers. The birds of Africa have already told us what happened, but we want to hear the story from the horse's mouth. Ha ha ha!'

Granny was such a nuisance. She knew everything, yet she hadn't left her room in many years. Of my eight siblings, I was closest to her. She confided in me, told me stories, the secret of her powers as a seer. Neither of my parents lived with us. In fact, my father had died a long time ago. My mother worked for a white family in Johannesburg. She only came home during Easter and at Christmas time. Our homestead, therefore, was headed by my brother and me. I was the eldest – a cook, a provider, a nurse to the younger siblings and also to my bedridden grandmother. I was basically the matriarch of the home in the absence of my parents.

'I am not going to tell anyone about our secrets, little Lettie,' my grandmother said, laughing weakly from her lair. I call it a lair because her room was dark and smelly. No one was allowed to clean it. I was the only one who could enter it – to pick up her chamber pot.

Neighbours whispered that my father had been killed by my grandmother, my mother's mother. She had used bad medicine on him. She was a tall, wiry woman with a very dark complexion. She didn't have too many friends. She used to go to church every

Sunday before she exiled herself to her room. She was a member of the women's guild at the Methodist Church and could be seen resplendent in her red coat, white scarf, matching white headgear, black skirt and black pantyhose, walking gracefully down the dirt road.

Every Sunday, granny would wake us children up and get us ready for church. She would cook us an extra nice breakfast of spinach and porridge, which we would wash down with sweet tea. Then she would help us get dressed in our smartest attire.

'God doesn't want ugly looking children in His house of worship. When you go to important places you dress your best, don't you? You want to impress the people you're visiting, don't you? The same should apply to God. Dress up for Him. Look your best. He will bless you with more beautiful clothes and good food. He is the wisest of us all because He made us.'

At church, granny was popular with the priest. Members of the church choir deferred to her because she had studied music at school. She understood written music called staff notation – all those funny squiggles. She could sing up a storm. After church, on our way home, she would buy us sweets at the local shop. As a result, going to church was always a celebration. It always brought fond memories to our young impressionable minds.

'How did we miss this all along?' the women of the area exclaimed among themselves as they leaned across fences to share their suspicions about my grandmother. 'The real devils are the church-going women who wear uniforms. The ones who are always in the company of the priest. The ones who are always at the forefront of church activities. They are using these church activities as masks to hide their devilish ways. The witches are those who thump Bibles by day, and ride baboons by night, sprinkling bad medicines and ointments at the doors of law-abiding citizens. This woman should have been the prime suspect right from the onset.'

The story spread. Granny, a confirmed witch who had been seen naked, riding a baboon into so-and-so's yard one night not so long ago, had to be eliminated.

I recall that not so long after my father died, a new father moved in with us. He was a man from the neighbourhood who promised to take care of us – his late friend's family, as he called us. As I recall, he had not been particularly close to my father. They had on occasion sat under a huge tree that stood in our yard. They drank traditional beer, played cards, shared jokes, talked about manly matters such as the politics of the day and how the crops were doing in the fields.

Anyway, no sooner had Mofokeng, our new father, moved in than the rumour that the community was planning to burn down our house gained momentum. Ntate Mofokeng was told by friends to leave our house lest he be caught in the crossfire.

Ntate Mofokeng stood his ground. His friends then turned around and said he had been involved in the murder of my father in order to inherit his riches.

My father had been a foreman at one of the factories in Maseru, the capital city of our country. He was not rich. Okay, he had been among the first men in the village to demolish the traditional mud and grass huts and replace them with 'the white man's house' made of bricks and mortar, complete with a zinc roof. He also drove a car, a decrepit VW Beetle. Perhaps by village standards this was an exhibition of wealth.

Suspicion and ignorance were swaggering across the length and breadth of the land those days. Witches were to be eliminated because they were causing political conflict in the land. Purges were carried out in many parts of the country. If your granny was very dark in complexion and did not have many friends, she was a potential witch. She had to die.

In rural areas, where lightning tended to strike and burn houses, livestock, and kill people, the fear of witches was higher. It was said that witches with strong medicine could send lightning to an enemy.

Kill the witch!

It was during that time that my granny disappeared from the public eye. She hibernated in her room. The community's excitement ebbed. They looked elsewhere for an outlet for their frustrations, suspicions and anger.

In all the years that she had taken exile in that gloomy bedroom, not once had she left the bed, except to relieve herself in the chamber pot that had been placed at the foot of her bed. I served her meals in the morning and late in the evening. I also left her something for lunch before I went to school. There was also fruit and other morsels of food she could nibble on during the course of the day. I left her enough water and soft drinks to see her through the day. The chamber pot was emptied and cleaned faithfully everyday. At the beginning of her hibernation, I never heard granny utter more than one word, or phrase. 'Water!' 'Orange!' 'Some sweet smell!'

Over the years the flowers that I placed in the room had formed an impressive display on her dressing table and on the floor near the head of her bed. The flowers, in tiny colourful vases, never died.

Granny forbade me from taking away the orange peels once she had eaten the flesh of the fruit. The peels, together with rinds of other fruit that she consumed, were spread all over the room. They seemed to sparkle in the dark room, suffusing it with a subtle, ghastly glow.

Over the years, colonies of butterflies, bees and locusts had made their home among the ever-living flowers. The bees occasionally buzzed out of the room using the ventilation holes that were set high in the wall, close to the ceiling. After the flirtation with the outside world, the bees always came back into the room, bringing with them the intoxicating scent of honey.

For hours on end, butterflies with huge vibrating wings, colourful as the rainbow, would sit on the bed cover under which the old lady lay, turning it into a Garden of Eden. Some of the butterflies sat on her face. Not once did she bother to swipe them away. The only indication that she was still alive were her flaring nostrils, her blinking eyes, and her heaving chest. Occasionally, she would move to take a drink of water.

In the early years of her hibernation, she never spoke a word to me. Just stared at me, stared through me. She didn't mind me sitting in her room, watching the slow grind of time in this other-worldly place.

Over the years, the body of the old lady had taken on a new dimension. She had grown big – not fat, but huge as if she was an inflatable doll. Her eyes, which glowed under the subtle illumination offered by the colourful flowers and the orange peels, were dimly visible above her huge cheeks.

The orange peels never seemed to dry out, nor did the rinds of other fruit rot. They remained as fresh as the day they had been consumed, their pungent aroma hanging thick in the room.

Sometimes she would break into a long series of dry coughs. The silences that followed would be long and haunting.

Beneath the colourful glow of the flowers, beneath the noise of the bees as they buzzed about, beneath the subtle flapping sound of the wings of butterflies, beneath the pungent smell of the orange peels and other fruit, beneath all this, there was a smell. It was the sickly smell of death. It was reminiscent of the bodies of people who were close to death, or who were recently deceased.

It was only on those occasions, when the smell became too overpowering, that I would stay away from my grandmother's room. As I turned my back, closing the door behind me, I would feel her sharp eyes stabbing my back. But she never said a word.

Four

The Troublesome Glass Eye

WHEN MY FATHER WAS STILL ALIVE, he doted on me.

'When everyone has left this house,' he would say, 'Lettie will be the only one left behind to look after her father. I don't want a boy casting naughty glances at my princess.'

The love between father and daughter was strong. When the old man passed away, I was deeply affected. I became a different person, always absent-minded and sad-faced. My school grades dropped. I stumbled into things like a blind person. Twice I was nearly hit by a tractor because I had tried to cross the road without looking. Whenever I was sent to the distant shop in the next village, I always brought back the wrong things. When I was asked to make tea for Ntate Mofokeng I either did not wait for the water to boil, or put too much sugar into the tea.

Ntate Mofokeng thought I was being deliberately disrespectful and spiteful. He started using his thick belt on me. On one occasion he smacked me across the face with his big hand. He was a giant of a man, with a tummy that hung over his belt like a sack of maize. When he belched and farted, which he did a lot at meals, you could almost feel the table rumbling. He had a big rubbery face that was very dark in complexion. He had lost one eye in a car accident, and wore a glass eye.

I think my stepfather was a good person at heart. But the frustrations that had been heaped upon him as a result of my grandmother's state and because I was proving to be a burden on him, turned him into a short-tempered violent person. Of late, when he beat me, it was as if he was fighting against a person his own age. He put all his anger and energy behind the blows he rained on me.

But things were to get worse. One day we were sitting in the lounge listening to the radio when the vase sitting on top of the

33

coffee table suddenly jumped from where it was sitting and smashed itself against the face of the radio. It was as if somebody had hurled it at the radio. We screamed in horror, ducking for cover. We didn't sleep that night.

Because there was no fridge in the house, Ntate Mofokeng kept his beers in the cupboard. A strange thing happened one day as he reached for a beer. It simply exploded in his hands. There were more sounds of breaking glass inside the cupboard. When he opened the cupboard door, he saw that all six beers inside had exploded.

It was clear that there was a bad spirit in the house. The bad spirit would sometimes turn the heat of the stove up to full blast, burning the food. Sometimes, it would play with the paraffin lamp. At first the family decided to keep these attacks under wraps, suffering in silence. After all, it is said in Africa that no elephant finds its trunk too heavy to carry. But it soon became obvious that this particular trunk was too heavy for the elephant, so we had to enlist the help of others. Ntate Mofokeng and my mother went looking for a traditional healer to come and exorcise the ghost that was troubling us.

The traditional healer came with all the confidence that matched his reputation. No sooner had he walked past the gate than stones from nowhere started pelting his head. One stone hit him on the forehead. He fell down. Once he was down, he started wriggling about, groaning as if an invisible force was kicking him. He managed to get up and dashed for the gate.

Now the story swirled around the village that the notorious house that once harboured a witch was now being haunted by a ghost.

'That family must be chased out of the village once and for all,' one of the prominent community leaders observed to a group of men gathered at his house to discuss the matter.

'I am sure that this is the ghost of the old witch. She is coming back for them. Maybe they did something to her. Maybe they killed her. Or she's just being spiteful as all bad ghosts are.'

'But how did she die, and where was she buried, by the way?'

'They say she was knocked down by a bus...'

'Good for her, the bloody witch...'

'But she's come back to haunt the poor family…'

'Why did she take so long to come back?'

'She was probably still trying to negotiate entry into heaven.'

'Maybe she sneaked into heaven unnoticed, but now they have caught her out and thrown her out…'

'Something must be done about this issue. It's bringing the village a bad reputation…'

It was ultimately decided that a delegation of men would be dispatched to visit our house. The intention of the visit was to evacuate the family from the house, which had put a blight on the image of the village.

On the appointed day, a group of five men walked to the house. I did not witness the things that people say happened. One version says that as soon as the leader of the delegation touched the gate, an explosion of fire descended on the group of men from nowhere.

Another version says that the car in which the men were travelling suddenly burst into flames. Whatever the truth, the ultimate result of the visit saw one man catching fire and dying. After that, no one bothered even to consider taking steps against our family.

One day Ntate Mofokeng was sitting in the lounge drinking beer, and listening to some programme on his new radio. I seem to think he was listening to a broadcast of a boxing fight. I can't be sure. When the announcer's voice suddenly reached a crescendo of excitement, Ntate Mofokeng jumped from his seat and started punching the air. But in the excitement, his artificial eye jumped from its socket and plunged into the beer mug. I chuckled. My mother gave me an angry stare. Ntate Mofokeng shot me a piercing look with his one good eye.

Ntate Mofokeng retrieved his artificial eye from the beer. He licked it with his tongue before putting it back into the socket. This time I guffawed, rocking back and forth with mirth.

Ntate Mofokeng leaned forward and gave me a big smack in the middle of the face. My nose started bleeding. I bleed easily.

'But there was no need for that,' my mother cried out, standing up to her full height, her hands planted on her waist, challenging him. 'She's only a child but you are fighting her as if you are up against another man! If you want a fight go out in the street and pick a fight with other men who have balls like yours. I'm sick and tired of you harassing my child as if she were an orphan with no parent to protect her.'

He picked up his beer mug and hurled it at my mama. She ducked just in time. The mug missed her by inches.

Then he moved with lightning speed from his seat, his big tummy wiggling this way and that as he waddled towards mother and me.

He punched her heavily in the tummy. She doubled over, screaming from the pain. Then he punched her in the middle of the face. I had by now managed to negotiate myself out of harm's way. I picked up a flower vase that was on top of the display cabinet and smashed it into the back of Ntate Mofokeng's head. The man went down like a sack of maize.

'My eye! My eye! You broke my eye!' he cried, instinctively covering his socket with his hands.

My mother staggered to her feet. We started for the door. But we didn't make it. The man was up on his feet again, blood oozing from his clean-shaven head. He lunged forward, grabbing each of us by the scruff of our necks. He banged our heads together, but he lost his grip on me. I ran to the neighbours to ask for help.

The following day, Ntate Mofokeng packed his things and left. My mother, who had been dependent on him for money, went to Johannesburg to look for work, which she found. She worked as a domestic servant for a white family. She wrote moving letters to me about how, one day, she would come back home for good with enough money to last us a lifetime.

My mother sent us generous amounts of money for the upkeep of the home. We never starved. We had enough money for school. Granny started talking again; but she still refused to leave her room. Luckily, Ntate Mofokeng had not told a soul that granny was alive and hibernating in the dark room. Maybe he feared her legendary powers of witchcraft.

Five

Destiny's Dance

A FEW DAYS AFTER THABISO FORCED himself upon me, I was taking my early morning ablutions in my bedroom when a child came bursting into the house: 'Ousie Lettie! Ousie Lettie! There is a very beautiful man asking for you outside. He's wearing some nice city clothes and...'

'Save your words and go tell him to go away.'

The child bounded out of the door. A few minutes later, the child came back and said: 'He won't go away. Besides, he showed me lots of money and...'

'Tell him to go to hell!'

But the visitor didn't go to hell. He got into the room where he found me naked, working on my body with a wet face towel. It was Thabiso, as I had guessed.

He hesitated for a moment on the threshold, but dug his hands into his pockets, saying: 'I've come to tell you how happy I am that your heart is singing in unison with mine, that your dreams have become part of mine, that your thoughts course the highways and byways of my own mind. Darling, I've come...'

'If you try anything nasty, I'll scream. The neighbours will be here in a minute. I will scream!' I said, my voice already rising.

'Angel of my heart, is that the way you wish to say goodbye to your Romeo, the king who reigns over your heart? Is that the way to treat the one who loves you like no one else?'

I felt like laughing. But then he leapt at me, I ducked, and was out of the house and into the yard – in my birthday suit, screaming my lungs out. He bounded out of the house, and ran for his life.

When I came back to the house, embarrassed by my nakedness, I heard granny's raucous laughter from the other side of the wall.

'He sounds like a love poet, your man,' she said.

'He's not my man. I don't want him now. I never wanted him anyway.'

'You are old enough now, my dear Lettie, to begin to understand matters of the heart. Give the young man a chance, be calm with him, he will reciprocate. He doesn't sound like a rough one to me. He didn't mean to hurt you the other day. You failed to listen to your heart. You failed to allow your heart to speak honestly to his. He is not a bad man, from what I can see.'

'You can't see anything from that... that... that cave of yours!' I regretted the words the minute I uttered them.

There was immediate silence from the other side of the wall.

That weekend I attended a wedding just across the river. Matlakala, a local girl, was getting married to a man from Maseru. It was always advisable for young unmarried women to attend weddings so they could be spotted and talked to by men. Weddings always led to other weddings. However, I harboured no ambitions of being spotted and talked to by any man. I went to the wedding simply because I hoped to bump into some of my school friends. And, indeed, I wanted to eat meat. I hadn't eaten good, freshly-slaughtered meat in a long time. I wanted to see people from Maseru; they were always good entertainment, with their pretensions – women wearing wigs made out of white women's hair, their lips bleeding red with lipstick, men walking in a bouncy manner that made them look like cripples.

By the looks of things, the groom was a rich man. His people had come in two buses and several cars to witness and celebrate the wedding.

Earlier in the morning, vows had been exchanged at the local church. By the time I joined the ceremony, the opposing sides – one from the bride's area and the others from the groom's – were jabbering at each other in song, as is custom at such ceremonies.

The bride's side was complaining that the groom was so cheap he couldn't even afford to buy cows for his new wife. The groom, they sang, had instead brought a handful of smelly pigs as part of the bride price! What a shame, what a shame! But, if truth be told, the groom had delivered a herd of nine cattle to her family in exchange for her hand in the time-tested *ilobolo* tradition.

The groom's side was singing how sad they were to see their son getting married to Matlakala who, as her own name suggested, was so lazy she lived in filth; their son was going to starve indeed, and his house infested with bed bugs and lice. What a shame!

Which brings me to something else. Matlakala is SeSotho for rubbish. I've always wondered why some parents are so cruel to give their children such horrible names. I'd also heard of Dikeledi (Tears), Mampi (The Ugly One), Tsietsie (Danger), Mahlomola (Trouble).

Anyway, back to the singing at the wedding. Each of the singing sides had spent weeks, months, practising these songs. After the singing, we settled down to tuck into mounds of samp and beef.

Now that the traditional singing was over, it was time for 'modern' music to be played. This came from a gumba gumba, the record-playing precursor to the hi-fi. In his lifetime, my father could have afforded this music-making wonder, but he wasn't a musical type. True, he did love some songs – especially songs by the smooth-voiced Nat King Cole. He listened to these on radio during a programme for music called Jazz and Blues. But generally, my father thought music and dancing were for lazy types who didn't want to go and work in the fields, tending their crops. Music and dancing were for idle people who couldn't sit down to a well-thought out debate on the state of the country's politics. Anyway, they started playing music from the gumba gumba at the wedding that day. I found the music quite moving, I must admit. Then as if out of nowhere a group of young men dressed in the traditional way – with their blankets wrapped intricately around their bodies, holding their traditional fighting sticks, and traditional conical hats made of grass – took the prominent spot that had not so long ago been occupied by the opposing singing groups.

'These are the MaRashiya,' somebody whispered, telling us that these young men called The Russians were some kind of gang that reigned supreme in some of the townships of Johannesburg.

The Russians had originally come from different parts of Lesotho. But in their migration to the white man's cities, they had fashioned themselves into a gang, which, we had been told, terrorised people in the townships. Their specialty was robbing shebeens and mugging people as they got off the trains in the big cities. They were also good at running protection rackets like all well-established extortionists and gangs.

In the numerous fights they had with other gangs over territory they were said to be good with their pangas. Guns were scarce those days. Pangas, knives and lead pipes were the weapons of choice.

In their visits to the shebeens where they not only picked the pockets of the patrons, but sometimes held up everybody including the host, the MaRashiya were always accompanied by their women. They dressed in traditional *seshweshwe* pinafores like respectable Basotho women. But they also wore stylish berets and other kinds of headgear. The women's faces usually bore the scars of numerous fights they'd had among themselves or with their men folk. But those faces also showed the observer that these women were in love with their skin lightening creams – Super Rose, Ambi, Memafoza and others. What self-respecting young woman from the cities hadn't tried to scrub the blackness from her face? These women wanted to impress citified men with their complexions, which made them look almost white, or at least coloured. It was said that the women of MaRashiya were tough. They carried knives in their purses or tucked inside their bras. They were the ones who had also mastered the art of settling scores using a sharpened bicycle spoke, which in expert hands was sure to paralyse an adversary.

Anyway, on the wedding day, the MaRashiya took to the 'dance floor', promptly joined by their women in their finery of flowing terylene dresses, *seshweshwe* pinafores, colourful high-heeled shoes. The music started. Swirls of dust rose into the air as the feet stamped the stubborn earth. Their dance routine was lewd, at least by our standards. There was a lot of movement around the pelvic area from the men. The women would suddenly kick into the air, in the process exposing their panties to the sweating men. In one or two instances I actually caught a glimpse of a woman's genitals as she kicked in the air. She wasn't wearing panties. A true Mosotho woman just like me.

This lewd dance, we were to learn later, was called Famo Sesh. I don't know what the words meant, but it was apparently a popular dance style in the city of Johannesburg where the MaRashiya held sway. In the cities, we were told, Famo Sesh was sold to the gullible public as a traditional Sotho dance routine. We were disgusted that these people had the temerity to misrepresent the essence of Sotho culture in the cities.

The dancing continued: wiggling pelvises, the wide kicks in the air, flashes of white, red and black panties; glimpses of female genitals and so on, women thrusting their tongues out in a suggestive manner.

Male spectators and admirers moved into strategic positions so they could get a better view of the flashing panties and genitals.

As soon as it started getting dark, couples began to disappear behind bushes, behind houses. A person innocently on her way to take a pee behind a hut would stumble upon a couple hard at work.

At some stage, the music from the gumba gumba stopped. Somebody started playing the organ. Almost every Basotho house whose breadwinner had been to the cities has a house organ and at least one harmonica. I don't know where this tradition came from, but somebody has suggested that the French missionaries had something to do with it. Anyway, the organ started groaning and the harmonicas wailed, and the feet thudded on the stubborn ground. Shrieks of excitement were heard from the women of the MaRashiya.

'Eu! Eu! Eu! Eu!' one woman ululated, spinning around to the rhythm of the music.

Disgusted and embarrassed, those of us from the surrounding areas slunk away from the dancing area to a spot under a tree where more meat was on the offing. Huge fires had been lit all over the yard to offer illumination and warmth. The tongues of fire cast ghastly shadows on the faces of the merry-makers who stood in clusters, eating meat, drinking traditional beer, telling stories, laughing raucously. What's a traditional African feast without a fire?

There was a cool summer breeze whispering in our ears. The moon looked down approvingly at the proceedings, and at the lovers doing their things behind the bushes.

A group of men stood aloof, smoking and drinking alcohol. They made catcalls at every passing girl. If the girl didn't respond positively to their calls, they would curse, calling her a bitch who didn't know what she was missing. The tongues of drunken people are like riderless horses. They gallop and trot about without purpose. Most of the time these riderless horses end up colliding against each other, injuring themselves, as happened with these young men who started hurling abusive language at each other.

Yes, tongues of drunken people are riderless horses. How many times have you heard a drunk waking up the following morning, crying in shame at the things he allowed his tongue to say the previous night, crying at the loss of a relationship or a friendship thanks to his drunken tongue, galloping about like a riderless horse?

It was while I was sitting with some girls eating meat that I spotted my friend Maki coming my way, a broad smile on her face.

'Lettie, my friend, how happy I am to see you again! You are looking good in this yellow terylene dress of yours!'

'Ah, thank you my friend. My aunt who works in Maseru made it for me, from material she bought in the town. I couldn't wait for an occasion like this to wear it.'

'Shine shine, my friend, how many boyfriends have you attracted so far today?'

'They are buzzing around me like bees, I must say. But there's this one from the groom's side who I think will win the day. We've exchanged addresses, and we will be writing to each other…'

'By and by you will be joining him in Maseru, I suppose.'

There was a gale of laughter from the girls standing around us. Every one of them was on their best behaviour in the hope of attracting the attention of the 'civilised' beaux from Maseru and other cities. Landing a good, well-dressed, well-spoken boyfriend from the cities was the height of achievement for girls in my village.

Girls were standing in clusters, showing each other pieces of paper on which the names and addresses of the boys they'd spoken to were written. But you had to be careful. Some of the girls who had not been spoken to could steal the name and address of the boy you had spoken to, and later write to him and steal him from you!

Each boy spoke to as many girls as possible, exchanging his name and address with all of them; the first girl to write to him stood a better chance of winning the boy's heart. Every girl knew this. They couldn't wait to get home so they could start writing those letters promising undying love to their citified dandies.

We were still standing in our circle, eating meat and talking when Maki said: 'Your man was supposed to attend this wedding. It's his cousin getting married anyway, but he had to leave urgently for the cities. The white man wants him back. He's off to make more money so he can marry you.'

'You seem to know him so well!'

'I have to look out for you, my friend, make sure nobody touches your man.'

The other girls were all ears, wanting to know who this man was. When his name was mentioned, they were green with envy.

'Lettie, you have hit the jackpot!' one of the girls said, 'Run after your man. Join him there in the cities, otherwise the girls there will bewitch him, turn him into a zombie whom they can control and milk.'

I had to act.

Six

Peace, Perfect Peace

It did not help that a few days after the wedding, the bad spirit came back to our house. Plates flew across the room of their own volition. The brother who came after me in age decided that was it for him. He left home in the middle of the night and never came back. A few weeks later my two sisters disappeared. There were now only six of us left. Although all of us had seen the works of the bad spirits before, we were still scared.

And then there was the matter of my thing with Thabiso. I missed my periods. When I told Maki about this, she was overjoyed for me: 'You are carrying his baby, can't you see? You must celebrate; thank your gods for such good luck! It is now definitely time to go and find him and share the good news with him. He'll buy you the best dresses in town. He'll spoil you with the most expensive perfume; he will buy you shiny earrings, and a big shiny ring. He will buy you the shoes with the highest heels in town, and he will buy you the best creams for your face – even though you are so light you don't need any skin lightening. Once you are in the city, in your beautiful clothes, people will think you are a white madam. Or at least a coloured. What honour, my friend! What pride! Don't say I never told you. This man loves you to bits, in case you didn't know. He will be on cloud nine if he were to learn that you are carrying his baby.'

'But, Maki, I do not think I am ready for all of this,' I said, 'I want to finish school first.'

I was doing standard seven, although I was already eighteen.

'School!' Maki exclaimed, 'Who wants to finish school when there's a man waiting impatiently for you to join him in the cities where you can start a family. If you must carry on with your schooling, you can always ask him to take you to one of their night

49

schools in the city. I've heard that a lot of people have improved their lives attending these night schools after they've done their bit working for the white man in the kitchens and factories. Your worry and focus for now should be on getting to the city before your man changes his mind, before they snatch him.'

'Let's say I do manage to go to the city, how do I find him? I believe the city of Durban is so big one can get lost for the whole year without finding one's bearings.'

'Stop thinking of excuses, Lettie! If you want to find your man, you will. I will go to his place and get an address for where he is based.'

I closed my eyes briefly, trying to conjure up his face. It wouldn't come to my mind's eye. I wanted to ask Maki to get me a photograph of him so I could look at it properly but I was too ashamed to make this request.

I couldn't sleep that night. I kept trying to picture the city. The images that assailed my mind were not attractive. There were too many people, too many cars, too many tall buildings, too many roads that I found myself already lost in this concrete jungle – even before I laid my eyes on a real city.

Did I really want to go to that madness? Or rather, did I really want to see this man? The thought of him evoked no emotion in me. Indeed, he didn't exist in my mind and soul. He was just a ghost from the past, a wraith whose face I couldn't even conjure up. But, as Maki had remarked, and my granny after her, I was carrying the man's child. Something had to be done. That was reason enough for me to go and see him. But then how does one make oneself love someone whose face she can't even remember?

I fell asleep to granny's voice from the other room: 'You are two months pregnant. Better move fast now, before it's too late. Your mother is not here to help you. She has not been home in such a long time that I cannot even see her face in my mind's eye – what a shame for a daughter to abandon her ailing mother like that; what a shame for a mother to abandon her starving, lonely, fatherless children like that! I advise you to go to the city and find your man.

That way, you will be able to pave the way for your brothers and sisters so they can join you there later. There is nothing to live for in this house of bad spirits. The village itself is dying. The crops are failing. The goats are all dead. So are the chickens. The amount of money that your mother has been sending has been dwindling; it has been coming at irregular intervals, as you know. The future of this house is upon your shoulders now, little girl. The house is crumbling bit by bit. You don't want to wait until it collapses on us. Listen to your granny, walk away from this stinking poverty. Go and find a new life out there. Most importantly, your own future is in your hands.'

There was some truth in what granny had said. Our money had run low. Whereas in the past we could eat our stiff porridge with meat, these days we had to be content with porridge and cabbage leaves. On other days things were so bad we didn't even have cabbage. We simply had to shove the balls of stiff porridge into our mouths, and wash them down with water just to fill our stomachs.

The coal stove, which had been our pride, had long been repossessed by the furniture shop for non-payment. The sofas were also gone. We now did our cooking on an open fire like most villagers. Of course they laughed us, pointing out how the mighty had fallen. In the past they had derisively called us whites in black skins – on account of our coal stove and other pieces of modern furniture that were to be found in our house. Now we couldn't even afford to buy coal. Because forests with good wood were too far away from our village, we had to use dry cow dung as our source of fuel. As if the forces of nature had joined in this conspiracy against us, our borehole had run dry a long time ago. We now had to fetch the brackish water from the communal stream, where animals also drank and shat.

The sun was shining brightly the morning I left home. The shimmering faces of the mountains looked sad as I boarded a bus at the Maseru terminus. Armed with a piece of paper with Thabiso's address and telephone numbers scribbled roughly in Maki's handwriting, I was headed for the city of Durban. In her kindness,

Maki had given me her own passport to use. Luckily, we shared the same surname – Motaung – and had strikingly similar features, which is why Maki got mad at the fact that boys always preferred me.

'What do they see in you that I don't have?' she used to complain, 'Besides being beautiful as you are, I also have style,' she used to say jokingly.

When I left that morning, she had accompanied me to the bus stop in the village. I was picked up by a truck going in the direction of Maseru, where I boarded the connecting bus to Durban. Even as I sat in the truck, I knew in my heart that I wasn't going to the city to find Thabiso. I was willing fate not to reveal him to me. I was leaving my home simply because I needed to turn my back on my family, my grandmother and her visions, and my past. It wasn't as if I had a deep-seated need to start a new life either. My decision to leave was propelled by instincts, and not logic.

Now I was sitting in the bus packed with passengers – most of them young men headed for the factories and coal mines of Dundee, in the northern parts of the Natal province. From the careless banter that was passed between them like a gourd of traditional beer, the young men were familiar with the ways of the city. In fact, although I could tell they were Basotho, they were speaking a strange patois that was a mixture of English, isiZulu, SeSotho and some other languages I didn't recognise.

Even so early in the morning, it was around 10am, the young men were drinking brandy straight from the bottle, passing the bottle from one pair of lips to the next.

Thankfully, I was seated next to an old woman who was impatient to get to her destination. The only words that were exchanged between the two of us were the greetings when we boarded. And then she retreated into silence. I was in no mood for small talk myself.

The bus meandered between the numerous mountains that have given our country the name of the Mountain Kingdom. Now and then the landscape would flatten so we could behold a dull brown blanket of vegetation interspersed with stunted thorn trees, aloe plants and other semi-desert species. Our landscape has always been stark, hard on the eye that is hoping for some greenery and tall trees.

As soon as we had crossed the border the mood in the bus changed. It was as if the bantering young men had sobered up to the reality that they would not be seeing their homes, their families and their loved ones for six months or a year, as their contracts usually demanded of them. While the young men slunk into silence and sadness, the landscape became cheerful. There was a thick carpet of vegetation on either side of the road. In contrast to the gravel road on which we had been rattling, the road we had just entered was wide and tarred. Now and then, I spotted huge farms on the side of the road, with hundreds of cattle grazing in the lush fields. The excitement in my heart was palpable. Many of the passengers disembarked at the next few towns that we passed. The oppressive heat that had burdened the inside of the bus eased. At Harrismith, the woman sitting next to me said her goodbyes and got off. She was cheerful at last.

I must have dozed off at some stage, because when I woke up there was a man sitting next to me. When he realised that I was awake, he greeted me in a booming voice – speaking in isiZulu. I responded gruffly in my own language. Smiling, he said in SeSotho how glad he was to meet me, and offered me a cold drink after my peaceful nap. I wanted to say no thank you, but my throat was parched. I accepted his offer of a can of Coke. He opened one for himself. We drank in silence.

We had just passed Newcastle when he broke the silence, speaking in my language: 'In my culture, it's very rude to sit next to someone in a bus without introducing yourself properly. So, in keeping with what I am used to, I am going to introduce myself as Peace Ndaba.'

I sniggered to myself at the name Peace. It reminded me of what Maki had told me. She said Zulus who had just a basic grasp of the English language, in a display of their familiarity with the Queen's tongue, liked to give strange English names to their children. There were Zulu boys called Lovemore. Girls called Precious, Pretty, Perseverance, Fortunate. Boys called Knowledge, Innocent, Gift, Moreblessing, Lucky.

Although I still was in no mood for talk, I had to accede to his request for my name. After all, he had been kind enough to offer me a cold drink. He was glad to hear where I came from.

'I have been to Maseru itself, but have never ventured to the hinterland,' he said.

'What are you then, a travelling salesman? I see you are carrying some suitcases; what's in there? Some skin lightening creams for ladies?' I asked him jokingly.

'In one sense I am a travelling salesman. But what I sell has nothing to do with skin lightening creams. I sell love.'

'Show me the love that you are selling?' I played along with his riddle.

He loved it. 'What I mean is that I sell emotions. I am a musician. I play the trumpet, sometimes the saxophone.'

'But do you play by yourself then?'

'No, I have a band. Let me correct that; I had a band. We had a fallout in Harrismith where we've been playing at the local hotel for the past week. I was the bandleader. But the other guys were approached by the hotel manager, a boer boy, who complained that I was too arrogant. If the band didn't fire me, he would kick the whole band off his premises and we would lose the hotel job. My comrades in the band decided I should go. They gave me a parting of ways fee, I took my trumpet,' he touched the box on his lap, 'and here I am. I know it wasn't personal. The guys have families to feed, bills to pay. I, on the other hand, don't have a wife or kids. It was convenient for all of us, for the future of our friendship that I go. I had to sell my clothes to people in town. I hate carrying bags. Which is why I have only this baby with me.' Again he touched his prized box.

'Oh, I am sorry to hear that Peace.'

'Peace is my given name, but my friends and fans call me Zakes. You can also call me that if you don't mind.'

'So, Zakes, what's your next step?'

'I'll go back home to Chesterville, and think this thing over.'

'How far is Chesterville from Clermont?'

'Not very far. Are you headed for Clermont?'

'Yes, my relatives are there. But I've never been to Durban, let alone Clermont, myself. In fact, this is first time I've ever left my country.'

I showed him the pieces of paper with my relatives' and Thabiso's addresses scribbled on them. He said he would help me locate the places. Thabiso lived in a place called KwaMashu, which Zakes said was to the north of Durban – whatever that meant. Clermont was much closer to the city itself, and he was more familiar with it having played a number of times at shebeens there. Shebeen. There was another new word. He explained its meaning to me. It conjured up the image of those Russians doing their lewd dance at the wedding a long time ago. I began to worry about sitting next to this man.

Seven

A Roomful of Boxes

Zakes,

It was late at night when the bus finally stopped at Durban station. We disembarked. For the umpteenth time, you offered to take me to your place for the night. 'It's too late now to go pounding the streets of either Clermont or KwaMashu. Spend the night at my place and we can wake up tomorrow and find the addresses you're looking for.'

I said no. Can you trust a man who travels around with only a small box to his name, a man who sells his clothes just because he hates to carry bags, a man who associates with those terrible MaRashiya and their girls who throw their legs in the air for the whole world to see their panties and slivers of womanhood?

'Okay, fine,' you said bitterly, 'you're on your own.'

With those words you started walking hastily into the night. For a moment I stood there with my two bags, looking this way and that, people bumping past me as they hurried to their respective bus ranks. Panic suddenly gripped me. I ran in the direction in which you had disappeared. There were so many shadows crowding the pavements I had no hope of spotting you. Tall buildings all around me. Traffic noises drowned my thoughts. I stood there with my mouth agape.

'Zakes! Zakes! Where are you?' I shouted. But my voice seemed to be drowned by the hum of traffic noises, and voices of people bantering as they walked home.

I turned to a man leaning against a lamppost: 'Mister, where do they park buses going to Coasterville?'

'You must mean Chesterville, ma'am?'

'Oh, yes, Chesterville.'

'That way, ma'am. If you can't find a bus, you can always come back to me. I'll be waiting patiently for you. Hhhm, I love your smell.'

I ran in the direction he had pointed out. When I got to the bus rank, I shouted unashamedly again, 'Zakes, Zakes, where are you?'

'Shut up, you bitch. You're breaking our ear drums,' some men muttered.

A figure broke away from the line of passengers ready to climb on the next bus.

'Listen, girl,' you hissed, 'I made you a decent offer and you turned me down. Now, don't go shouting my name at bus ranks. There are people who I don't want to see.'

'Hey Zakes,' a voice said, and a man approached us, 'I didn't realise you were back in town, until your bitch shouted your name. What's happening, my brother?'

You turned to study the face in the darkness: 'Ah, Matewu, it's you!'

'Yes, man, yes. Are you going to Blekes (I was to later learn that this was the affectionate name they'd given to Chesterville) or are you hanging around town?'

'I'm going home, man.'

'What are you waiting for then? Climb on the bus.' The man led us to the head of the queue. Those who had been waiting patiently complained. But, as I later learnt, Matewu was the driver of the bus and a feared thug; he could call the shots.

The bus was packed with well-dressed people. Most of them had that smell that reminded me of Thabiso. It seemed to me that after performing those heavy tasks at their various places of work, these people had taken the trouble to wash themselves and smothered bad work smells with this thing they called perfume.

I noticed that several people were sitting comfortably in their chairs reading books! I suddenly remembered what Maki had said about night schools. I took a mental note to make sure I registered at one of these schools as soon as possible so I could start reading my books on the bus. I wonder what my friends and siblings back home would say seeing me reading a book inside a moving bus. Books were things to be read in the comfort of your classroom, at your desk, or in warmth of your stationary bed. Not inside moving buses. The city was amazing me already.

'Are you comfortable?' you asked me. You had regained your cool. Our elbows touched. I felt a shiver run through my entire right side.

'Yes, I am fine. I am sorry about my behaviour.'

'No, it's okay. You have every right to be distrustful.' You touched my knee in reassurance. Again I shivered.

I watched in fascination as we whizzed past well-lit houses and buildings.

'This is the white part of town,' you told me. 'The suburb of Glenwood.'

'Amazing! I've never seen so many houses clustered around each other. So well-lit. So imposing.'

'Ag, don't worry. You'll see more tomorrow, when there's enough light.'

You said goodbye to your bus driver friend Matewu as we alighted.

'This is our part of the township. Road 11,' you said.

I looked disbelievingly at the rows of houses. Lined up the way they were, they looked like a train. Not that I had ever seen a real train, but pictures in books gave me an idea of what a train would look like.

'But the houses look like a train, the way they are set one next to the other, like train coaches!'

You laughed. 'In a way, we blacks do live inside a train. A train to nowhere.'

Finally, we reached a gate, which you opened for me. I was by now carrying your small trumpet box, and you my two bags. We reached the door. You unlocked it and let me in. You fumbled somewhere in the darkness, and the room was suddenly bathed in bright light.

Wow! I'd never before been inside a house with electricity. It was the stuff I had read about; even then, I was told that electricity was for white people. Blacks had to be content with paraffin lamps and candles.

After my eyes had adjusted to the sudden brightness of light, I looked around the room. Sure enough, it looked like a kitchen. But there was something odd about it. Then I realised what it was. All the pieces of furniture were covered in white cloth. As I was to learn later you, short of real furniture, had painstakingly looked for cardboard boxes, stuffed these with newspapers, books, and other hard objects, and arranged them into squares, oblongs, rectangles of various heights and other shapes of various heights, then covered them neatly in cloth. It must have taxed your imagination, almost like putting pieces of a puzzle together, to get the dimensions right. Also, you had to be very neat to keep the place in the exquisite state I found it.

'Please sit down,' you said, motioning me to a box convincingly shaped like a stool. It had a black cushion on top of it.

You reached underneath one of the boxes and emerged with a kettle, two mugs, a bottle of coffee and sugar and placed these on the 'table'. As the water was hissing to boiling point, you had laid out four bread rolls and a slab of cheese that you'd fished out of the fridge. The fridge was the only real piece of furniture. You buttered the rolls, sliced the cheese, poured the coffee.

'I'm sorry this is all I can offer you at this late hour,' you said as we tucked into the rolls and sipped our coffee.

After the meal, you led me to another room that turned out to be your own bedroom. There was a bed, a huge bookcase with the most books I'd seen in one place – except for the first and last time my mother took me to a bookshop in Maseru.

You put my bags at the foot of the bed and said, 'This is where you're going to sleep. I'll rest on the couch in the other room.'

'Why don't you sleep here, and I take the couch. After all this is your house, this is your bed.'

'Exactly my point. You're the guest, I am the host.'

Our arms touched as you walked out of the room.

You called out from the kitchen: 'Lettie, I'm going out for a quick drink. You sleep tight, I'll be back in a jiffy.'

'No, no, no!' I cried out in panic, 'You can't leave me here all alone!'

'You can come with me if you like, then.'

'But what kind of drink are you going to have at such a late hour?'

'Ag, it's only 10:30, and it's Friday. No one is going to work tomorrow,' you said. I noticed you had your trumpet box under your arm.

I had no choice but to go with you.

Eight

The Majesty of the Blues

IN THE MINUTES WE'D SPENT in your kitchen, I had taken furtive glances at you as you ate hungrily. You had a sharp beard like that of a mountain goat. The more I looked at you, the more I expected to hear you go: 'Meehhh!' like a goat. Your face was deep black, the skin smooth and shiny. Your forehead had three ripples of lines that accentuated themselves when you concentrated on something.

Again, like all the city people you carried that sweet smell about you. Whereas it had infuriated me when I first encountered Thabiso, now it beguiled me so that I found myself looking long and hard at your face. There was just a hint of a moustache above your upper lip.

Feeling that you were being watched as you ate, you lifted your eyes to me and smiled. Your eyes were huge as if you had been startled by the sight of a ghost. Your lips were thick as if you had been punched recently. Your head was clean-shaven. But your voice was surprisingly soft for one with such loud facial features.

'You're here chasing after your husband,' you'd said.

'Who told you that?'

'The one address is that of your relatives, and the other is for the hubby.'

'Who told you that?'

'You're here to tell the hubby that you are pregnant now. He hasn't been writing or sending money home?'

I looked at my tummy. It wasn't so big as to be noticed by others, I thought.

'You don't need to tell me you are pregnant. Everyone who's got eyes can see. Especially a person with eyes as big as mine.' You laughed.

'In a way, you're right. I am pregnant.'

'Interesting way of putting it – in a way you're right. You can't be half pregnant. You are just pregnant. Full stop.'

We both laughed.

'I am pregnant. But he is not my husband, and I am not running after him. I am here to find a new life for myself.'

'I guess that's what we always say when we're trying to fool ourselves, when we find ourselves in tight corners. We flee the familiar surroundings for new locations in an attempt to 'find ourselves'.'

'But honestly, if I do bump into him, fine. I will tell him I am carrying his child. If I don't I'll continue with my own life. Possibly find a job, go to night school and continue with my education. Find my own place, and so on and so on.'

You took hold of my hand and spread out my fingers across the white cloth covering the 'table'.

'Look what beautiful, graceful hands you have,' you said softly. 'Well sculpted, firm yet not harsh.'

That shiver again. I looked up and our eyes met. You finished your coffee in a hurry.

Now we were on the street, going to your shebeen, which you called Sis Jane's.

'It's a jazz and blues shebeen,' you said, 'we've got all kinds of shebeens around here. *Tsotsi* shebeens, where patrons produce knives at the slightest provocation – mostly without any provocation whatsoever. Then you have *skokiaan* shebeens where the folks drink lethal home-brewed concoctions that leave their lips pink, their skin flaky, their hair spiky. Then you have the jazz and blues shebeens where they play good music, sometimes, live. The music is just loud enough for patrons to continue with their conversations if they feel like it. I am not saying there's no fighting at these jazz and blues shebeens either. People around here have a predisposition to violence. Black people all over the place like killing each other. We've argued about this obsession with violence, about where it comes from.'

I didn't know what you were talking about; where I came from, people rarely fought. And when they did, they used their fists. After the fight was over, the victor would take the vanquished to the tap or stream where he would help wash the blood off. They would be friends again. But you were talking about deadly violence here, where people cut each other with knives, where they blew each other's brains out with bullets, where they sliced each other to pieces with pangas.

'Anyway,' you said, 'This is the place here.'

We detoured into a gate with two cars parked in front of it.

The yard was littered with people standing in groups, glasses in hand, talking and laughing. Couples standing against the walls, kissing. From the house came the music full of horns and drums and screaming guitars. Now and then a plaintive voice would cry out, wailing about lost love – at least that's what I could understand with my limited English vocabulary.

We entered a huge room with a big table in the middle, people sitting in chairs around it, smoking and drinking and talking. Now and then an appreciative 'Yeah, man! Yeah, man!' from the drinkers as the singer finished making his statement. When we stepped into the room, the music had subsided somewhat so that only the sound of the harmonica could be heard – with some drum shuffles in the background. I later learnt that this was called the solo. The harmonica man was taking a solo. A soon as he finished, you jumped in, blowing your trumpet furiously. Heads turned our way. Then there were howls: 'Zakes is back in town! Blow, Zakes, blow!'

And you blew. Blew until I got embarrassed, standing there near the door, wondering where to sit as all the visible seats had been taken. A man motioned me to join him. I looked away. After you were finished playing, you came to join me.

A whirlwind of a woman, tall, very light in complexion, with long hair like that of a white woman, came hurtling towards us.

'Oh, my baby is back!' she shrieked, giving Zakes a bear hug. I say she was a whirlwind of a woman because she left men dazed in her wake.

Now she stood back, looked at your face, and kissed you smack on the lips. I looked away.

Anyway as an afterthought, the woman turned towards me, bored holes into my face with her eyes, then turned to you and said: 'Is she with you, baby?'

'Ah, yes, my friend Lettie.'

'It's always good to meet little Zakes' friends,' she said. Then, in a conspiratorial whisper she said to me, 'He is a shark, my darling, so you have to be careful. That's if you still haven't been bitten already. Ha ha ha! A nice shark nevertheless.'

She threw her head back and laughed. Her laughter sounded almost like your trumpet.

'My name is Jane, my darling.' She was all business again. She was quite a beautiful woman – bulbous eyes, nice lips painted a subtle purple, an oval-shaped face, a pointed chin. I suppose I had a soft spot for her because she reminded me of the way I looked. In her I saw an older, elegant version of myself. Someone once said we invent ourselves in the manner in which others see us, perceive us and, by the same token, we see others in the manner in which we perceive ourselves.

We settled into an easy chair, next to each other. Sis Jane ordered one of the serving girls to bring a 'straight of the red one' – which turned out to be a full bottle of brandy. I knew it was brandy because that's what it said on the bottle: Bols brandy. Besides, I had seen this kind of alcohol because my father used to buy it around Christmas time to share with his friends and neighbours.

Sis Jane poured me a glass of Coke. Then she poured you a generous slug of the drink, which you duly gulped down, closing your teary eyes and smacking your lips.

'You must have been thirsty,' she said, smiling.

'Every time I see you I get very thirsty,' you said, kissing her on the cheek. She winked at me. She poured him another slug; this one you nursed for a long time while you talked to Sis Jane.

Sis Jane had positioned herself in front of us, and chewed the fat with you, to use her expression. You told her about the breakup of the band. And she told you about who'd been visiting the place since your departure from the township.

'I don't think you should feel sore at them,' she said finally, 'Most of them can't afford to go without an income.'

'True. But now I have to figure out what to do with my life.'

'That shouldn't be a problem. You are always welcome to come play daddy in this house, run the errands, make sure everything is in order.' She smiled at me again. 'Starting tomorrow, I could use a pair of extra hands seeing that it's the end of the month the drinkers will be very thirsty and loaded.'

'Thanks for the offer, but first thing in the morning I'll have to help Lettie here find her husband in KwaMashu.'

'Husband?' she asked, bemused, 'I thought you two were an item.'

'I so wish we were,' you said, smiling and touching my arm. Shiver.

Now and then, patrons would come and pay homage to Sis Jane as they departed for home. Others, it seemed to me, wanted to make sure that Sis Jane had noticed their presence in her place. Later, I learnt that this was important because on rainy days, she would extend credit to those who were loyal patrons of the place.

Nat King Cole was singing 'Sunny Side of the Street'. I knew the song because it had been my father's favourite. You picked up your trumpet and started blowing softly, placing a saucer at the mouth of your instrument to produce an eerie, distorted sound.

A woman in a black, sleeveless evening gown and matching gloves got up from her chair and started dancing to the music, swaying like a cobra under the snake charmer's spell.

More sleepy, sorrowful music was played. You explained that the sound was called The Blues. The way you said it I could tell that you would have written it in capital letters were you asked to put those words on paper. You seemed to have a special reverence for the sound. You kept going on about the majesty of the blues, the sound of angels.

People kept coming to our table to welcome you back from your travels. I could sense that you were well respected and well loved. You wore the mantle of fame with humility.

Much later, we said our goodbyes and left the house. You tucked me in bed, kissed me good night and went to the lounge where you were to sleep.

The dream came immediately. I was back home, sleeping in my room. Granny was talking to me from the other side of the wall: 'Beware of city men, my child. Go on with your mission of finding your man, that charming Thabiso of yours. He needs you.'

'But I don't want him, granny,' I remonstrated.

'It doesn't matter if you want him or not. What matters is that you are carrying his child. You should respect that.'

It was clear to me right there and then that no matter what I did, I couldn't wipe my past from my mind. It would follow me wherever I went.

There and then, granny suddenly appeared in front of me, at the foot of my bed.

I woke up with a start. You were standing at the foot of the bed in black shorts and a white T-shirt. You were carrying a tray with tea things on it.

'You are one of those who talk in their sleep,' you said. The sun was already up, I realised.

I drank my tea in bed. I hadn't slept in such a comfortable bed before, with a foamy mattress – instead of the thin sponge that I had left back home. There were clean sheets too, instead of mielie meal sacks that my mother had fashioned into sleeping sheets. I finished my tea. I was drifting back to sleep when I heard traffic noises outside in the street. I remembered that I was in somebody else's house. I got up to join you in the kitchen.

Nine

The Song of Butterflies

ZAKES,

You will have noticed, by now, that I name most of my letters to you after your favourite songs, songs that you shared with me over the time we spent together. I guess by remembering the song titles I am trying my best to relive the past.

Anyway, back to that first morning with you.

When I finally left the bedroom, I joined you in the kitchen. The house was redolent with the smell of fried bacon and eggs. You were sitting at the table, eating your breakfast steadily. You encouraged me to dish up for myself, which I gladly did. I was famished.

'Sis Jane is quite an interesting character,' I heard myself say as I speared a rind of bacon.

You laughed happily at the mention of her name.

'A shark of a woman, if there ever was one.'

'That's the expression she used to describe you. A shark of a man, she said last night.'

'Jane and I go back a long way. A long way indeed.'

Your eyes had a distant look in them. You took a bite from a slice of bread, chewed slowly, your eyes getting misty. Then you continued: 'I've known her for ages, growing up in this neighbourhood as a boy. She wasn't born in this neighbourhood, for sure, but she arrived here when I was a school-going boy of about thirteen, fourteen. I remember very vividly the first time I laid my eyes on her.'

You used your slice of bread to scoop the egg yolk from your plate.

Then you continued telling me about Sis Jane: 'You see, I was walking down the street that runs next to our football stadium.

Then I spotted her. She was, you see, wearing a tomato red dress that reached just above her knees. Her legs – you didn't see her legs last night, wow – her legs were milky white. She had on red high-heeled shoes. Her head was covered in a red hat with a big brim, you see, and her lips were painted red.

'She looked just like a white woman with that complexion of hers! Not just any white woman, mind you, but a white woman with style; a white woman straight from the pages of those stylish magazines. For a moment I wondered what a white woman was doing in our neighbourhood. But then I realised that underneath her hat, her hair was black and curly. I continued staring unashamedly and continued walking. You see, she was smiling at me.

'Just up the road there was a group of men playing cards. They stopped playing and stared.

'Hey, boy, look out!' she said. But she was too late. With my eyes still glued to her, I fell into a ditch filled with green scummy water. When I emerged from the ditch my clothes and my face were covered in green slime. The card players had a good laugh.

The woman was smiling sadly at me: 'You must watch where you're going, boy, otherwise you are going to hurt yourself seriously one of these days. Come here, let me clean your face.' She reached into her red purse and fished out a white handkerchief. She wiped my whole face with it. Then – now wait for it – she kissed me full on the lips. I staggered, almost falling back into the scummy water. She steadied me on my feet as she realised I was still dizzy.

'The card players stopped laughing, and stared at us. She patted me on my head. Then she was on her way again, swaying her hips in a manner that announced to the card players: 'Eat your hearts out, boys. You can look but not touch!'

'As an afterthought, she wheeled around and gave me the soiled handkerchief. "Keep it," she said, and then walked away.'

At that stage, you paused, took a sip from your coffee, and continued: 'I held the handkerchief in my hands. The kiss she'd given me came back to me. I always think of that kiss as the first time I made love to a woman. From that moment I had an idea what it felt like to be in love.'

You paused again, your eyes avoiding mine. At that very moment I knew you were attracted to me. I had sensed this the previous day. No words need to be spoken when Cupid's arrow hits home. I had sensed the emotion of love when our bodies touched the previous night as you showed me to the bedroom. Your refusal to look me straight in the eye told me about your love for me. It was a new sensation for me as well, something I hadn't felt when I told Thabiso I loved him.

'Well then,' I said, 'what happened after that?'

'Well, over the next few days I learnt that the lady in red was one of our new neighbours. Her name was Sis Jane. She was called Sis Jane because she ran a shebeen. I was disappointed. How could one so pure, one so beautiful and graceful run a drinking place, a place of sin? Oh, by the way, my father is an Anglican minister.'

'Is he still alive?'

'Very much so. It's just that we don't get along very well. He disapproves of the life I lead.'

'What? Playing music? Is there anything wrong with that?'

You paused, finished your coffee, looked at the ceiling, in search of words. Then you spoke slowly, carefully: 'I hope you'll find it in your heart to understand that I have lived a terrible life. I've done some horrible things in my life apart from quitting university and playing music, against my parents' advice.'

'You don't have to tell me if it makes you uncomfortable.'

'There will be a day when you will get to hear my life story. But for now, let me just tell you how disappointed I was at the fact that the angel in red was a woman of sin, a woman who relieved family men of their hard-earned money. She was a breaker of families.'

There was a knock on the door. Before we could respond, the door opened. In walked Sis Jane.

'Speak of the devil!' you beamed at her.

'I hope he hasn't been telling you bad things about me,' Sis Jane said, smiling at me. 'How are you this morning, my angel?'

She touched me lightly on the shoulder. I said I was fine. She had an easy air about her. I knew that I would be a very happy woman if I were to stay with one so warm and humble. Sis Jane went right ahead and poured herself some coffee and then joined us at the table. We exchanged some small talk. She told us that she would drive us in her own car to Clermont or KwaMashu – wherever I wanted to go.

'You must hasten to find your own man, so I can have Zakes all to myself again,' she said, laughing. I knew she was joking, but I felt a twinge of jealousy nevertheless.

I suddenly felt the urge to go to the toilet. 'May I please go and use myself?'

The two of you looked at each other, bemused. It was Sis Jane who got my meaning first: 'Oh, you want to go to the toilet?'

'Yes,' I said shyly.

'Just turn to your right,' you said pointing at a door just outside the kitchen door.

A sense of disgust and amazement overwhelmed me. I couldn't believe that people in the cities relieved themselves right inside the house! Right next to the kitchen. Back home, we relieved ourselves about a kilometre away from the house, deep in the bush. Those of us who'd been to the cities dug pit latrines. But even these were located a respectable distance from the house.

I was self-conscious as I did my thing in the toilet. The place smelled like flowers. Amazing! There was even a roll of soft paper that my private parts had never had the pleasure of being pampered with. All I had to do to get rid of my waste was to pull a chain, and water gurgled, and the smelly bits went away! Ayi, ayi, this city life!

When I came out of the toilet you directed me to the bedroom in which I'd slept. There I found a bath tub with warm water in it. Next to it, there was a saucer with a cake of soap in it. I quickly did my ablutions, luxuriating in the warmth of the water, and the sweet smell of soap. I was more familiar with blue soap whose smell reminded me of petrol, or paraffin. It was a pungent smell that stayed on your body for days on end.

After I'd done my ablutions, I picked one of my best dresses from my suitcase and put it on. I then stood in front of a mirror I'd found in the room. It was the biggest mirror I'd ever seen in my life. As big and round as the plate from which I had eaten my breakfast. Back home, I had to be content with a mirror as big as the palm of my hand – just big enough to take a peak at my profile as I made sure there were no cobwebs around my eyes after I had finished washing my face. I looked myself in the mirror and smiled. My light-complexioned face was radiant with some inexplicable happiness. For a moment I wondered what you, Zakes, thought of me, of my beautiful face. I closed my eyes and reconstructed Sis Jane's face in my mind. True, she was a beautiful woman. But not as stunningly beautiful as you had described her the first time you laid your eyes on her. The ravages of age and a protracted struggle with alcohol had manifested themselves in the sagging bags below her eyes. I wondered what you, Zakes, had seen in her. Oh, true, she had big breasts. But in due course I concluded that those big breasts would soon be rubbing themselves around her knees.

I, on the other hand, still had a trim figure, firm breasts, and flawless facial skin. What did you think of me? I suddenly felt embarrassed by these thoughts. I opened my eyes and looked at my face in the mirror. For a moment I thought I caught a glimpse of my grandmother's face in the mirror. I blinked repeatedly. The mirror was blank. There was no image of my face there! I opened and closed my eyes repeatedly, alarmed. Then the mirror seemed to crack in half. From the crack emerged a pink butterfly. Followed by a yellow one. Then a white one. A blue one. Another pink one. Suddenly the room was suffused with colour that reminded me of my grandmother's lair back home. The butterflies filled the room with the flapping sound of their wings. It wasn't just a discordant flapping noise. It had a melody to it. It was musical. I wanted to scream. But I couldn't. My mouth kept opening, but no sound came out. I began swatting at the butterflies.

From the kitchen I could hear Sis Jane shouting: 'Where are these butterflies coming from?'

79

I joined the two of you in the kitchen. You were on your feet, swatting frantically at the butterflies.

Suddenly my grandmother's face appeared in my mind's eye. I remembered how one day I had confronted her, demanding to know why her butterflies had an everlasting life; they didn't die. Of course, as one committed to her vow of silence, she didn't respond to my question. But later that night, as I was teetering on the brink of sleep, her voice was loud and clear, penetrating the thin wall separating my room from hers.

'I am happy that you are a curious little girl, Lettie. You ask questions. That's healthy. A mind that doesn't ask questions is as good as dead. About the butterflies. That's what I want to talk to you about. They are lovely, aren't they? That's why you keep asking questions about them. They are fascinating little creatures of beauty and mystery, aren't they? That's why they are flapping their tiny wings inside your mind and soul. Powerful little creatures they are. And you know why? I'll tell you why. Our elders in the spirit world have chosen butterflies as our guardian angels to look after us in this world. Butterflies are beautiful, vulnerable creatures. But that's also where their strength lies – in their vulnerability. Only a mean-spirited person sees a butterfly as a threat. As such, only a mean-spirited person would deem it fit to kill a butterfly. A butterfly is a thing of beauty that needs to be admired, to be allowed the freedom to fly away at liberty, to add splashes of colour and vivacity to the atmosphere. Unlike a bird, a butterfly cannot be caged. It cannot be captured, tamed and trained to perform, like owls, cranes and other species of bird, which in African lore can be trained to perform evil deeds among human beings. They can be used as familiars. When you see butterflies in your midst, know that you are close to the spirit world and you are in benevolent company. But when the butterflies disappear, know that beauty and splendour have forsaken you; that you are vulnerable, that the clouds of doom are hovering above you, replacing the dashes of colour that come with the butterflies. A world without butterflies is a desert of the heart, where spiritual death looms large and menacing.'

Over the years, Lettie would come to understand that the butterflies were an indication that she was in a good place and that her grandmother was with her. Without them in the immediate vicinity, she would feel vulnerable, with no guardian and no protection from evil.

★★★

It's one thing to meet a stranger, spend a night at his place; sleep on real sheets, on a real bed, wake up to a breakfast of bacon and eggs – all in a matter of a few hours. It's quite something else to wake up in a strange land to be confronted by the biggest concentration of modern houses you have ever seen, and streets teeming with children and cars.

We left the butterfly-infested house and got into Sis Jane's car. I sat in the front and you plonked yourself in the back.

After turning a few corners, the car came to a stop in front of a house with three cars parked in front of it. I recognised the house as Sis Jane's shebeen we'd visited the previous night. Sis Jane asked me to give her the piece of paper where my friend, Maki, had scribbled the telephone numbers of both my distant Aunt Lizbeth, and my… my… my lover, Thabiso.

'I'll phone your aunt so she can give us directions to her place,' Sis Jane said as a parting shot as she got out of the car and went inside.

In her absence the two of us, you, Zakes, and I, maintained our silence. She came back within a few minutes, confident that she had a rough idea of where my aunt lived. In a section of Clermont called Fannin. Fine. We drove off.

I kept looking this way and that as Sis Jane drove her car down the street from your house and we meandered out of the township on our way to look for my distant relative's place in Clermont.

There were too many sights assailing my eyes. Arriving in Chesterville the previous night, the township had been cloaked in darkness. It had been difficult for me to even imagine what a township looked like. Townships were peculiar to South Africa. Back home in Lesotho people lived either in the rural areas, or in the cities and towns – not these monstrosities called townships where people lived so close to each other they could almost smell each other's breath.

The houses were made of red brick. With asbestos roofs. Nice little windows. True, they looked too small for the typical African family with father, mother and an average of eight children. But they were so modern and, by Lesotho standards, they looked like white people's homes.

The other downside was that they had no gardens. Where were the children supposed to play? My question was soon answered. I saw a group of children – the biggest concentration of children I'd seen outside church or school. They were playing all manner of games right in the middle of the street. Sis Jane had to honk the horn of her car repeatedly before they grudgingly made way for us to drive through.

'That's the soccer stadium I was telling you about,' you said excitedly, leaning forward to point at the football ground.

'Oh, you mean where you first saw Sis Jane in her red outfit?' I asked.

'He's told you that story?' Sis Jane exclaimed, her face melting into a wide smile as she stole a glance at me. 'But you mustn't read too much into what he's been saying about me. We are just good old friends.' Another warm smile and a glance in my direction. 'Isn't that so, Zakes?'

You just smiled.

Ten

There is no Hell

DEAR LETTIE,

Music composers say the essence of a song lies in what is left out of it. The gaps in between the notes; the yawning spaces in between phrases; the brief spells of silence between words and melodies; the hesitation between the stanzas. That is the music. What is left unsaid. The rest is noise. I guess what I'm saying is that the canvas I'm trying to fill is too small for what has happened to me in this lifetime. So, listen to the music of what's left unsaid. The songs of my heart. The melodies of my emotions. The screaming, howling, piercing Charlie Parker wails from the depth of my being. To keep the tone you've set through your letters, I've also decided to name my letters after the songs we used to share.

You see, from the moment I laid my eyes on you that very first time in the bus, I felt moved by your presence. It wasn't just the physical beauty, but something more than that. Yeah, you were, and still are, beautiful. But what pulled me to you was the spiritual magnet in you. One moment you had this brooding look about your face, this intense stare-into-the-distance thing that made you look melancholy. Then within moments your face radiated an amazing innocence and a sense of vulnerability. A look so tender I sometimes felt like hugging you. Felt like rocking you as one would a small, heartbroken baby.

But you see. The minute I thought of wrapping my protective arms around you, you started talking. You told me about your past, about the man who was going to marry you, the man you were going to join in the city. I felt so hurt that there was a man out there who could have what I, Zakes, the famous trumpeter, could not. I vowed that I would bide my time. That I would have you all to myself sooner or later.

When we arrived at Sis Jane's place that night, the intention was to give you a doctored drink that would soften you so I could ravish you. The thought did cross my mind. But the more I consumed my liquor, the more lucid and guilty I felt at the very thought of taking advantage of you. I invited you to sleep peacefully in my bedroom while I crashed on my couch, with visions of your innocent face looming large in my mind's eye. Painful desire burdened my heart, slowly pushing me into the bottomless pit of troubled sleep.

I dreamt of butterflies. I dreamt of an old woman whose face looked like yours. Except it was darker, wrinkled. When I woke up I realised I was truly besotted. I cried in my heart on the very morning I would be delivering you into the hands of your man.

You made me laugh, the way you kept exclaiming every time we saw a beautiful car. The elegant Valiant, the splendorous Zephyr, the stylish Buick. I laughed repeatedly when you said you hadn't seen so many beautiful cars in one place. You couldn't believe the cars were being driven by black people.

'Who's that important-looking man?' you asked, pointing out at a man standing next to a maroon Cadillac with an open top. The man had a huge cigar in his right hand. And what looked like a brandy glass in the other. It wasn't unusual for township people to have a liquid breakfast. You can't eat on a dry stomach, was the motto of these fast-living, hard-drinking men of the townships. Except that the man we were seeing was no ordinary Joe.

'Oh, that man is a cousin of AWG Champion, the famous politician,' I said.

When you pestered me with questions, I had to explain that Champion had been one of those wealthy, educated black people. Those who were highly involved in the struggle for the liberation of black people. But apart from that, he had been one of the first black people to be allowed to drink white people's liquor. But in order to qualify for that privilege, he had had to dump his Zulu surname, Msomi, for Champion. Changing the surname to this English one not only gave him the right to consume white people's liquor, but it also exempted him from laws applied to black people. He could live among coloured people if he so chose. He could also buy land for he was an honorary white. Ordinary blacks could not own property.

At that stage Sis Jane told a story I had forgotten. You see, it was about a man who had been arrested and appeared in a court of law where he was told that as a European, as white people were called at that time, he was not allowed to live amongst coloureds.

So he moved to a European area where he was treated as a European by everyone, you see. One day he was involved in an accident at work. He then claimed compensation as a white man. Fine. They compensated him accordingly. Fine.

But then one day he went to buy fifty bottles of beer as a European. Now, he found himself on the wrong side of the law. They arrested him for playing white, for buying white man's liquor under false pretences.

Evidence was led in court, and an uncle of the man testified. The magistrate was satisfied that the man was coloured, found him guilty, but discharged him with a warning.

But the lawyer for the defence argued vehemently that the appearance of the man was so European that there was no reason why he could not continue to live as a white man, among white people, and occupy a white man's position at work... provided he didn't buy any more white man's liquor.

We all laughed, all three of us.

Then I continued to tell you that Champion himself had long since died. His land had been expropriated by the white government. But his progenitors still lived large from their inheritances.

'Just like this show-off we've just passed,' I said, at which Sis Jane laughed uproariously, and said: 'Oh, I think we're being jealous now. Jealous of the successful Champion family.'

If the truth be told, Sis Jane and the Champion man had had something going between them a long time before, and I had been jealous of them.

'I don't think I'm following you,' Lettie, said. 'Are you telling me that black people are still not allowed, by law, to drink beer and other so-called white people's liquor?'

'No, no,' Sis Jane said, 'blacks can drink whatever they want. You saw the people at my place last night, drinking beer, brandy, wine, what have you. It's just that the white establishment has made drinking an expensive habit. They have pushed the prices very high. In the process, they are making a killing, considering the fact that the darkies, long deprived of this booze, are doing their damndest to prove to the white man that they are not poor, that they can afford to drink white man's liquor. They blow their hard-earned money buying white man's liquor – just to prove this stupid point. But when they are down and out they go back to the cheap concoctions from the townships.'

I leaned forward to listen to her give you the low-down of these gut-corroding concoctions. As I leaned forward, my chin brushed against your shoulder. You turned to look at me, in the mistaken belief that I had touched you deliberately, wanting to say something. As you turned, our lips almost touched. The musky smell of you filled my nostrils.

'Did you say something, Zakes?' you wanted to know.

'No,' said I, 'I just wanted to hear what tall tales Jane was telling you about our lovely down-to-earth brews from our humble townships.'

There was a moment's silence in the car. The soft hum of the engine was soothing.

It was hot inside the car. I rolled down my window. You followed suit. Soon, the car was filled with the noises of the streets – children and dogs and radios from the different houses competed for dominance.

We drove on in relative silence until we entered the huge settlement of Clermont. The streets of Clermont were worse than those of Chesterville. Not only were they a parading ground for a mixed salad of all shades of human beings, cars, goats, pigs and buses, but on the sides of the streets were nauseatingly green blocked drains. We spotted a dog floating in one of these pools of scum. Horrible smells flooded into the inside of the car. We hastily rolled up our windows and Sis Jane put the fan on in a desperate attempt to chase away the bad smells.

The streets had given you more ammunition to throw at us. You started talking again: 'Tell me, people, how can you call yourself a human being when you are wallowing at the bottom of this smelly mound pretending to be humanity? Children who play in the middle of the street, and make rude gestures to you when you tell them to get out of the way. Women who get drunk with their men in public so early in the day?'

You were getting on my nerves, but I decided to leave you be. I knew that with time, you would soon find answers to your questions. You would soon be part of what you called the 'smelly mound pretending to be humanity'.

I knew your type. Many had come from the outlying areas of the country to the city. Upon arrival, and seeing how people in the township lived, their heads were suddenly full of questions. But after a while, those questions were answered. They adjusted to township life and became a part of the 'smelly mound pretending to be humanity'. Those who found the answers too bitter to swallow simply left and went back to their ancestral homes. I didn't know if you would stay. And if you did, would you be able to triumph over the vicissitudes of township life.

You were excited when you spotted the first church steeple pointing its holy finger to the heavens. The church was located near the Ndunduma taxi rank. I suppose the church embodied hope and salvation from its immediate surroundings. At least those who had been kicked in the teeth by life could seek the warmth of the heart and comfort from within the confines of the church.

'A church! Oh, what a beautiful church,' you cried out.

Sis Jane stopped the car so you could marvel at the holy edifice. We rolled down our windows. The air outside was laden with the soothing smell of the eucalyptus trees, which formed a green wall around the church, protecting it from the malodorous world of sin.

Music from the church hit our faces with ferocity. I found it strange that these people were having a church service on a Saturday. But after listening to a few bars of their music, I realised that the holy ones behind the thick walls of the church were singing a funeral song. From the sound of it, they were members of the controversial church called KwaSihogo Kasikho (There is no Hell).

When one of their members passed on, members of this church held a colourful, party-like service where they celebrated, singing out loud how they envied the departed one because he was now going to sit at the throne with the Almighty.

Uzongibiza nini Nkosi yami (When are you going to call out my name, oh Lord), they sang hoping that the Lord would beckon them to come over to the throne sooner rather than later. And they sang very loudly – just to be sure the Lord heard them. The Lord was known to ignore those who prayed silently. He wanted to be hollered at until he lost His temper – and acceded to whatever request was being made.

When the song died down, I asked Sis Jane to start the car so we could go. But then a voice boomed from a speaker strategically positioned at the entrance to the church. It was a voice so captivating it arrested our attention, and we couldn't help but listen: 'As I said earlier, we are here to celebrate beauty, the beauty of a brother of ours who's passing on to sit by the Creator's throne. Now, we can't choose the day on which to die. That's God's duty. But what we can choose is how we look while we are still alive. Looking ugly and unattractive is a kind of death, can I hear an Amen?'

'Ameeen!'

'This sermon is about beauty this side of the grave. And it is about the beauty on the other side of the grave. You're in the wrong place if you came here thinking we celebrate pain and ugliness. My sermon is not pie in the sky before you die. This is something sound on the ground while you are still around. While we're choosing what's best for you, and while we're bidding bye, bye to the departed brother, we must celebrate beauty, ahhhhhh, can I get an Amen?'

'Amen!'

'It is the height of blasphemy for people to waddle around with oversized tummies. There are ways of controlling weight. Our bodies are the Lord's temple, allelujah! Temples need to be worshipped and protected. Temples need to be respected. Ease down on that ice cream, my dear sister. Ease down on that chocolate, my dear child. I said ease down on what?'

'Ease down on the ice cream!'

'And ease down on what else?'

'On the chocolate!'

'Yes, children of God, run away from those mounds of stiff porridge. Show disdain for those bottles of beer, my dear brother. Respect your body. Show respect for the Lord's temple. No, no, no, children of God, I am not referring to anyone in this house. Let me close my eyes so no one will think the pastor is making remarks about them. Can I get an Amen?'

'Amen!'

'When you die and you're overweight, don't expect love from the Almighty. That's not how He brought you into this world. You ate too much and defiled your body. You defiled the Lord's temple and that's a shame. What is it, children of God?'

'A shame, Reverend!'

'A mighty shame indeed! The brother who's passed on was a well known weight lifter. A man who will impress those angels up there. I know in my heart of hearts he will be rewarded accordingly. Oh, children of God, I can see those beautiful angels. Can I get an Amen?'

'Amen!'

'The beautiful angels massaging the brother's well-toned body; the angels burdening that firm body with their heavenly kisses, can I get an Amen?'

We were rolling in our seats by that time. Later we learnt that the man who had passed away was indeed a well-known bodybuilder and comedian called Makhanda.

We drove away from the church.

A few blocks later we spotted the next church, and another one, and the next one. You couldn't help opening your mouth again: 'Why are there so many churches in this place?'

'City people have got too many sins; that's why they need so many churches,' I responded without even thinking about it.

We all laughed.

What I didn't tell you was that religion was big business in the cities. Almost every month, a new church was launched when a disgruntled deacon broke away from the main church to found his own joint. The names of the churches were themselves a farce: Mount Zion Primitive Baptist Church. Old Order Bishops Congregational Church. New Generation Synagogue in Africa Church of Zion. Holy Baptist Church of Zion in Africa. New Pentecostal Catholic Church of South Africa. African Roots Church in the Spirit of Jesus.

The ministers and pastors drove big cars: Cadillacs, Bentleys, Dodge Monacos, Zephyrs, Fords, etc. It was also not uncommon for church men to find themselves in the newspapers – for the wrong reasons. One of the stories that had shaken the city at the time had been published a month or so ago in *Ilanga* newspaper under the headline: *Umfundisi weZayoni edilini lesinene* (Zionist priest in sex orgy). The newspaper told of a famous priest who had had sex with almost one hundred women over a number of days. He had taken them to bed, with their permission, to rid their bodies and souls of demons and bad spirits. Injecting them with the Holy Spirit, it was said.

As we drove on, I realised, with much trepidation, that the street we had entered was very familiar to me. I had been here many times. And the memories that this street brought back, memories of one of its denizens in particular, made my heart go boom, boom, boom. And then boom-boom-boom. I wanted to say something, but decided against it.

Sis Jane parked in front of a house painted yellow. Consulting the piece of paper with the address written on it, she said: 'According to the directions written here, this is the house where we are going to find your aunt.'

Sitting in front of the house was the very man I was scared to face after so many years. The man who made my heart go boom, boom, boom.

His name was Bhazabhaza.

He was sitting in his wheelchair, a beer mug in his hand. It was before noon, yet there were four empty beer bottles standing at his feet, still glistening with moisture indicating that they had been drained of their contents not so long ago, and in quick succession.

I looked at Bhazabhaza now. The past we had shared together came flashing back in my mind's eye.

For a moment, I closed my eyes. I saw a younger version of Bhazabhaza. He was sitting on the hood of his shiny black Cadillac with the top down. He was wearing a neatly pressed powder blue Saville Row suit, a black Viyella shirt and a powder blue cravat to match the suit and a black Stetson hat to match the shirt, a pair of black and white two-tone Nunn Bush shoes. A cigarette dangled from the left corner of his mouth, smoke rising to his eyes. Lurking behind those eyes was a ghost of a nasty smile.

His right hand was playing with a half-full whisky glass. Two girls, one in a shocking pink dress and the other in a yellow two piece trouser-and-jacket ensemble, flanked him. The girls had drinks of their own, enjoying every moment of basking in the presence of the one and only boss of all bosses, Bhazabhaza.

An hour later after this colourful frolicking in front of his car, one of the girls was found outside his house. Her throat had been slashed. Bhazabhaza and other girls and boys were having a party inside the house. Every now and then a person would walk outside to have a leak in the toilet, which was in the backyard. They would cry out in shock at the sight of the bloody corpse, only to recover very quickly. 'Ag, it's only that bitch,' they would mutter drunkenly to themselves, prodding the corpse out of the way with their feet, before proceeding to the toilet.

This mental picture was just one of many that I could easily retrieve from my memory at the mere mention of the name Bhazabhaza.

This was the man I had lived and had fun with. A man who was to leave a lasting impression on me. He fitted those times. It's said men are made by the times they live in. But again, men make the times they live in.

But this wheelchair-bound creature that was now looking fixedly at our car was a far cry from the Bhazabhaza I could conjure with ease in my mind. Lord, I wanted to flee the place.

'Are you sure this is the place?' I asked Sis Jane.

She turned to look at me, her face bearing the question: 'Is there something wrong with you?' But she didn't say anything. She just got out of the car and said: 'Let's go.'

Bhazabhaza's eyes widened when he saw me. I looked fixedly at him, my face melting into a sad smile. Even as I smiled, I could feel his presence striking a dark chord in my heart.

Eleven

Burnin' & Lootin'

THEMBA 'BHAZABHAZA' DLAMINI was only 14 years old when he got into trouble with the law. This was to change the course of his life forever. When you are caught breaking the law, there is always a price to be paid.

Nobody knows for sure what sparked the war between Indians and Africans in Durban in 1949. Political analysts and historians have said that Indians, forever the money-hungry hustlers had, for a long time, been exploiting Africans. They overcharged them at the shops that they owned. They made them pay exorbitant rent for the shacks that they had created on the periphery of the city of Durban. Like the Nazi's portrayal of the Jews in Germany, the Indians were considered exploitative interlopers stripping the indigenous people of their dignity and closing all business opportunities for these people. There could be an element of truth in this, but it doesn't answer the question: what really ignited these emotions, which had obviously been simmering under the surface? Many versions of the story have been told.

According to one, a young African man was seen kissing his Indian girlfriend at the corner of Victoria and Grey streets. A gaggle of young Indian males, green with jealousy, turned on him and started punching and kicking him.

African passers-by who witnessed the attack thought they just wouldn't be able to live with their consciences were they to leave the poor African boy to his devices. So they fell in and launched ferocious blows on the Indians who in turn, disappeared into the nearby avenues to call for reinforcements. Blood flowed freely in the avenues and arcades of the city.

Yet another version of the story maintains that on a warm Wednesday afternoon (Wednesdays were market days), one of the African boys who worked at the main green grocer market, where Berea Road train station stands today, accidentally bumped an Indian gentleman with the trolley he had been pushing. Infuriated by this outrage on his person, the gentleman cursed at the boy – whose apologies fell on deaf ears – and spat in his face.

An African woman who witnessed the attack on the boy decided it would be impolite and uncivilised of her to pass the scene without making a contribution. So, like the conscientious citizen that she was, she fell on the Indian gentleman, hitting him in the face with her handbag.

But then the Indian's wife, who had been standing by watching her husband teach the uncivilised African boy some manners, came to her husband's rescue. She threw a handful of curry powder into the face of the African lady, who, coughing and rubbing her eyes, was inspired to cry out: 'Curry-farting coolie bitch!'

'Banana-shitting kaffir baboon!' the Indian lady responded.

The humid, warm Durban air was suddenly burdened with racial insults. The two women tore into each other, punching, clawing, biting. The Indian woman had huge breasts, which she used to her advantage, knocking her opponent to the ground. African boys who worked at the market laughed briefly. But civilisation overcame them, and they moved to help the African woman to her feet.

The Indian wife, in turn, was screaming her lungs out. She was running around, semi-naked. Her purple sari had been torn to shreds in her scuffle with the African woman. Her torn black panties were not offering her much protection from the passers-by who were watching, their eyes wide open.

But the onlookers soon regained their composure, and sanity, and joined the great mission at hand – the fighting. They pummelled the Indian. But then other Indians working at the market couldn't stand by while one of their own was being attacked. Serious fighting ensued.

These are just two of many versions of what really sparked the fighting. It has, however, been reported that as the violence gained momentum, marauding gangs of Indians piled into African passers-by with bush knives, their weapons of choice. It was said a good Indian man had three hands – two ordinary ones, and the bush knife was the third.

By 1949, Indians were highly prosperous, owning property in the city itself. But their dominion extended beyond the metropolis. They owned vast tracts of land in the settlements on the periphery of the city, most notably in the Cato Manor settlement just northwest of the city. Cato Manor was one of those multiracial settlements where Indians, blacks and whites lived cheek by jowl. Indians, the enterprising businesspeople that they have always been, held the lion's share of the land. On this land, they built houses, which they rented out, mostly to Africans. Because Cato Manor had the highest concentration of Indians, this settlement bore the brunt of most of the fighting between Indians and Africans.

Zulus from far and near came to Cato Manor to help defend the motherland from the Indians who were armed with guns. However, it must be pointed out that many of these Zulus didn't understand what the fighting was all about. But they didn't care. If you wanted to offend a Zulu man, you would start a fight in a corner of town and not invite him to join you. A Zulu man stumbling upon a street fight always saw it as his duty to join in – on the losing side, mind you, because he loved a challenge. He would ask questions later. Sometimes he would not even ask questions. Fighting was its own reward.

By the second day of the riots, the fighting had spread to other parts of the city, to the adjoining shacklands, and further afield. Africans were looting and burning Indian shops and properties. Outrages were committed on women from both sides of the conflict. Buses belonging to Indians were stoned and set alight. Indians were pounced upon and lynched on sight. In turn, Indians barricaded themselves behind their huge doors, raining sniper fire on passing Africans from the safety of their windows.

When the Zulus poured into Indian neighbourhoods, the women could be heard pleading with marauders: '*Hhayi bulala zonke, baba, shiya lombewu!*' (Don't kill us all, daddy, at least leave the seed) – asking them to spare the children.

The fighting was in its third day when 14-year-old Bhazabhaza – so-called because he had a big tummy even at a young age – was walking home from school, whistling nonchalantly as he unwrapped a toffee and threw it into his salivating mouth. He had just passed the ruins of kwaMadala eJuteni, the legendary shop that had belonged to a Jewish man. The shop had also been torched as some Africans thought the old Jew was partial to Indians, that he was as exploitative as the Indians themselves.

In their blind rage, these Africans had forgotten how the Jew had been so kind to them, giving them credit when times were tough. But most importantly, Madala had been so kind that he had written off a lot of debt from his book. He could afford to do this because the core of his business was the wholesale aspect; he made most of his money from selling directly to Indian shopkeepers.

Bhazabhaza wrinkled his nose irritably at the smell of the ruins of Madala's shop. Suddenly, he faced an agitated group of people armed to the teeth with knobkerries, bush knives, sjamboks and stones. The first instinct was to turn on his heel and run for safety. But then he realised that these were his own people, Africans. He even spotted children of his own age in the group. And more importantly, some of the children were holding cold drinks and other morsels of food. It was clear that some unlucky Indian had just had his shop looted and burned down. His mother had warned Bhazabhaza against taking part in the madness of looting. 'If you see the looters, run for your life,' his mother had said.

Bhazabhaza weighed his mother's warning against the cold drinks and other delicacies he saw in evidence among the running crowd. A warning was just a collection of words, an abstraction, whereas cold drinks and morsels were tangible things he could see, touch and smell. And eat! He voted with his palate. But his conscience spoke to him again: honour thy parents…

He woke up from his stupor when the humming swarm of people whizzed past him, leaving him standing there on the side of the road.

'Bhazabhaza, you fat fool, a voice stung his ears, 'why don't you come and join us? We are hitting the other shops up the road!'

He recognised one of the boys from his neighbourhood waving a whole family-size bottle of Coke. His palate suddenly wanted to keep its appointment with the contents of that bottle of Coke. Bhazabhaza made a mental note to later punish the boy for calling him a fat fool. But for now, he was joining the crowd if there was much to be earned by being part of this mass of humanity flowing down the dusty road. A whole bottle of Coke, some cream buns, perhaps? Or even a new collection of marbles. He took a deep breath and waddled in the wake of the angry crowd.

More people were coming out of their houses to join the sensible crowd moving up the road to participate in the business of putting the Indians in their place. The damn exploitative bastards needed to be reminded that this was Africa, for crying out loud. Africans had to hold sway. Even beer brewers agreed with this notion. Or so said street philosophers from the country's black townships. Having consumed a couple of quarts of beer, the philosophers used to sit down to analyse the hidden meaning behind the name Lion Lager, the popular beer brand at the time. LION stood for Let Indians Own Nothing. Full stop. And LAGER was short for Let Africans Get Equal Rights. See, even beer brewers understood the fact that Africans had to be on top and were being undermined by the Indians!

Mind you, these very philosophers from the dusty streets of black townships and shacklands were consuming clear beer illegally as it was still classified as white man's liquor.

But Bhazabhaza wasn't thinking about all these things as he ran after the horde of people.

'Africa!' cried the leader.

'For Africans!' responded the running, panting followers. The fists of those who were not carrying weapons punched the air.

As the human hurricane swept through the streets it sucked more people into its ranks. As the crowd grew, so did the levels of anger. Eventually they arrived in the more affluent section of the settlement, obviously dominated by the Indians.

'Niyabesaba na?' the leader chanted, wanting to know 'are you afraid of them?', an old Zulu war cry.

To which the followers responded gallantly: 'Hhayi, asibesabi siyabafuna!' (Shit, we are not scared of them; we want them!)

And then stones started raining on the nearest house, which was painted a bilious green, with a purple roof and yellow window frames. Windows started breaking. Part of the crowd poured into the house, ransacking it. Others moved to a tiny shop next door and fell on bags of sugar. For a moment, time seemed to freeze in Bhazabhaza's mind. He did not know what to do, which group to follow – those ransacking the house, or those feasting on the goodies inside the shop. How stupid of him to even think he was facing a dilemma! All he wanted was a collection of toffees, at least one family size bottle of Coke; the rest would be a bonus. So he dumped his school bag, which was beginning to be nuisance and ran towards the shop.

The sound of gunfire resounded from inside just as he crossed the threshold. For a moment the looters paused and sized up the Indian shop owner who was training his rifle at them, getting ready to squeeze off another round.

Somebody in the crowd threw a missile which hit the shopkeeper on his head. As he fell, his finger trembled around the trigger, involuntarily releasing a few shots. One of them hit a looter, while others peppered the ceiling. The looter, who had been hit by the bullet, died instantly.

Undeterred by this turn of events, one of the men broke from the group and jumped for the cash register. Two of his friends rushed to help him carry the register away. They ran for their lives. Bhazabhaza was on his knees, stuffing his pockets with coins which had fallen on the ground; stuffing his other pockets with toffees.

Finally, he reached into the rickety fridge and retrieved a bottle of Coke. His whole expedition couldn't have taken him three minutes, but by the time he got up and made to run for it, the other looters had long left. Inside the shop, it was just him, the dead looter and the Indian shopkeeper who was bleeding profusely, groaning in pain.

He was barely five metres out of the door when a loud-hailer ordered him to stop or be shot.

The police!

Twelve

Shattered

BEFORE HE DIED, THE INDIAN shopkeeper made a brief statement in which, as he recalled the events of the day, the dominant image was that of a fat black boy. The fat boy throwing a huge stone, which hit him on his forehead. Then a deluge of people pouring into his shop, looting it. And later, the image of the fat boy towering above him as he lay on the ground, bleeding, slowly slipping into unconsciousness. The brief description fitted Bhazabhaza.

In those days courts were not rigorous in their investigations, especially if the accused was a black person. Blacks were natural law breakers. The law naturally had to break them.

After going through the motions of trying the young Bhazabhaza, the magistrate found him guilty. The snag was that he was still a minor. The magistrate therefore could not have the ultimate sentence – death – imposed upon him. The death sentence was quite common those days. Bhazabhaza was sentenced to an effective ten-year sentence, five of which were suspended. Considering his age, he was to serve his sentence at a reformatory just outside Pietermaritzburg. All things considered, five years in the reformatory wasn't that bad. He would be 20 by the time he came out, still a young man with a whole, productive life ahead of him. Reformatory, it was hoped, would make a man of him, a focused black person who didn't fuck with the white man's law, thank you very much.

'O, *Jesu Mariya Josefa*, what have I done to deserve this?' his mother MaThabethe cried bitterly as her son was led away from the court to the underground cells.

His father, Dlamini, who had left his family two years previously to work in the mines in Johannesburg, wasn't in court. In fact the last letter from him had arrived a year ago. He had even stopped sending money home.

MaThabethe, who had been raising the boy to be a pillar of strength in her old age, had been devastated by the news of his arrest. Now, she was standing helplessly in the court as her precious son was being led away into the cavernous darkness of prison life.

Thirteen

Counterpoint

DEAR ZAKES,

All these things you are saying about Bhazabhaza are truly amazing. Now let me tell you what I remember about Bhazabhaza from that very first day I saw him. I can't say I liked him or did not like him. But the sheer experience of being introduced to him was an occasion all its own. No sooner had we stepped out of the car than the yard in which Bhazabhaza was relaxing in his wheelchair was abuzz with people. Many of these people had just spotted you, Zakes. They wanted to greet the famous musician. Beers were brought to the courtyard, and a spirit of merrymaking suddenly permeated the air.

'Oh, my dear little Lettie, how big you've grown!' that was my aunt shouting as soon as she landed her eyes on me. 'Girl, I have been dreaming about you for the past few months! This is the girl I have been dreaming about, baby.' She was addressing the man in the wheelchair.

'Ag, you and your booze-inspired dreams! What haven't you dreamt about? I bet you've even dreamt about Jesus Christ himself making a pass at you!'

'Ag, *suka wena* Bhaza,' my aunt said, 'you're always harbouring thoughts of jealousy!'

Chairs were brought over to the courtyard. We all sat down. It seemed to us that our arrival had offered Bhazabhaza and my aunt, and the countless other families with whom they shared the yard, a great excuse to throw a party. Case after case of beer was brought through. The throng of people grew in volume. Many of the people were not just miserly gatecrashers. They brought their own beer and their own money to join the party.

The man from next door told all and sundry that he had slaughtered a lamb the previous night and was prepared to share with the rest of us.

'So when were you going to offer us the meat, you miserly piece of shit?' Bhazabhaza wanted to know.

'I think my gods could tell that a great man like Zakes would be coming to pay us a visit. So, people of Clermont, I offer this side of lamb in honour of this auspicious visit by the one and only, Zakes.'

The music that had been playing in the background suddenly grew in volume. People took to the floor, doing the marabi dance.

As the atmosphere warmed up around the courtyard you, Zakes, suddenly got up to dance. After a few turns on the dance floor, you systematically moved towards me. You reached for my hand and without saying a word, asked me for a dance. I did not refuse you, even though God knew I couldn't dance to save my life. You moved with such ease and grace that a person watching us couldn't tell that you were teaching me how to dance.

Zakes, my heart was constricted. I found it hard to breathe. I felt waterfalls of sweat dripping underneath my armpits, a ringing noise in my ears. My throat was parched. I licked my dry lips repeatedly to stop myself dying of dehydration.

For a brief moment, I thought I could see butterflies through the open door. You turned me around gracefully. I felt your body suddenly freezing.

'What the hell is wrong with the world now?' you said, slurring your words, 'What the hell is it with these butterflies?'

At that particular moment the music had stopped, and someone was trying to change the record.

'These butterflies are getting to me!' you said.

'What butterflies?' someone asked.

'There, out there floating about,' you said.

People looked outside the door, threw their heads back and laughed out loud: 'This booze must be good, it's making him see butterflies.'

There were swarms of butterflies in the streets, and children were shouting excitedly, chasing them. But the drunken fools inside couldn't see the butterflies.

But then, it suddenly dawned on me that only you, Zakes, the children and I could see the butterflies. Not even Sis Jane could see them. She thought you were still thinking about the butterflies we had seen at your house earlier that day. But there were hundreds of butterflies outside. This was very puzzling. Earlier, back in Chesterville, Sis Jane had been able to see the butterflies; but now she couldn't. I stopped dancing and went outside. What I observed there confirmed what I already knew: that adult people couldn't see the butterflies. They kept saying irritably, 'Why are these crazy children making noise about butterflies?'

'Ah, leave them alone. Maybe it's a new game they are playing.'

Bhazabhaza, who'd disappeared into the house, rejoined us in the courtyard. He had in his hands a shiny instrument which you called the alto saxophone. Remember how beautiful the music sounded? Tears welled in your eyes.

When he finished playing his saxophone, Bhazabhaza said in a clear voice, and with a stupid smile on his face: 'That number was for the pregnant lady over here,' he said pointing at me. People stopped talking, looking at me.

Bhazabhaza continued: 'But where is the father of the child? Ha ha ha ha. Is it going to be another bastard? Please don't tell me the drunken fool who sees butterflies where there are none is the father!'

Fourteen

Big Hugh

Dear Lettie,

Now, you see, that was the Bhazabhaza I knew. Always looking for a fight. But let me tell you how he started playing the saxophone.

During the second week of his stay at the reformatory, he was with a group of boys washing in one of the communal showers. By that time they had tired of making fun of his fatty disposition, the layers of unattractive meat around his girth. But there was a boy, much older than him, who could not seem to remove his eyes from Bhazabhaza's nakedness. That boy should have been sent to adult prison, but had gotten away with it by lying about his age.

At last, he just couldn't help himself but touched fat Bhazabhaza's bum as they were showering. Bhazabhaza dismissed it as an accident. But the other guy touched him again. Now the other boys were looking at the two, some of them tittering nervously. The other boy touched Bhazabhaza again. And that was it. Bhazabhaza punched him in the gut, knocking the wind out of him. The older boy came back with a punch to Bhazabhaza's chin. He slipped and fell on the floor. The older boy waited patiently for him saying: 'Now you've started it, fatty-boom-boom. I am going to fuck you with my fists, and fuck you with my dick as well. And I want all these other boys to watch.'

Bhazabhaza remembered his style of fighting that had never failed him in the school playground. He bent forward and charged like an enraged bull. He rammed his head right in the middle of the bigger boy's tummy. They collapsed on the wet floor, to excited ululations from the spectators. Bhazabhaza moved fast to pin his adversary to the ground, spitting repeatedly into his face. But then he remembered the code of the street: winning the fight wasn't important, just as long as your enemy knew you could fight. Anyone can win a fight

– it's just the timing and the circumstances that determine it. He was about to release the adversary when one of the male teachers came running into the showering area and started caning the boys. They got up and ran out of the bathrooms, still naked. There was whistling and ululating from the girls' section of the reformatory on the other side of the fence.

As punishment, the two boys were locked together in a cell. Within a day of being confined there, they were the best of friends. Big Hugh, for that was the name of the other boy, was a juvenile of unremitting delinquency who had been to institutions such as these a number of times. He had broken into shops, picked people's pockets, had forced his sister to have sex with another man for money.

'When we get out of this place,' Bhazabhaza was saying, 'we can make a good team, you and me. There are many opportunities. We can get into cars. We can get into robbing the dockyards.'

'Why do you want to go for the risky stuff that can result in the spilling of blood? Let's go sell bitches,' said Hugh.

'My man, that's the spirit!' exclaimed Bhazabhaza. 'Imagination! But that kind of shit takes a lot out of you. You have to train the bitches. You have to watch them otherwise they eat your money. When they are sick, you don't eat. Sometimes they run away, or get stolen by the bigger pussy pedlars.'

'Man, look at the positive side of things,' replied Hugh. 'Bitches bring you glamour. Have you seen how popular pimps can be? Everyone loves a pimp. I've got another way of attracting fame and glamour. I am a shit hot musician; I play the saxophone and can sing too.'

'See? We're getting somewhere now. You attract those bitches with your saxophone, I take some of them and start putting them on the street. Those will be tasty bitches, man, hanging out with a well-known musician!'

A week after their release from punitive confinement, they started frequenting the reformatory school's music laboratory. The lab was well-stocked with music books, a piano, two guitars, a drum kit, a trumpet and a saxophone. Playfully, Big Hugh started teaching his new-found friend how to play the saxophone. They were becoming close friends. But what irritated Bhazabhaza was that his friend was known to bother other boys at night, crawling into their beds and doing outrages to them. But, hey, thought Bhazabhaza, that's the price some people have to pay for finding themselves on the wrong side of the law.

In the second year of his stay at the reformatory, Bhazabhaza was a competent saxophone player. A band had been started, with Big Hugh as the leader. They played on special days such as Easter, Christmas day and so on. They were also occasionally made to perform for important visitors such as magistrates and other top government officials when they made inspection visits.

But disaster struck the following year: Big Hugh was released. Suddenly Bhazabhaza was alone again. His last year in prison was long. By the time he got out, he had been in so many fights he had lost count. His violent nature, and the fact that he had outgrown the reformatory, saw him being transferred to a real prison where he became a hardened fighter.

He was 19 when he was finally released from jail.

Fifteen

Lonely Road

THE EARLY SIXTIES WERE A DRY, mean and lean season for the black people of South Africa. In fact, the decade started on the wrong foot right from the beginning. In 1960, the major black political organisations, notably the African National Congress and the Pan Africanist Congress were outlawed. Their leaders, including Nelson Mandela, spent long spells in jail.

South Africa was kicked out of the United Nations for its apartheid policies. The country was a dreary place to be.

But none of these momentous political developments had any relevance or direct bearing on the life of Bhazabhaza. What was important to him was that he was being released from jail on August 8, 1960. Having spent the larger part of his teenage years at reformatory school, and his early adult life in jail, he couldn't even begin to imagine how much the world outside had changed.

While inside he had followed, albeit with not much interest, the news of what was happening out there. For example, he knew that Cato Manor, the settlement in which he had been born, had been demolished by government edict. Former inhabitants were carted off to various racially segregated neighbourhoods: Indians were shipped off to a newly created suburb called Chatsworth; Africans were sent to various townships with names such as Umlazi, KwaMashu and so on; whites were distributed around the suburbs of Malvern, Cavendish and so on; while coloureds were resettled in Wentworth.

More than anything else, it was the depressing collapse of the great Cato Manor that unsettled him about the world beyond the tall prison walls. He had no intention of going back to that world. It was now alien to him. Prison life was what he knew and understood best. It was a year after the Pan Africanist Congress had broken away from the African National Congress, the dominant political voice of the black people at the time. Historical records will show that the PAC felt that the white people within the ranks of the ANC had neutralised black anger and were thus delaying black liberation. The PAC leaders thought that no sane white person could sincerely forgo the privileges he enjoyed solely because of his race and throw in his lot with the oppressed black people. PAC leaders wanted to take the fight to the apartheid rulers. One of the avenues they pursued to translate their anger into action was calling on all black people to burn their identification documents, the very documents that they felt were tangible proof of their status as second class citizens in their own country. These documents restricted their movements in the country of their own birth; these documents, in a way, spelt out black people's station in life. The documents indirectly implied as to what kind of jobs black people could perform — as the rest were reserved for whites. The burning of their identification documents would culminate in the banning of the ANC and the PAC, and the beginning of the armed struggle by these two major black parties. But all these things did not mean much to Bhazabhaza; he was concerned with locating his mother.

It didn't take him long to locate his mother and his uncle in KwaMashu. He stayed with them for a few months, doing odd jobs in the neighbourhood while he considered the next step he could take to find himself something to do now that he was outside of jail. He knew he wouldn't lead a nine to five existence like other ordinary human beings. But he nevertheless stayed with his uncle for a while, biding his time. It was around this period in his wanderings that I encountered him.

Sixteen

The Big Payday

THIS WAS GOING TO BE THE big payday for Bhazabhaza and the crew. Big Hugh, his prison mate with whom he had hooked up, had done thorough research at the dockyards and knew that a huge consignment of merchandise from China had just landed.

Radios, calculators, watches, torches and other paraphernalia had been off-loaded from the ship and transferred to a waiting goods train. The goods train would then transport the goods to the main dispatching area at Rossburgh station where they would be loaded onto trucks that would distribute them countrywide. The plan, then, was for Bhazabhaza's crew to intercept the goods while they were still in the dockyards where the security wasn't that tight.

Late that Friday night, they sat outside Big Hugh's shack going through the finer points of the visit to the dockyards.

'You're sure there's only one security guard in that specific corner of the dockyard?' Bhazabhaza asked.

'Positive,' said Big Hugh taking a long puff on his dagga pipe. 'In fact, the poor sod spends most of his time sitting in front of a brazier, smoking cigarette after cigarette. The only snag is that he carries a gun.'

'We have to immobilise him before we can even begin to do our job,' suggested Makinati, who had been quiet all along.

Around eight o'clock they got into Big Hugh's Dodge bakkie.

Twenty minutes later, they were parked outside the dockyard, watching the security guard on the other side of the fence putting more wood into his brazier. He lit a cigarette, took a huge puff and sat comfortably on his wooden chair and enjoyed the fire.

He had no way of knowing that on the other side of the fence, predators were getting ready to pounce.

Even if the guard turned towards them, he would not be able to see the car, it was so dark on the other side of the fence. There were also trees in the shadows that provided cover.

'It's time to spring into action, boys,' said Big Hugh, picking up his huge pliers. Bhazabhaza picked up his baseball bat and Makinati touched his axe. They left the car and walked quietly towards the fence between them and the huge wealth lurking inside the containers.

Big Hugh started cutting a huge hole through the fence. The security guard stood up, stretched, and walked around the well-lit area immediately next to the fire. He touched his holster and turned to look directly at the spot where the young men were crouching. For a moment, the three young men thought he could see them. But the guard went back to his perch in front of the fire, smoking his cigarette peacefully.

Bhazabhaza was the first to walk through the huge hole his mate had cut. His heart was throbbing with anxiety, his palms sweating as he tightened his grip around the baseball bat.

This is no way to make a living, thought Bhazabhaza, I am approaching a man armed with a gun and what have I got? A fucking baseball bat!

His foot stepped on a handful of dry leaves. Alerted by the noise, the security guard turned... but was too late.

Bhazabhaza swung the bat smack into the middle of the guard's face. The guard fell backwards, the back of his head almost landing in the middle of the burning brazier.

'Quick, Bhazabhaza,' said Hugh, 'one slug is enough. You don't want to kill the arsehole. Just paralyse him long enough for us to finish our job.'

In that instant, Bhazabhaza was overwhelmed with rare anger. He thought of the years he had spent in prison for a killing he never committed. White justice. He saw himself taking another slug at the prone figure.

'Are you crazy, arsehole?' the other was screaming. 'You kill that man and we are in shit!'

'Who gives a damn?' Bhazabhaza was hitting the guard all over his body, breaking his kneecaps, ribs. The fury was unbelievable. In all of this, he was seeing the face of the magistrate who had sent him to jail. The magistrate had been white. The guard was white. White justice, black anger.

He had to be dragged away from the corpse, for the guard was certainly dead now. He quickly reached for the guard's gun while his friends were not watching. The gun would come in handy one day. With a gun he felt more powerful – invincible.

By that time, Makinati had broken the lock of the container and was busy unloading boxes filled with watches and calculators.

'Gentlemen,' Big Hugh was saying, 'We are made! We are rich. We won't need to work for a long time. Joe-the-Indian is gonna love us for this.'

'We are going to make two thousand rand easy,' Makinati said as he wiped sweat from his face and dropped the last box of watches into the back of the bakkie.

They drove away. Indeed, Joe-the-Indian, the fence who sold stolen goods, paid them two thousand rand. He, in turn, would be making double that amount.

From that hit, Bhazabhaza realised he would not be doing the dockyards again. He had killed. He would have to leave the yards for poor up-and-coming criminals from the ghetto. He had graduated to bigger, deadlier things.

Seventeen

Seven Steps to Heaven

Dear Lettie,

In 1970 two things happened that were to change my life forever. Two things. One, I found God. Two, I found God. God revealed Himself in His two incarnations. It is said God moves among us. He lives with us. He lives within us. He is us. Yet it takes some people a lifetime to find Him. Others never find him in their lifetime. Yes, many are called, few are chosen. I had spent thousands of hours reading theological texts; thousands of hours praying; thousands of hours listening to my own father's religious teachings; thousands of hours preaching to other people; yet God continued to elude me. But when I found Him, he revealed himself twice. He was a black man. A black man with two incarnations. Two souls. Two powers. His one face was that of a young black man with smooth ebony skin, a proud nose, thick lips and piercing eyes. The lips were moulded into a perpetual pout, as if he was always ready to blow the world. This face had been known to me for a lifetime, but it was only in 1970 that I found the true essence of this face. This one face, this one incarnation of God, was Miles Davis. The Miles Davis who released Bitches Brew in 1970. A year of revelation. A year of redemption.

The other face of God was that of a young black man with a brown complexion. He had high cheekbones. He had a noticeable gap between his top front teeth. A gap he had been born with, not a gap caused by some intrusive accident. This God had a goatee, and just a hint of sideburns. The hair was short and crinkly. The eyes were intense. There was a ready smile hovering about this face. This face of God was Steve Biko. The second incarnation of the God who revealed himself to me in 1970. This face of God had been studying at the same university as me, studying medicine, learning how to mend broken bodies – but finally excelling in mending broken souls and broken black pride. These were the two Gods who made me forsake the Bible I had been embracing as a torch, as a magic wand that helped me negotiate my way around this valley called life. These Gods said to me: 'Son of man, wake up and know who you are.' I left my studies at the university. I turned my back on my earthly parents for I had found salvation. My salvation was the duopoly of Miles and Biko.

You see, I come from a religious family, my father and his father before him having been ministers in the Salvation Army. Not only were they religious men, but they also had a weakness for things of a military nature, hence their affinity for the Salvation Army.

My grandfather, it is said, enlisted in the army during the First World War. To his chagrin, however, he discovered that black people could only serve as cooks and cleaners in the army. Now my grandfather was useless in the matter of making fires, which is why he didn't last long in the army. He was kicked out even before members of the South African Native Corps, the black unit he was to serve in, could leave South Africa for Europe. Disappointed and angry at the rejection, grandfather tried to take his own life. The only problem was that he chose a miserable way of exiting the world: he set himself alight. But he was useless making fires. So, he tried a number of times – and failed – to set himself on fire. Ultimately, he died a slow, painful death from burns sustained over a couple of hours and countless attempts at turning himself into a human torch.

Perhaps, inspired by his father's wishes, my own father decided to enlist in the army when the Second World War came around. Of the many acts of gallantry that he achieved while he served as a cook for the white soldiers in the army, was learning to play the trumpet and other wind instruments. He became a devout member of the Salvation Army, an affectation he instilled in the rest of his family when he was discharged from the army.

As a result, I learnt to play a few musical instruments at my father's knee. By the time I finished high school, I was proficient at a number of instruments, but my first love was the trumpet. At my father's insistence, when I finished high school, I enrolled at the University of Natal where I studied theology. I took private lessons in music – all in the service of the Lord.

But when 1970 came around, and Steve Biko told me what a fool I was wasting my time studying theology, an exercise meant to help me understand how to best sugar-coat the bitter pill of my oppression; when Miles Davis released Bitches Brew, a piece of music that ignited in me something that I never realised existed, I was ushered into another world altogether.

As I said, I had heard Miles, but it was only because of Bitches Brew that I listened to the oracle. He spoke to me. He spoke to my soul. He spoke to my muse. He said, fuck, Peace, you will never find peace as long as you continue shuffling along to the stupid Salvation Army Brass Band shit. You're up to your throat in the shit that's killing your spirit so get the shit out of the shit if you want to find me, your God. For I don't go to no place where there's predictable shit like your Salvation Army Brass Band shit.

Miles called me by my given name, he said Peace, lift up your head to the mountains and look at me, find me, find the paean to life. He said I'm revealing myself to you, Peace. Take this opportunity and come and touch the hem of my robe and you shall achieve redemption, or you shall forever drown in your own mediocre shit, he said to me. He said come glide, swagger and prance with me, motherfucker.

And so I turned my back on university, I turned my back on my father's house, and took to pounding the streets in search of the home that Miles Davis told me existed just beyond the horizon. It was a home inhabited by many like him, a home that would offer me a spiritual refuge. The home I was looking for was a good jazz band.

As a classically trained musician, I had listened to a lot of music in my lifetime – everything from classical music to jazz in all its incarnations. Everything from boogie-woogie to Dixieland; from the disturbing hollers of bebop to the mellow sounds of swing. But the stew that Miles Davis cooked on Bitches Brew was something out of this world, so out of this world it inspired me to rebel against my father, risk a serious beating and a possible expulsion from the family. Before my father could say anything about my decision to quit university, I beat him to it. I started walking the streets looking for the home that Miles Davis promised existed somewhere just over the horizon.

One of the hot bands of the time was Heshoo Beshoo – with the Sithole brothers on saxophones, the crippled Cyril Magubane on guitar, Ernest Motlhe on bass, and drummer Nelson Magwaza. It was during one of their concerts at Curries Fountain stadium that I decided to befriend them.

Because I had my trumpet with me, after the show they allowed me to join them for a jam session. We drove around in their kombi, hitting a number of drinking places in Clermont, Chesterville, KwaMashu. At almost all these places, they had a jam session. Because they were tired and drunk, they allowed me free reign. I played my lungs out. My efforts didn't go unnoticed by Bhazabhaza, who was playing host to members of this band that came all the way from Johannesburg. Bhazabhaza the man about town himself joined the band during the heady jam sessions, and proved his mettle as a saxophonist and powerful singer.

When it was time for the Johannesburgers to go back home, the generous Bhazabhaza who had supplied the visitors with food, booze, accommodation and women suddenly found himself stuck with me, a shy little religious boy whose sheltered life had denied him exposure to the debauchery that had taken place during that eventful weekend.

Bhazabhaza was at the peak of his career around this time. A well-known jazz saxophonist who always had a bevy of women at his beck and call. But it soon turned out that apart from being a musician, he was also an entrepreneur engaged in shady business.

Just a street from Bhazabhaza's yard was a famous shebeen called Mountain Dew. It was frequented by people who were new in town, country bumpkins working for the municipality picking up night-soil buckets and rubbish bins. These were love-starved men who were so lonely they flung themselves into the arms of local girls no matter what notorious bitches they were. One of the women who frequented Mountain Dew was a girl called Thandi who would sleep with as many as five men per night – as long as they bought her beer.

One Friday night, a few years before when he was still in the business of robbing dockyards, Bhazabhaza had decided to go to Mountain Dew to have a beer. But he had more on his mind than just a couple of beers.

He spotted Thandi as she walked into the yard. She was wearing a sleeveless summer dress that accentuated her lean waist. Her tiny breasts were surprisingly firm and pointed for one who had been a mattress on which so many men had lolled in her young life. She wore no bra. She wore red panties which showed prominently beneath her see-through, pale yellow dress.

'Hey, Thandi, how are you?' he said, feeling his manhood harden.

'Good, my man, what are you doing here? I thought people in your line of business get very busy on Friday evenings.'

'I've quit that line, you know. I am exploring a whole new line of business now. And you are going to help me get started,' he said simply, as he poured her a glass of beer.

She emptied the glass in one long gulp, then sat back, smiling at Bhazabhaza.

'You gotta tell me more, sweetheart.'

Later that evening, both of them more than a little tipsy, they ended up at Thandi's shack. They made passionate love for hours, smoking huge quantities of dagga in between. Finally spent, they collapsed into each other's arms and fell asleep.

In the middle of the night, Bhazabhaza got up and started shaking Thandi urgently.

'Hey, bitch, get up, get up!'

Thandi was angry with the sudden commotion. 'Hey, what's happening? Why are you disturbing my sleep?'

She didn't finish those words. He slapped her hard across the face. She opened her mouth to say: 'What's happening?' Another slap as loud as thunder. Blood began to run from one of her nostrils. A tough street fighter herself, she tried to sink her sharp nails into him, but he moved just slightly out of her reach and punched her hard in the tummy. That's how you temporarily cripple a bitch, his prison friends had told him. You punch her hard in the tummy before she can reach your balls and slice them open with her sharp nails.

He reached underneath the bed for his gun, the same gun he'd stolen from the dockyard security guard he'd killed. He pressed it tightly against her temple.

'You know what this is?' he asked through clenched teeth. 'Do you, bitch?'

'Yes,' she said. Her bowels gave.

'Shit, bitch, go on shit, bitch! Whenever you see me you must shit in your pants. Do you hear? I want you to shit and piss in your pants when you see me!'

While she was gasping for air, he climbed on her and drove his hard penis into her violently. For hours, he rammed her, enjoying her pain. At daybreak he left her house, leaving her almost unconscious.

As an afterthought, he came back to the house and said to her: 'If I were you, I wouldn't leave this house at all today. I would clean myself up and relax in bed for there is a big assignment ahead of us. Do you hear me?'

'Yes, Bhuti Bhazabhaza,' she said weakly.

'Yes, I like it when young girls call me big brother. We are beginning to speak the same language. So long, I will see you later, nice, clean and relaxed, remember?'

'Yes, Bhuti Bhazabhaza.'

He left. Later that afternoon, he came back to her house bearing a packet of fresh fruit, yoghurt and a packet of dagga. They ate and smoked. But she was tense, not knowing his intentions.

He deliberately put the gun on the table, to drive more fear into her.

And that, in a nutshell, was how Bhazabhaza started his empire as a pimp those many years ago. In the months that followed, more girls joined him, and he got them working hard.

His place came to be known as Seven Steps to Heaven, after his favourite Miles Davis number.

My relationship with Bhazabhaza moved seamlessly from one of simple friendship to business partner. I never asked him for work, nor did he ever officially appoint me as his business partner. Things just fell into place as if our destinies had been decided by some powerful force somewhere in the ether, that we were destined to be with each other. This symbiosis was to last until he died. Our paths would keep crossing, for better or for worse.

While Bhazabhaza concentrated on making sure the girls were doing their work, I started a steady and highly lucrative business selling booze from the premises. Next, we ventured into the business of promoting live music. We hosted numerous live jazz gigs – ranging from small local outfits such as the Keynotes to big motherfuckers with players such as Kippie Moeketsie, who occasionally came down to the coast from the big city of gold.

All these interactions with the important musicians of the time offered me an opportunity to practise my music regularly. I never was a permanent member of any band, but I played with many of them. This helped me experiment, keep in touch with the latest, and, of course, communicate with my Miles whose music had become a staple diet at our house and wherever we travelled.

Bhazabhaza and I called our music promotions company BP Promotions. (Bhazabhaza and Peace, dig?) After live music, our second speciality became hosting beauty pageants. These were quite popular and drew big crowds, and were cheap to host. All we needed were the prizes: a lounge suite, a clothing hamper and a cosmetics hamper for the winning girl, and prize money of R500. The first and second princesses received clothing and cosmetics hampers, and consolation purses of R200 each. At the beginning we supplied all

139

of these prizes from our own pockets. But as our fame spread around the province, big furniture shops such as Ellerines and Town Talk were knocking on our doors, offering to sponsor the prizes in exchange for publicity. So our contests had to have the name of the sponsor thrown in somewhere: Miss Durban Ellerines, Miss Natal Ellerines and so on. We made lots of money from the door takings.

A few weeks after each contest, after all the hype had died down, Bhazabhaza and I would get in touch with the girls for some fun. Others simply abandoned whatever dreams they had been pursuing in their small boring lives, happy to live with us, chasing the glamorous life of beauty queens. Each person, I decided, worshipped their own gods. My gods were Miles and Biko, while the girls believed in the god of money and leisure. Except that the god of money and leisure didn't stay with them for a long time because after a few months of having fun with them, we threw them out. Sometime Bhazabhaza found other uses for them – in his ever-burgeoning crew of prostitutes.

Those days, if you were running a business in the township you had to have the backing and the protection of powerful and feared gangsters. Even though Bhazabhaza was himself a feared killer, he hired members of the Makwaito as additional security. Not only did they patrol the street on which Seven Steps to Heaven was situated, but they also acted as security guards whenever we had jazz concerts.

Their mythical leader was SomJerry, a big fellow whose reputation as a fighter preceded him. I get irritated and utterly exasperated these days when people tell me stories about contemporary brawlers. I say to them, bring me SomJerry any time and you will see the essence of street fighting. In the heyday of street fighting, SomJerry strutted the streets like a prize cock – and everyone avoided the streets like the plague. He was apparently as tall as a lamp-post, but as thick as a tractor. His arms dangled just below his knees when he was at ease and not pummelling some poor sod with his sledgehammer hands. SomJerry may have existed in the past, but he was long dead. But in the popular mind, he continued to live. He was a legend, and his name was invoked as a warning to anyone who threatened Bhazabhaza's business.

His feet were so big that no factory-made shoe fitted him. When he was still a kid, the kind monks at the Marianhill Monastery, where he had grown up as an orphan, had made him shoes in order to accommodate his giant feet.

While many of the street fighters swore by their knives, SomJerry apparently preferred a butcher's meat cleaver. Whenever he happened to be in pursuit of some thief who had offended one of his many clients, the big man did not hesitate to demolish the whole street of shacks single-handedly in search of the thief's hiding place. With this kind of mythical fighter on our side, we were safe.

In addition to his old kombi and a maroon Buick, Bhazabhaza bought himself an open-top Pontiac. In due course, I was driving the car, ferrying girls to and from their assignments on the streets of Durban.

If my father could only see his son driving such a smart car. Things were looking good. What could go wrong?

Eighteen

'Round Midnight

FROM THE PROCEEDS OF OUR beauty pageants and music concerts, we had become so rich that we could buy, for cash, a spanking new minibus, which we immediately put to use ferrying musicians from all over the place to the big halls of Durban where they performed to big crowds.

'This shit is a real money spinner,' Bhazabhaza said excitedly, 'Why didn't we think of the idea earlier? Go right ahead and get some of these up and coming bands around the province. Whenever you need transport, you can use my own transport.'

The entertainment-starved townships around Durban enjoyed the shows, which brought a number of acts including the Shange brothers from KwaMashu, Ronnie Madonsela from Umlazi, Dalton Khanyile, and many others. I made the most of these shows because not only was I the promoter, but I also managed to squeeze myself in, playing with whichever band would have me.

It was Easter Friday when Drive, one of the hot new outfits, honoured our invitation to play at the Ndunduma community hall. The bonhomie that accompanied the arrival of the band was palpable.

All through the night, they were playing great jazz – ranging from old American standards, to South African-inspired shit.

'And now, ladies and gentlemen, we are happy to invite on stage our hosts Bhazabhaza and Peace. These gentlemen are not only good hosts who are doing wonders for the promotion of the arts in this province, but they are accomplished musicians themselves, as you will soon see.'

That night, Bhazabhaza was wearing tight black leather pants, black high-heeled boots, a white shirt buttoned up to the neck and a knee-length black leather coat. He finished the smooth image with a leather cap and dark sunglasses.

I, on the other hand, had on red leather pants and a matching sleeveless leather vest, which allowed me to show off my muscles. I had begun lifting weights, and my body was well-toned, which didn't go unnoticed with the girls. I also had on a red leather cap and dark Chinese style glasses.

Bhazabhaza and I gave each other a high five, and started sauntering to the stage where our instruments were waiting for us. There were cheers from the audience, and a resounding drum roll from the band on stage.

The first number we did was Coltrane's 'Afro Blue'. Despite his lack of discipline and practice, Bhazabhaza was a technically accomplished player. He was playing a soprano saxophone for this particular segment of the show. He was more at home on the tenor and trumpet, but I had on occasion listened to him take his chances on the soprano and alto. I love that in a man. A person who takes chances. Isn't that what life is all about, taking chances? Isn't life itself a gamble? Bhazabhaza wasn't bad at all. He played clean and competently. But when he ran out of ideas — and you are bound to run out of ideas if you don't practice regularly — he would glide into the land of vibrato. Now I hate that shit. But the crowd just loved it when he blew one long, vibrating note.

He had his eyes closed, head thrown back in intense concentration, lips wrapped around the mouthpiece, veins standing out on his neck, and he was luxuriating in the experience of the thunderous cheers that accompanied the long vibrating note he was coaxing out of his horn.

I jumped in before he even indicated he was done with his solo. He opened his eyes abruptly, looking at me dirtily. I paid no mind to him and eased gently into the rhythm. I glided and I soared; I bobbed and I weaved, moving from low-low register to pitched, ear-splitting hollers.

The hall went quiet when I used the palm of my hand to mute my horn, creating a distorted sound. Then, still blowing, I walked towards the nearest wall. I brought my horn as close to the wall as possible, and blew a series of warbled riffs. I turned to look at Bhazabhaza. He was visibly stunned. He hadn't realised that while he was gallivanting with the girls, I took every available minute to experiment, to listen to Miles telling me how to break the boundaries. I wished I could be sitting in the audience, watching and listening to myself. I wished I could behold my sound as it ricocheted off the wall, hitting me in the face with its ferocity. I wondered what I sounded and looked like from the point of view of the audience.

Bhazabhaza was the first one to clap and holler when I finished my solo.

We played a few more numbers, with Bhazabhaza dropping the soprano sax in preference for the tenor. He eased into a slow groove and immediately got into a breathy vibrato. Amazingly, the vibrato on tenor sax was not as irritating as it had been on soprano. In fact the more he played, the more I thought I could hear the earthy tones of Stanley Turrentine in his phrasing.

Bhazabhaza and the organist moved into that realm of tenor-organ duet à la Jimmy Smith and Turrentine, swaggering and galloping along the undulating plains of mellow music. The drummer and bassist were there somewhere in the background, but the groove was being dominated by the tenor-organ combination. Man, we were cruising. We were loving it, and the audience was loving it.

It was sometime around midnight. I was in the middle of a solo when there was pandemonium at the door. Somebody shouted that some armed gangsters had taken the door money at gun point. The Makwaitos gang, our protectors, sprang into action. Blades flashed dimly as the Makwaitos took the fight to the new invaders. One of the marauders shot at a light bulb. Fire broke out.

'Where's SomJerry, somebody call SomJerry!' I heard Bhazabhaza's voice crying out.

The air was suddenly filled with the name of SomJerry.

But the fire intensified. There were screams of anguish and panic. I saw a man, who had turned into a human torch, running around in confused circles. Someone managed to knock him down to the floor in order to extinguish the flames. The smell of burning flesh hit my nostrils as I went about rescuing people, pushing them out of the inferno. The hall was gutted that night.

Early the following morning Bhazabhaza, myself and some members of the Makwaito stood surveying what remained of the hall. Some pieces of rubble were still smouldering. A lady's high-heeled shoe just nearby; a purse not far away; the remains of a chair. The place smelled of destruction, of pain, of loss, of anger.

'I am really disappointed in you boys,' Bhazabhaza spoke softly to the four members of the Makwaito. Other members of this once sizeable gang, which usually numbered around 30, seemed to have disappeared.

'Bra Bee, we are terribly sorry about what happened. We will pay you back your money for the mess. Besides, we are ready to give those thugs payback. We have a reputation to protect. A man of your stature should get the respect he deserves. What those thugs did was a loud and clear exhibition of disrespect and rudeness. Now they must pay, and will pay.'

'I hear you,' said I, 'but where was SomJerry last night? This wouldn't have happened had he been present. He must be made to pay!' I said vehemently.

The four gangsters, their guns in their hands, looked at each other. I couldn't help noticing that their eyes avoided mine.

After a long time, Bhazabhaza looked at me. Slowly, his face melted into a shy smile. Then he threw his head back and broke out into a loud guffaw.

As if on cue, the other members of the gang joined him, laughing raucously.

'Where was SomJerry?' Bhazabhaza repeated the line, laughing until tears streamed from his eyes. 'Where was SomJerry?'

SomJerry didn't exist. He was just a legendary figure conjured up to drive the fear of God into the hearts of those who thought of doing us harm! Somebody with the name of SomJerry had indeed existed in the Durban underworld. But he had died a long time ago. His memory was invoked by people in the underworld with such sincerity that some people, including me, actually thought the man still existed. His physical attributes and prowess as a fighter were highly exaggerated. Only the seasoned thugs of Durban knew the truth about SomJerry. And clearly I didn't.

'But all is not lost,' Jackson, who seemed to be the leader of the gang, said after he had recovered from his fit of laughter, 'Boys, come with me. Let me show you what Makwaitos can do.'

He led us to his bakkie that was packed with baseball bats.

'Put your guns away, and take these,' he said as he handed each of us a baseball bat.

We followed him to the basement underneath the gutted hall. It was dark and damp there. Cowering in the corner were two young men who had been tied so tightly together that they couldn't move. Wads of tape were pasted across their mouths to stop them from screaming and attracting unnecessary attention. The basement smelled of fear and the products of their bowels.

'These are the punks who were part of the posse that fucked-up Bra Bee's money last night,' Jackson spat out. He roughly peeled the bands of tape from the mouths of the punks.

'If you let us go, we can tell you where they are hiding the money,' one of the boys said.

'We'll give you the addresses and all,' said the other.

My anger was growing by the minute. It wasn't that I was angry at the loss of money. I was angry because these punks had disturbed me while I was just getting into the groove of playing. You see, for me music wasn't just the act of entertaining crowds of people; for me, music was a spiritual journey. I felt the more I played the more I understood who I was, and what my mission was on this Earth. Parting me from my music then, or disturbing me while I played was not only the height of insolence, but it was a threat to my very sanity, my very life. True, I was an easy-going chap who could converse with all classes of people, but I was happiest on stage.

Every time I got on stage, I recalled something I had heard about Charles Mingus, that son of a gun who could play the bass like an angel. Or like the devil himself.

Mingus, the story goes, was sitting with Charlie 'Bird' Parker, the great alto saxophonist, inside a jazz club where they were due to play. The subject under discussion was Buddhism, the religion with which both cats were fascinated. Suddenly the club owner raised his hand, indicating it was time for them to get on stage and start playing. Getting up, Bird said to Mingus: 'Well, it's time to go. Let's finish the discussion on the bandstand.'

And they did just that – got on stage and continued their discussion there through their music. Over the years of playing, I have found that these discussions on stage are much deeper, more soul-searching, more spiritual, more probing, more satisfying than normal discussions that people ordinarily hold over bottles of booze or plates of food. Music is not just the technical competence of playing an instrument, or projecting a voice in a majestic manner; music is a conversation with the self; a continuous process of self-discovery and revelation; a conversation with a higher power. That's what I've found out.

I suppose this is what sparked my anger at the boys who were cowering in the basement; they had deprived me of yet another leg of my spiritual journey. They had violated me. They had to be punished accordingly.

Stix, one of the boys in our crew, a skinny little boy who had that distant gaze that you see in the eyes of habitual killers, moved slowly forward. He lifted his baseball bat and brought it down hard on the kneecap of one of the youths. The kid yelped in pain, then fainted.

The other youth gave us all the names and addresses that we needed. Satisfied with the information, Bhazabhaza said it was time to go. I was the first to turn away from the miserable sight of the boys.

'And just where do you think you are going?' Bhazabhaza asked.

'I'm out of here. Let's hit the road and leave these miserable sods here.'

They all looked at me as if I was mad.

'Here,' Bhazabhaza said, giving me his own baseball bat as if the one I was carrying wasn't enough. 'Put the buggers out of their misery.'

That day I surprised myself because not once did I hesitate. I took the bat and moved calmly to the teenager who was crying, pleading for his life. Memories of me communicating with my demons through my trumpet the previous night flashed in my mind; the anger of this intuitive moment being snatched from me by these gun-toting punks welled within me.

I smashed the face of the youth once, twice, three times. Teeth and fragments of bone scattered around the floor. I turned to the next kid, the one who'd fainted, and delivered blows to his head with equal vehemence.

After the dull thud of my bat against the boy's skull, a great silence settled over the damp basement. We could hear dogs barking in the distance. From the depth of the basement, traffic noises were muted.

I walked away. I was ascending the steps out of the basement when I heard a dull thud as someone finished off the other boy. There was a short clapping of hands.

Over the next few days, we systematically raided the homes of members of the amaPhela, the gang that had had the temerity to rob us of so much money and then go on to ruin our reputation by burning down the hall.

When people say your life can change overnight, it is always hard to believe them. But the events of that weekend plunged me into a dark realm that I had only read about in books, or seen in movies; an abyss that was to colour the rest of my life. All I ever wanted was to be a tenant in the house that accommodated the likes of Miles Davis, the house of good music.

But look where I was now.

Nineteen

Lakutshon'ilanga

THE HOUSE ITSELF WAS NOTHING to write home about. A simple red brick government-issue four-roomed hovel just like any other in Soweto. It was set on a tiny piece of ground that was more repulsive than remarkable. A profusion of weeds all around. Uneven stubbles of lawn fighting for survival among the giant weeds. I entered the gate and stepped over a grey dog turd.

Then it hit me: a sweet, slow melody wafting from somewhere in the lugubrious little hovel. My trumpet case in one hand and my suitcase in the other suddenly felt heavy. What was I doing here? I wanted to run away from it all. I paused briefly, took a deep breath. I dragged myself forward nevertheless, succumbing to the pull of the clinking notes from the piano.

And then I was standing on the threshold, looking into the dim confines of what looked like the lounge. I put my suitcase down. I wanted to knock on the door to announce my presence, but I didn't want to interrupt the man playing the piano. So I just stood there awkwardly, and watched, and listened.

While the exterior had been repulsive, the interior was alluring. There was a riot of big paintings hanging on the walls: a Gerard Sekoto here, a George Pemba, a Cecil Skotnes linocut. Then there were masks populating whatever space they could find. The floor wore an exquisite zebra hide mat. The sofas were draped in kudu skins.

The man at the piano, with his back to me, continued playing even though I knew he was now aware of my presence. He was wearing denim shorts but naked from the waist up. His feet were bare. A huge cream fedora hat sat at a rakish angle on his head.

He continued playing the familiar tune.

155

Then he said: 'Are you going to just stand there at the door, or are you coming in?' He said this in a calm voice that didn't betray the fact that he was concentrating hard on the keyboard.

Like one waking up, I stepped inside the room and looked around for a place to sit.

'Let's get cooking then!' he raised his voice as his fingers weaved a cluster of notes.

I hesitated for a moment before I removed my horn from its case. I started blowing. Initially, my phrasing was rushed, eager to impress.

But then I regained my composure, started strutting and swaggering in the spirit of Mackay Davashe's *Lakutshon'ilanga*. We played for a long time, and I was bopping, howling with joy, sinking to low notes of pain of loss that the great piece was all about. *Lakutshon'ilanga* – when the sun goes down. When the sun goes down I will be looking for you, scouring the hospital wards, asking after you from the prison authorities. *Lakutshon'ilanga* – when the sun goes down. When the sun goes down, I'll pound the pavements looking for you, until I find you. *Lakutshon'ilanga*.

At last we faded out. For a long time the man sat with his back to me, his fingers poised on the keyboard as if he was about to launch onto another song. But he turned slowly towards me. He peered at me from behind dark glasses. His face was tiny, slightly fair in complexion, intense of demeanour. An angry scar ran along the left-hand side of his jaw.

'So you're the boy from Durban, Bhazabhaza's boy?' he grunted.

'Yes, Bra Bhazabhaza sent me.'

'I don't know why the arsehole keeps sending me impressionable kids who think Miles is the best thing since sliced bread, the piece of manure. I run the best school of music and drama performance in the southern hemisphere, you hear?'

'Yes, I am listening sir.'

'This here is the Vivian Qunta music academy. Are you listening to me, baby?'

'Yes, sir, I am listening.'

'And stop calling me fucking sir, I am not some fucking honky, you hear?'

'Yes, s...'

'What I am telling you is that this is the Qunta academy, and we don't want no half-baked pseudo-Miles Davis bopping shit. We play pure African shit. You understand where I'm coming from? If you want to join us you better learn that immediately. No fucking screaming Miles Davis shit. You will blow the way our ancestors used to blow their horns during their traditional ceremonies, no fancy shit.'

So, in a nutshell, that's how I was introduced to Vivian Qunta, the great playwright and composer. His tone of voice hurt me. But the fact that a trained musician like him could already tell what I was trying to do musically, that I was taking my cue from the great Miles Davis, flattered me. It told me I was well on my way to creating my own sound.

After that memorably violent weekend in the township, Bhazabhaza had decided that I should make myself scarce for my own safety because friends and comrades of the boys we'd killed were likely to want payback.

Bhazabhaza felt the logical place to go to would be Soweto, the biggest township in the country. He arranged for his friend Vivian Qunta not only to take care of me, but to utilise my musical talents in his dramatic troupe, which had made a name for itself by producing a number of powerful musicals such as *The Jazz Prophets, Kudala* and others.

On the first day after we'd finished playing, we sat down to a couple of bottles of beer. We spoke about politics, music and life in general.

Later that evening, he showed me to a room at the back. That's where I was going to sleep; that's where I was going to dream my dreams, regret my regrets, curse at my fucked failures in the company of my own fucked-up self, cry myself to sleep about lost love, at love unfulfilled because I never had time to nurture such love.

Because I am made of flesh and blood, and not steel and mortar, I had my regrets, my moments of self doubt. Why was it that a young man of my age wasn't having what was called a steady affair? Why was it that I had almost forgotten that somewhere on planet Earth was a woman who called herself my mother; a man who had sweated his way into bringing me into this world, a man who called himself my father. Suddenly I felt like I was a lone star in the sky, with no relationships, no attachment to the rest of the constellation of stars. All that had mattered to me was my music. I gravitated only towards those who offered the promise to help nurture my art.

All my life, my association with women had been technical. First, there was the woman who brought me into the world. As soon as I could do things for myself, clean myself, feed myself, go to the toilet by myself, a distance grew between the two of us. There was no hostility, and our drifting apart was an unconscious phenomenon. I greeted her politely, talked about my school work with her, and listened to her religious teachings. But I made it a point that I spoke only when spoken to; no, I am wrong. I never made it a point to do that; it just happened by itself.

After I'd already left home, and started working with Bhazabhaza, my interaction with women was again technical. I would go hunting for them when we were just starting out with our beauty pageants; would cajole them into taking part in the contests, make money out of them, then move on. Sometimes I would get them when there were pressing carnal needs to be fulfilled, sweat with them, scream with them, laugh at them privately as they declared their love for me, and finally kick them out of my bed the following day. That's what my life had been. It didn't look like it was about to change.

The difference between Bhazabhaza and I was that even though his heart was never dedicated to any woman, he liked to cling to them. He would have as many as ten women attached to him at any given time – that's excluding the girls who were walking the streets for him. He would squeeze every little drop of enjoyment from their company, from their suffering. And the more they suffered at his hands the more pleased he seemed to be. He drove his prostitutes hard, even when they were sick, or even when they were experiencing women's monthly troubles. He maintained that some tricks derived pleasure in sleeping with a woman experiencing her monthly problems. And I guess he was right because some of the girls attracted lots of repeat business during the time of their monthly troubles.

All these things were coming back to me now as Bra Viv was showing me to the little hovel in which I was going to live my life.

'This is going to be your home, for as long as you want to stay with us,' he said.

'Thank you very much, Bra Viv. I will repay you for being so kind to me.'

'You can't afford to repay me; I'm too big for you, my boy.' He said this with a straight face. Then he broke out in a guffaw. Just as quickly, he knitted his face into a scowl and quickly walked away from me. This was a funny man.

The following afternoon a group of young men and women came to the house. They were members of the Qunta dramatic crew. The afternoon started with voice exercises, with the girls going through the scales. Doh ray me fah soh… and so on.

Then one fat girl with a piercing soprano broke into a spiritual, and the rest of the group joined in. All of a sudden, members of the band joined in with their instruments as well, the organ, the piano, guitars, the bass, the drums, the trumpets. It was all so spontaneous and easy going. To the untrained ear it was all groovy music. But there was something I didn't like. I couldn't tell what it was, but it was there. It was like eating a delicate dish of nicely roasted vegetables, only to keep encountering grains of sand in the dish. It was grating. But I couldn't pinpoint the source of my irritation with the playing. I listened harder.

The trumpet players were energetic but unrefined except for one guy known as Stompie. When it was his time to solo, I listened attentively.

But in the middle of his wail, Bra Viv stepped in: 'Come on Stompie, come on, don't be shy with that vibrato. Give it more volume! Vibrate, my boy, vibrate, the masses love it.'

The whole room suddenly exploded in vibratos. It was only then that I realised what had been bothering me with the singing and the playing. Everyone was trying to out-vibrate the next person.

Over the next few sessions, I got into the groove of the music they were playing. But I simply refused to vibrate. Bra Viv noticed this, and tried to get me to remedy the situation. I ignored him.

In an attempt to hurt me and humiliate in front of the others, he said one afternoon: 'You must go for more music lessons, baby, so they can teach you the intricacies and beauty of your horn when you make it vibrate.' In a way he was suggesting that vibrato was the pinnacle of musical achievement. He knew that wasn't true.

While the world thought of him as a musical genius, Bra Viv was a cantankerous old fart who throttled other people's musical ideas and dreams. Actors who enlisted with him were browbeaten into accepting his way of acting and singing. Long after an actor had left the Vivian Qunta stable, you could point him out easily from the way he contorted his face whenever he had to deliver a line, the eyes bulging out furiously to make a dramatic point. There was no room for subtlety and creativity at the Vivian Qunta stable. And it was his way or the highway. Later accounts of the history of South African theatre portrayed him as a revolutionary. In fact, the man was a reactionary right from the onset, a person who didn't give his artists, or even other ordinary human beings for that matter, any breathing space, any opportunity to express themselves, to question his judgment, to look at the world around them through their own eyes, not his, to discover things for themselves.

At the Vivian Qunta stable I saw the best theatrical brains and talent going down the drain, being pummelled into submission by an autocrat. There was Ndabazabantu, a genius comedian whose wit and creativity were so hammered out of shape that in the end he became something of a circus clown instead of being nurtured and allowed the space to explore his comical genius.

Musicians such as Sipho Qwabe, who was to later become a dog on the bass guitar, couldn't last long at the Qunta stable because they were independent individuals who couldn't take shit from an artistically-challenged megalomaniac.

But, that having been said, Qunta had his own personal appeal. Everything he touched turned to gold. Most of his productions were sell-outs. Critics, both locally and internationally, called him the Father of Black South African Theatre. In the end, it was his hard-headedness and narrow take on life and the arts that catapulted him to fame and recognition. I don't know what one should read into that. I'll just leave it for you to judge.

Look, I know that in many artistic fields, formulae are of great importance. Every writer or director or producer has his own style, his own outlook, his own signature. But I maintain that having one's own signature doesn't mean these artists should stop dreaming, stop pushing the boundaries. Pushing the envelope is the essence of art. And that wasn't allowed at the Qunta school, and the man made this clear to me the first day we met. For Vivian Qunta, the formula was 'for a story to sink and seep into souls, sing a song'. He used his musicians and performers, his compositions, texts and choreography as social messengers, he said. And they were just that: messengers delivering to the world what he had dreamt up as he had dreamt it up, with no input from others.

But it was a formula doomed to consign its practitioner into a rut. I wasn't prepared to be part of an artistic corpus caught in a rut. I was young and ambitious. And let it be said, I was a classically trained musician while most of those who came around to the school were highly innovative, artistic cats whose limitation was their inadequate education. Their limited education made them insecure, I suppose, and they were grateful to genuflect at the artistic feet of the one and only Vivian Qunta. It is true that many great artists realise their greatness as a result of serving under a great master. At the risk of belabouring the point, Vivian Qunta was no benevolent master.

Nevertheless, I had no option but to hang around. After all, the man was providing me with accommodation, contributing towards some of my meals and booze, thanks to Bhazabhaza who adored Vivian and had put in a good word for me.

Despite all my misgivings about the direction my musical career was taking, the stay with the Qunta crew was an eye opener. Not only was I playing in the biggest band I had ever been exposed to – there were four trumpets, four saxophones, a trombone, an organ, a piano, drums, bongo drums and percussions, bass, lead guitar, rhythm guitar, acoustic guitar, and about 20 singers, I also had a speaking part in the play. Just a couple of politically inane lines; Bra Viv considered himself a politically inspired revolutionary playwright. I happened to have good English diction and had the training not to forget what I had been taught. I therefore had the potential of being turned into some class of actor.

'While others use guns to fight for their liberation, through music we shall overcome. Listen to the thunderous anger of the oppressed coming out of our horns…' some shit like that, which I recited before I launched into a solo on my trumpet and so on.

There were cats in the band who could indeed play. All that they lacked was vision and guts. They were happy to enlist with Bra Viv because he provided them with shelter – many of them were from out of town and lived in houses that he paid rent for. And they were guaranteed some form of income at the end of the month. These people were weak and couldn't stand on their own feet. They were meek, and couldn't take the heat. Also, none of them had any management skills. When you are not in charge of your financial affairs, it kills you.

Somebody, I think it was Nsanga, so-called because of his squinty eyes, suggested that we start a small band of our own on the side. We could play the townships around Johannesburg, he suggested.

Clement, one of our guitarists, started laughing. He was not right in the head, always laughing for no reason. Once he started laughing, it was difficult to stop him. The only way to silence him was to give him a guitar. Then he would close his eyes and take a deep breath. And play.

To cut a long story short, it was agreed over a few drinks that we should start a small band that would play in the neighbouring townships whenever we had time off from our obligations with Bra Viv.

'Maybe we should tell Bra Viv about this idea, he might think we are going behind his back,' I ventured.

'Shit no,' exclaimed Stompie the trumpeter, 'We are men in our own right. There's no need to tell him about our every move, just as long as we don't eat into his time or interfere with his programme. He doesn't consult us whenever he wants to submit a drama to one of the radio stations. He chows that money all by himself...'

'Those of us who have a bit of drama education can tell that he gets some of his radio drama ideas from interacting with us,' jumped in Scotch, the bassist.

It was decided that I should be in charge of the band's management issues. We christened our band Zakes' Zeppelins. By that time they had already started calling me Zakes. I think this had to do with the fact that I was listening a lot to a guy called Zacks Nkosi, a dog on alto saxophone.

We played in the East Rand townships because, for some reason, that part of the province always seemed to be receptive to new innovative jazz. We played mostly standards – American and local; some of us ventured into writing.

All of my guys played by ear, but they were imaginative and ambitious. As a result, they would come to me with some ideas for a song, some phrases, and we would sit down and write.

Through all this activity, Bra Viv never said a word. He neither voiced his disapproval, nor heaped praises on us. Our name had started appearing in the press.

But shit clouds were gathering on the horizon.

Twenty

Straight, No Chaser

ON A FRIDAY AFTERNOON sometime around August, we were on a truck with our instruments. This time we were not just playing the local townships, but our destination was the Orange Free State province where we'd been told there was money to be made.

I had raised my reservations to other members of the band earlier.

'Shit, gents, I'm concerned about this trip to the Free State. Those *moegoes* in the mountains and forests will not understand jazz in the first place. Secondly, I don't see where they will get their money from. Those of them who've got brains are stuck here in Joburg, wasting their lives away on the gold mines. Those who were left behind were fools, blind enough not to realise how miserable their lives really are.'

'I don't like the way you're talking,' Clement spoke in a lucid voice for the first time since I had encountered him. 'Look me in the face while I'm talking to you. Look at me! I am from that province, and you know what I'm capable of playing. This attitude of looking down on people who don't come from Johannesburg or other major cities must stop, *barena*.'

After much debate, I was overruled. It was agreed that we would be going to the Free State after all.

By midnight on Friday, we were inside a hall in Mangaung township. The crowd was big. I was truly amazed at the sophistication I saw there – the people walking into the hall in the latest fashions. Unlike the loud mouths of Johannesburg who sometimes forced their way into the hall with bottles of booze even though the normal rule was no booze during performances, the people of the Free State walked solemnly into the hall, took their seats and waited for us to start performing. Some of them were mildly drunk, but they were

167

restrained and didn't attract attention to themselves for all the wrong reasons.

We had been playing for a solid hour non-stop, when I suddenly got the urge to speak to the audience. People generally believed that jazz musicians spoke through their instruments, or to introduce pieces in their repertoire.

'We're standing on this stage not because we are hungry monkeys eager to steal the few peanuts you have in your pockets,' I started speaking angrily into the mike.

There was stunned silence as I proceeded: 'We are here as prophets, the bringers of the soothing music that liberates. After all we can't entertain an oppressed people. Think of our music as a message for liberation. This horn here, this trumpet, is my gun.'

I paused. There was a nervous silence, before someone started clapping. Then the whole hall started clapping thunderously.

After the show some of my comrades were angry with me.

'Look, man,' Scotch said, 'We are not politicians, we are musicians. Ours is to play, get paid and fuck-off. If we start talking politics, we will end up like the Hugh Masekelas and Miriam Makebas of this world.'

'Yeah,' said Stompie, 'And look where they are now. Languishing somewhere in exile. I don't think that's what I want do, attract police attention to myself.'

'Look, guys, what I said up there on that stage wasn't something I had planned. It was just like a voice, a power higher than all of us speaking through me. But that doesn't mean I am apologising. Some of these things have to be said, to remind the people to remember that even though they are enjoying music, they are not living in a normal society.'

I continued talking, quoting one of my favourite philosopher-musicians, John Coltrane: 'The main thing a musician would like to do is to give a picture to the listener of the many wonderful things he knows of and senses in the universe. That's what I would like to do. I think that's one of the greatest things you can do in life and we all try to do it in some way.'

Yeah, gents, we try.

The talking went on, but the anger of the guys had lost its edge, neutralised by the fact that we had had a hugely successful show.

'You see what I told you guys?' Clement was grinning broadly as we packed our instruments after the show, 'I can bet you my bottom rand, which I don't have until I get paid by Bra Viv, that none of you have ever performed for such a well-behaved audience. Those losers in Joburg think the world and all its inhabitants owe them a favour. They think they are God's gifts to man.'

And it was true. In addition to being a good audience, the cats of the Free State didn't raise objections to the fact that local ladies were fond of us. In many townships where we'd performed, the local cats tended to be overly protective of their ladies. In fact they were mostly violently opposed to the idea of a musician walking away from a concert with a local girl hanging onto one of his arms. Not so with the Free Staters.

From the time we'd started setting up the stage, a particular lady who was all by herself had caught my eye. She was dressed in a cream tweed coat and pants suit, elegantly cut. Her hair was done in the latest braid style, and her ears sparkled with the biggest diamond earrings I'd ever seen. She was very light in complexion. It was clear that there was some white blood in her family tree. But she spoke SeSotho like a Mosotho woman. She had that deep husky voice that always brings a tingling sensation to my spine.

I had spoken to her during our break and she had responded positively to my advances. Now, it was time to go home and she offered to take me to her home, which was just as well considering that our lodgings at the home of one of Clement's distant relatives were overcrowded.

There was something wrong with the way she walked. But that didn't bother me. After all I wasn't here to be a judge in one of those beauty pageants I had been in charge of back in Durban. All I needed here was the company, the smell, the warmth of a woman that night. Fuck the walk.

I had my band mates drop me at her place.

'Don't forget to pick me up around nine in the morning so we can start preparing for the next destination.'

'No problem, Zakes. Have fun,' said Scotch.

They flung themselves into the night.

The woman lived in a back room that was part of a cluster of buildings in what, at that time of the morning, looked like a huge yard inhabited by many other families. I spotted about three cars in the yard, which told me that this neighbourhood was relatively well off as cars were scarce among many black communities.

When we finally reached her door, she unlocked it and walked inside.

She groped somewhere in the dark, then a light came on. I couldn't help noting that her room was exquisitely furnished. A small fridge, a nice double bed, a dresser groaning under the weight of lotions, perfumes and other paraphernalia that could be expected from a woman of her class. I had decided that she was top *shayela*, as we called those on the upper rungs of society.

'In many townships people are still using candles and paraffin lamps, but I notice that you have electricity,' I said casually in SeSotho.

'Yes, your observation is accurate,' she responded in the highly modulated tones of an English woman, throwing me off balance. She had told me her name was Palesa, SeSotho for 'flower'. 'Even here in the Free State, black people still have no access to electricity. It's just the whites and us coloureds who have the privilege.'

So, she was coloured. She offered me a seat, reached for a beer in the fridge, found herself a chair and we started drinking and talking. Talking about segregation, music, education and so on. God knows I needed that beer. I had been blowing the whole night, and my throat was parched. I gulped it quickly and didn't wait for her to offer me another one; I helped myself from the fridge.

We talked some more about politics, race relations and stuff. I kept reminding myself that I wasn't here to explore the intricacies of race relations and social disparities. I yawned deliberately loudly.

I edged closer to her and we started kissing. She had the alluring smell of a mature woman. She was a good kisser. But there was a melancholic depth to her eyes, like life hadn't been too kind to her, like she wanted to break down there and then and tell me about the all the travails of her life.

'Honey,' she said, pushing me gently away from her, 'we need to sleep. You have a long day ahead of you.'

'Yep,' said I readily, as I started to undress.

She got up and switched off the light. I was disappointed because I had been hoping to have a good look at her body. I had never seen the body of a coloured woman before, except in magazine pictures.

I got into bed. She continued walking about in the darkness as I waited impatiently in bed, getting more excited by the minute. I hadn't had a woman in a long time. She was muttering to herself.

Finally, she joined me in bed. I moved towards her, wanting to start playing with her thighs. She moved out of reach just as my hand was about to reach her.

'What's wrong with you?'

'Nothing. It's just…'

This time I moved too fast for her. I was lying on my right side, and with my left hand I grabbed her left thigh. My hand moved logically towards the triangle between her thighs.

But I couldn't feel the other thigh. I froze. Got up and got out of bed, my heart thudding. She was up after me. She cut my way towards the door, and switched on the light.

'Okay' she said to me, 'This is what I look like, bloody black bastard. Do I scare you?'

She was standing there on her one leg. Her eyes were on fire. 'Look at me all you like, and get back to the fucking bed. I am a freak, all right, I have only one leg, but I am going to make you happy. I want to be made happy as well. How long are you black bastards going to shun me for just because I had an accident? Tell you what, motherfucker, you are going to fuck me until your friends come for you.'

I tried to reach for my trousers. She hit me hard in the ribs with her wooden leg, sending me sprawling on the bed. Before I knew it, she was on top of me. She was all gentle again as she coaxed my manhood, shrivelled by fear, back to its glorious hardness.

And she rode me. Steadily at first. Gently. Then with sudden fury. We galloped across the plains of the Free State, glided across the Atlantic Ocean and we were in Birdland and Charlie Parker and Miles Davis and Coltrane and Sonny Rollins and Dizzy Gillespie and Duke Ellington and Thelonius Monk and Billie Holiday and Sarah Vaughn and Duke Ellington and the other cats saw us and they said 'ride on, brother, ride on.'

And ride me she did. She rode me until we came across the King's Messengers and they were singing 'Ride on Moses, Ride on King Emmanuel, I want to see my Jesus in the morning...' And she still rode me. She rode me until I cried out for my mother, cried like a miserable baby, crying 'Maaaaah! Come take me out of this misery, out of this bondage!' But she ignored my bittersweet cries for mercy. She continued to ride me. Changing her pace every now and then from gentleness to sudden fury. She rode me until I screamed and vomited the names of all the women I've ever had in my life – those whose names I remembered. But she still rode me. She rode me until we came across Shadrack, Meshack and Abednego smiling and having fun while walking in huge flames of fire with their skins remaining unscathed, while my own body was burning all over, the searing pleasure-pain of her fire consuming me right down to my inner core. I said put out these flames, put out the fire, bring me water, bring me the sweet milk from the core of a coconut and put out this fire this very minute. But still she rode me.

And she drenched me with her sweat, and I choked and began to drown in our combined sweat. She rode me until I screamed her name: 'Palesa-flower, Palesa-flower, Palesa-flower', until my entire universe exploded into a profusion of flowers – yellow, pink, blue, scarlet, orange, white, lilac. And I was rolling, naked, in a bed of flower petals. And the flower petals held my body in such a tight embrace I could hardly breathe.

Palesa-flower, flower, flower, flower, flower, flower. Flower flower flower flower flower. Power power power power power power power power power. Flower power. Power to Palesa. Powerful Palesa. Palesaful power. Palesa palesa, palesa palesa palesa palesa palesa palesa. Pulse pulse impulse. Palesa-pulse-impulse-power-flower. Flow with the flowers. Have the power of flowers.

By the time the Zeppelins came to fetch me the following day, I could hardly walk. She had zapped me and sapped me until my back bent like a bow, my knees as wobbly as jelly.

Inside the truck the boys were drinking brandy and Coke.

'Your hangover needs a potent cure,' said Stompie, pouring me a generous slug of the amber drink, 'here take a shot.'

I accepted the glass.

'Here,' offered Scotch, 'get a dash of Coke.'

'Straight,' said I, 'no chaser.'

I gulped the drink all at once. Sat back in the chair as the laughter of the brothers swirled around me.

'Straight, no chaser, he says,' Scotch said, throwing back a slug of brandy.

I started telling them about my encounter with the one-legged lady the previous night.

'Sometimes, we men are real bastards,' Clement said quietly. 'How can you make fun of a woman who clearly gave you so much pleasure?'

'Speak, Mr Philosopher,' the guys chorused.

Clement had a point. How could I make fun of a woman who had taken me into the warmth of her bed and given me one of my most enjoyable sexual experiences?

Anyway, the conversation inevitably veered back to the issue of the cheap political speech I had given at the hall.

Stompie was talking: 'You educated guys tend to confuse things. You mix music with politics. You mix religion with politics. You are so mixed up in the head you want ordinary individuals like us to join you in your state of confusion.'

'When the white man came to Africa,' Clement spoke slowly, 'it is said he had the Bible, and we Africans had the land. He asked us to pray with our eyes closed. When we opened our eyes, we had the Bible, and he had the land – and the gun, just in case.'

Everyone laughed.

'I guess what I am saying,' continued Clement, 'is that all these things are linked. Life is a sum total of things – love, hate, religion, war, and so on. Each of these elements is, in some way, the antidote of the other, or it complements the other. In this country the whites have used religion to justify their rule over us. They say we are heathens who have to be ruled and gradually weaned off our barbaric, uncivilised ways. It's therefore our duty to take up the challenge back to them – use whatever avenues are available to us to fight back the tyranny. Bra Zakes here, is taking over from where the likes of Paul Robeson, Miriam Makeba, Hugh Masekela left off. Using music not as opium to pacify the people, but as a weapon through which they can express themselves.'

This was the most profound thing I had ever heard about music and society. From then on, it became my habit to say a thing or two about the state of our nation wherever and whenever we performed.

Later that afternoon, we found ourselves in the middle of a rural village.

We were sitting in front of a school hall, which, we were told, was the venue in which we were going to play. The good thing was that we had had the good sense to bring our own generator as there was no electricity at the school.

'But where are the people?' I asked the local chief who had organised the concert.

'Don't worry,' he said taking a swig from a gourd of foamy umqombothi, the potent local brew, 'the entire village will be here shortly. By the time they are finished with you, your hands will be full, I tell you.'

Because we were impatient, we proceeded and played to an empty hall. People started trickling in. They turned out to be one of the most appreciative audiences we had entertained in a long time. We played with all our hearts and minds. We were happy to be so appreciated. But there seemed to be a problem at the door. The doorman tried to get my attention, but we were all too absorbed in our playing to attend to whatever the problem was.

We continued playing for a few more minutes before taking a break. During the short break, the doorman came rushing to me.

'Bra Zakes, you better come and see what's happening outside. There are so many people out there I don't know what to do with them.'

'The hall is almost empty, why are you keeping them out?'

He took me by the hand and dragged me outside. The other band members followed.

'Jesus!' said I upon setting my eyes on the throng of people outside there. Some of them had fowls, others goats, others a variety of vegetables. All of these people wanted to come inside the hall to witness the musical spectacle that had been so well publicised in their village. But they had no money and they wanted to use their wealth – livestock and vegetables, in exchange for the right to see the show.

My cynical urban voice spoke to the other members of the band: 'See what I meant, these *moegoes* from the sticks will take a long time to take a healthy bite on the sweet fruit of civilisation. What do they think we are going to do with all this shit they are bringing us? We want money, not smelly goats.'

We all laughed. I had never seen anything like this before. We allowed the people into the hall and gave one of our most memorable performances. After the show we slaughtered some of the animals and had a feast that lasted until the following day, Sunday.

Although we knew that Bra Viv expected us home on Monday, the booze and the women made up our minds for us. We decided that we would only leave the following day, meaning we would be arriving in Johannesburg on Monday night.

As a result, the party continued unbridled on Sunday. Late into the night, we walked across the length and breadth of the village, accompanying the local women. A good many orgies were had on the side of the footpaths. The moon was out. In the distance we could see trees dotting the landscape. As we walked down the footpaths, suddenly there would be music coming out of the trees: guitars and voices. As if there were ghosts hidden there in the trees.

Then you would hear a concertina wailing, and a voice piercing the night at intervals from another side of the wilderness. Perhaps a man walking home from a party, massaging his concertina to make the walk home more bearable, unaware of the great music he was making.

Just across the river, we came upon a couple sitting on top of a rock singing praises to the moon. It wasn't some ritualistic singing. It seemed to us this was their spontaneous appreciation of the moon, a song that sprang from their hearts, a song known only by them, a song that they wouldn't be able to remember the following day. Improvisation. A song for that particular moment in time. A song, no doubt, that made them happy human beings at one with nature and God's other creatures.

Further up the hill, a man was walking home, pinching his guitar strings and singing. His dog kept barking at intervals, its barking becoming part of the musical mosaic the guitar man was making. This was more soulful and original music than we'd performed up there on stage. To these people music was just a part of life.

It was therefore a pity to leave this village behind and head back home on Monday. To find a murderously angry Bra Viv waiting for us.

Twenty
One

So What?

'GUYS, GUYS, GUYS,' that's how Bra Viv started his monologue as we stood in front of him inside his garage where we normally held our rehearsals. 'Guys, guys, guys. You have fucked me over, do you know that?'

He was pacing up and down, his eyes downcast. His voice was a low, intense rumble. His temper was famous. He didn't hesitate to punch an actor who fluffed his lines. Whippings were a daily occurrence at the Qunta school. He ran the place like some kind of reformatory school. He dealt with his crew as a prison warder would with juvenile delinquents. The shocking thing was that these people, talented singers and actors, some of them family men and women in their own right, never challenged the unprofessional and callous manner in which he treated them.

'Eyi, Bra Viv has a temper,' actresses could be heard saying. 'You must never cross him.'

They sounded like an abused woman who believes her man is expressing his love for her by beating her up.

'Guys, guys, guys,' Bra Viv was saying now, 'you really fucked me over. Not only have you been fucking my reputation all over town, but you are now beginning to miss rehearsals. Just where were you when your dedicated, focused and hard-working comrades were rehearsing this afternoon? No, you don't need to answer that. It's what educated people call a rhetorical question. I know exactly where you were. I know all of that. You were somewhere in some smelly village sinking my good name in shit. I feed your poor selves, I house you, I even give you booze and drugs, and now you think you are bigger than me. Shiiit!'

We could all see his gun sitting on the table next to the door of the garage. His sjambok was also sitting on the same table, looking like a lethal angry snake.

'You've been using my name to land concert deals with some shady promotions company all over the place. By the time we launch our tour of the country, my name will be so deep in the mud I wonder if I'll be able to drag it out and restore it to its former glory. Instead of concentrating on the work that brought you to Joburg in the first place, you are gallivanting all over town playing some jazz shit, soiling my name, fucking up the reputation of the fucking Vivian Qunta academy! You know that it's just about time for the crew to get down to our next tour of the country, yet you are doing your damnedest to fuck everything up.

'You don't pitch for rehearsals, your names are all over the newspapers, saying members of the Viv Qunta academy have been making fools of themselves in some godforsaken village in the Free State. And you think I am going to sit by and allow my name to be driven in the mud just like that! I worked and fought hard to be where I am, and no one, and I say no one, no pseudo professor of music, no fucking half-baked university drop-out piece of shit is going to bring me down just like that. You think I am going to keep quiet while all that I have worked for all my life is being fucked-up by two-bit musical wonders? I hear some pieces of shit think making half-baked political statements on stage is going to make them musical geniuses. You think I am going to stand by and watch this nonsense? No, baby, Viv is going to fight back like an enraged lion!'

He stood in front of Scotch, and said: 'Scotch. We come a long way, baby, we really do. You know that, baby. We've been together for such a long time, I picked you up from the streets, rescued from prison so many times I've even lost count, but now all of a sudden you think you are bigger than me, going all over town bad-mouthing my sound, the sound of the Viv Qunta academy? What's gotten into you?'

Clement started laughing hysterically. Bra Viv turned around and punched him smack in the middle of his face. He went down like a sack of potatoes. The room was suddenly filled with the stink from his bowels.

Bra Viv then reached for his sjambok and started lashing us indiscriminately. For a moment I expected one of us to stand up to him, to stop the bully's foolishness. But big men were rolling on the floor like children, crying out for mercy, promising never to offend Bra Viv again.

After about an hour, with welts rising all over our skin, blood on the floor, Bra Viv dropped his sjambok on the ground.

'Get this fucking place cleaned up, you ungrateful bastards,' he rasped.

Turning to me, he said: 'If you continue misleading these people, I'll get you thrown out of this city. And those vultures in Durban are still baying for your blood. Ever since you got here you have been nothing but trouble. Now, if I were you I would start behaving appropriately and stop fooling myself into thinking I know shit about music. You know fuck all, my boy,' he said, picking up his gun and sliding it into its holster. 'You know fuck all. And you better get that into your fucking hard Zulu head. So what if you've got some university education? So what if you think you're the next musical legend after Miles? You all get out of my face!'

He stormed out of the garage. We remained behind, nursing our welts, washing our blood from the floor.

Two weeks after that incident, Bra Viv could feel the artistic restlessness among his crew. He could feel that we had rehearsed enough.

At the last minute, Bra Viv got me involved in the planning of the tour. This entailed liaising with the theatre promoters in the various provinces, getting them to book venues, organise accommodation for us. Publicity – by word of mouth, through the media, through street posters – was crucial. The contacts that I had established over the years during my early involvement with beauty pageants, and also my promotion of various jazz concerts, came in handy.

By the time the production we'd been working on, Hungry Earth, hit the road, audiences all over the country were waiting eagerly. Obviously, we launched the tour with three performances in Soweto. All of them were sold out. The rave reviews emanating from this ensured a smooth run all over the country.

We had just done the third and last performance at a small township called Hammarsdale, in the province of Natal, when the shit hit the fan.

'Zakes,' Bra Viv spoke to me as we stood behind Glazier Hall after the performance. 'The money is not adding up. All our shows have been sold out since we got on the road, but that is not reflected in the takings.'

'But Bra Viv I am not a money person. I am on stage performing most of the time while the money people are selling tickets at the door.'

'I know that, but you're still my link with the promoters and everyone else who's got anything to do with money.'

'In a way you are right, I've been liaising with them. But the person who's been directly involved from our side has been Nicky.' Nicky was his wife. 'She's the person you should be talking to about the money.'

'What the fuck are you saying? Boy, are you telling me not to trust my wife?' He lunged at me, trying to punch me to the ground. But I was too fast for him. I ducked out of the way just in time. He almost fell to the ground.

After regaining his balance, he came back grunting through clenched teeth, 'What is this? Are you fighting against me, boy? Standing up to me?'

He came for me again. I blocked his punch. This time I didn't stop there, but I punched him back. He fell to the ground.

Everyone was screaming now. 'Somebody stop them!'

Bra Viv whipped his gun out from the inside of his jacket. The bloody coward, producing a gun on an unarmed person whom he'd provoked in the first place.

There were more screams as some members of the crew pushed me to safety.

That marked the end of my stint with Bra Viv's crew. When they packed their things and trekked back to Johannesburg, I stayed behind. Scotch and Stompie, my two lieutenants from Zakes's Zeppelins, stayed with me in Durban.

A great, tortuous journey lay ahead of us.

Twenty
Two

Back at the Chicken Shack

IN THE TIME THAT I had been away, Bhazabhaza's house had been transformed completely. True, it was still called Seven Steps to Heaven. But the ramshackle chicken shack from which we had hosted sex and booze parties was nowhere to be found. In its place there now stood a sprawling piece of property, what we used to call *izulu labelungu* – white man's heaven.

'What I did was,' Bhazabhaza was telling me as we walked about the verdant lawn in front of the property, 'I bought all four ugly houses that were flanking the old shack I used to call home. I then had everything knocked down. And I mean everything. Then I had a couple of white architects come down here with designs. Of course we were not working from an existing model. I just told the white boys the picture that I had in mind, and they translated it into a plan. As a result, the plan kept changing, driven by my moods of course.' He laughed. 'Whenever I was angry, I felt I needed a roomier property with lots of windows to let in more light, to chase away the darkness in my heart and mind.'

What inspired confidence in Bhazabhaza's heart was the fact that Clermont was the only remaining place, at least in the province of Natal, where black people could buy and own property. In other parts of the province those rights had been revoked as a result of numerous racist land laws. He could build as he pleased without having to worry about the white government. But you never knew with those unpredictable bastards in Pretoria.

We were now standing in front of the house, the magnificent outcome of those endless meetings with the architects. The main house was a double-storey affair with so many windows it was almost entirely made of glass. The windows were such that you couldn't see through them from the outside, but the guy inside could see you.

There's a special name for these kinds of windows, but it's a name that I never cared to commit to memory. Anyway, this was a new innovation, something only white people could afford, or even think about for that matter. As it was, the black man had a lot of basic bread and butter issues to think about, and therefore could not afford to add some more sophisticated shit to his already unbearably heavy shit load.

Anyway, at the back of which was a huge swimming pool with deck chairs and umbrellas scattered around it. Being a weekend, a number of people were lazing around the pool, sipping their cold drinks. Waiters were swooping about, taking orders. In later years I was going to hear a lot of high rollers, such as Peggy 'Belair' Senne, and Nqola Mzimba, claiming that they owned the classiest drinking places. Bullshit. Bhazabhaza was in a class of his own. It's just that he was operating from the wrong city, Durban, whereas the people who claim to have the monopoly on all wisdom and class were based in Johannesburg. But I digress.

A swimming pool was a rarity in a black neighbourhood, but Bhazabhaza was moving in the realm of white opulence and achievement. In addition to the main house, which had countless rooms, there were other free-standing buildings which served various purposes. There were a number of free-standing guest rooms, a huge bar where ordinary patrons drank and listened to music. Next to this bar was a huge entertainment room partitioned into smaller cubicles where women entertained guests privately when necessary.

Then there was a music room in which Bhazabhaza kept his own baby grand piano and numerous horns, a guitar and set of conga drums. The walls were decorated with classy black and white photos of big name artists of the time – both local and international. This was the room me and my Zeppelins were going to use as our rehearsal room while we stayed with the big man.

The first few months at Bhazabhaza's place were sheer bliss. Not only did the man entertain us with booze and women, but we also got a lot of work done. We toured the townships around the province and were quite a hit. My boys were pleasantly amazed that my province, long reviled as a province of moegoes by the all-knowing arseholes of Johannesburg, was actually a civilised place.

'Fuck,' Stompie said as we sat around the swimming pool one weekend after a hot rehearsal, 'if your province has this to offer, I am not going back to Joburg in a hurry.'

'Not only is the place inspiring artistically,' said Scotch, 'the weather is good, there is no smog from millions of chimneys like we have back in Soweto; then there's the sea to keep you calm both bodily and spiritually.'

'And of course,' Clement whispered conspiratorially as he noticed a bevy of girls walking towards us, with Bhazabhaza leading them, 'the girls here are not privy to our bad reputations. They think we are angels!'

'Boys!' Bhazabhaza boomed, 'meet the girls! Girls, meet the boys!'

We got up to greet the girls and find chairs for them. After introductions had been exchanged, Bhazabhaza got straight to the point: 'Zakes and the boys here are all the way from Joburg. Zakes is the leader of the band, the Zeppelins, which has been causing a stir around our province of late.'

He paused, and then addressed me directly, pointing a finger at the girl who appeared to be the leader of the female crew: 'Zakes, this is Girlie and her crew. They have won a number of a capella competitions around the province. They call themselves the Hot Mamas.'

We smiled at each other. Then Bhazabhaza continued: 'Now I have a business proposal. I have discussed it in detail with Girlie, and she agrees with me in broad terms. And Zakes thought it was a good idea. But the devil is in the details, as they say. Now, this is why we are having this meeting.' He hadn't said a fucking thing to me about Girlie or any business proposal for that matter, but I nodded sagely while I was furiously trying to think what he was trying to get at.

189

'The idea here is to marry the talents of the two groups,' he said, bringing his palms together slowly to illustrate the coming together of the two sides. 'Zakes and the Zeppelins are not only accomplished jazz musicians, but they have a wealth of experience in conceptualising musical dramas, and Zakes himself is an actor. On the other hand, Girlie and her crew are singers of note. So,' he looked from Girlie to me, 'we are here to start a musical drama academy to blow Bra Vivian Qunta out of the water. We've got the talent, the experience, and a bit of money to get us started. There's nothing to stop us.'

'Look,' I started, careful not to offend Bhazabhaza and expose him as a liar, but also to protect myself from members of my band who would surely skin me alive when we were alone. 'When I spoke to you, Bra Bee, I thought we were just joking, throwing ideas around. I didn't realise that you would actually go out to get other outside people to get the thing started. These things need a bit of thought.'

'There's nothing to think about. All we have to do is start rehearsing. I've got the space; I've got the transport to drive you around. I've got some old scripts from Bra Viv's academy which we can use as a springboard to greater things, you get where I'm coming from. We'll take Bra Viv's scripts, tweak them a bit, and start working, while we continue to write our own scripts.'

'There is something called plagiarism,' Stompie warned, 'and I don't think any of us here, ambitious as we are, want to fuck with another person's work. Besides, until now, we hadn't been consulted about this whole musical drama thing.'

'Fuck that, I am consulting you now!' Bhazabhaza said. 'I'm saying to you, how about starting rehearsals as soon as possible. People are hungry for musical drama in this province. They don't have to wait for Bra Viv to come all the way from his province to steal bread from our mouths. Let's be smart about this and corner the market before he comes back next year with one of his own works. Let's take a work of his, turn it around. That's not plagiarism. It's called spoofing. It's called parody. You gentlemen are educated enough to know the difference between theft, and paying tribute to a bigger force, a bigger artist like Bra Viv.'

The discussion went on for another hour. No longer were we discussing the merits and demerits of venturing into musical drama, we were now working out specifics: when to start rehearsing, how often, which Vivian Qunta script to focus on. Later, Girlie and her women were driven away by Bhazabhaza himself.

Now we were sitting there facing each other, clearly with daggers drawn.

'What the fuck do you take us for, Zakes?' Scotch was the first to fire away, 'We come all the way from Joburg with you, and you are now selling us down the river.'

Stompie got up and started pacing up and down the room, his hand clutching his whisky glass so hard I thought he was going to crush it. He said: 'You were the one who inspired us to rebel against Bra Viv and his shitty musicals because you said we should be pursuing our real, noble musical dreams. And look what you're doing to us now! Is this how you treat your friends? Is this how you treat people who are like brothers to you, people who've entrusted you with their careers, their lives?'

'Calm down, gentlemen,' Clement said, his eyes focused on the floor. 'Please calm down. I am looking at this thing differently. But as you know, I am crazy, and crazy people have their own crazy way of looking at things. Let's give this thing a try...'

'Fuck you!' Scotch said, starting towards Clement.

'Hold it, hold it,' Clement said, without ever removing his gaze from the floor, 'from what I can see, Zakes had nothing to do with the whole plan. The whole shit is being imposed upon us by Bhazabhaza.'

'Bullshit!' bellowed Stompie, 'You heard Zakes admitting that he'd discussed the idea with Bhazabhaza. You heard him. And we are not talking behind his back. He is here, right in front of us and he's got a mouth big enough to speak for himself!'

'Okay,' I started slowly, 'I think we're getting heated up here...'

'Damn right we are! And justifiably so!' said Scotch.

'Look, I never discussed any idea, any plan with Bhazabhaza. Everything was as new to me as it was to you. But I didn't want to expose him as a liar, to embarrass him in front of those girls. Not for a minute did I think he was serious. I thought it was just one of his schemes to impress the girls, to get them to open their legs for us. It seems I underestimated his seriousness. Now we are in this situation. We can either reject it, which would mean us starting to look for accommodation and all the rest of it. Or we can work with him while we try to get our house in order, in other words just buying time...'

'That's exactly what I was trying to say,' said Clement, 'before I got shut down. This Bhazabhaza man has almost everything we need – accommodation, rehearsal space, transport, money...'

'Booze and girls,' Stompie and Scotch added, laughing.

'Right,' continued Clement, 'let's use him as much as we can. We can do his proposed musical, earn a few bucks that will come in handy when we finally decide to walk away from the arsehole.'

Twenty
Three

Ain't Misbehavin'

THE CHALLENGE OF STANDING at the helm of a jazz band cannot be overstated. Not only do you have to lay down the law and chart the musical direction of the group, but you also have to deal with the personal expectations, fears and plain bullshit from members of the band. Most artists are children in adults' bodies. They never grow up. They are forever finding reasons to complain, to compare their poor lot with their comrades in the band who are treated better than they are. This has to do mainly with money. Some of your band members cannot understand why their comrades get more privileges, more money than them. They forget that some of them are mere players, with no idea of how to compose a song. On their own, deprived of a leader, a guide, a father figure, they would be at sea. Yet they complain. True, as members of a group, they were excellent players and artists who could improvise and perform magical feats with their instruments. That was the reality I had been dealing with ever since we decided to form the band. I was forever harassed, challenged, insulted, drowned in tears.

These thoughts were boiling inside my head as I carefully tended to my dagga garden at the back of the house. When I wasn't rehearsing or reading, I spent my time tending to the dagga plants. When they had ripened, I harvested them and carefully placed them on a wooden tray. Then I would place the tray in the sun over a number of days while the plants dried, gradually turning an alluring golden colour.

Having finished my chores in the dagga garden, I continued ruminating on the responsibilities and challenges of heading the band. Things that interfered with my music truly irritated me. I was thinking of ways to deal with the brewing trouble within our music ensemble.

The situation was going to get worse with the incorporation of the Clermont girls into our band. You must remember that the idea was to set up a powerful cast for a musical to rival Bra Viv and all his imitators, who were beginning to mushroom in many townships around the country. Every young man and his toothless dog thought he was destined to be the next Bra Viv, writing the next musical blockbuster.

The money to feed and pay the members was there. The transport was easily available. When I had to take the group to one of the less sophisticated townships where we performed for free to test our impact and polish our skills, I had no worries whatsoever.

The problems, when they started surfacing, had everything to do with sex. My boys fighting over girls, and the girls fighting over my boys. Each girl thought she was destined to be the soprano lead, and tried to bad-mouth the current lead. This was amazing because when these girls were first introduced to us, they had projected the images of saints. After all they were members of one of the local churches.

But I soon realised that there were monsters lurking behind their sanctimonious façades. These kids soon turned out to be the most virulently double-crossing and divisive bitches I'd ever seen. They were fabricating stories about each others' sexual escapades with members of my band. One day two girls got involved in a knife fight over Clement.

'I had to fire two of the girls from the group,' I told Bhazabhaza as we sat sipping whisky one afternoon.

'Which two?'

'That's the painful part. Zodwa, one of our best sopranos, and Ntomb'futhi, another soprano. In as much as I respect and like them for their skills, I had to make a good example of them.'

'I agree with you. You have to be firm with these things otherwise they'll distract you with their pussies.'

'Not only are they bringing bad vibes to the group, but they are truly violent little pieces of shit.'

Bhazabhaza laughed long and hard. Then he turned serious and said: 'If that's what you say they are, I've got new assignments for them. I've got lots of work for little pieces of shit.'

From that week on, the two girls became Bhazabhaza's trophy girls who accompanied him to big glamorous parties. They seemed happy doing that. Not only were they making more money without the huge responsibility of having to learn and practise stupid songs everyday, they got to be driven around in Bhazabhaza's flashy cars to a variety of venues where they were wined and dined. They were passed around among Bhazabhaza's friends at the parties that the big boss hosted or attended.

But that was at the beginning. As soon as Bhazabhaza had acquired younger, fresher girls to entertain his friends who were rich and not shy about it, sporting gold-plated teeth and gold jewellery, the two singing girls were relegated to the streets. They hustled around the Point Road area. Under cover of shadows in the smelly dock area, they bowed to the demands of sailors and other sex-starved types. Bhazabhaza's look-out boys stood close by, ready to collect the money or beat up a trick who refused to pay. These look-out boys thought they were pimps when, in fact, the real pimp was Bhazabhaza himself. They were just disposable pieces of junk. When he got tired of them, he dumped them just like he did the girls. He also warned them not to even try pimping on his turf. Or else.

★★★

It was the summer of 1973 when my band embarked on our last tour. My memories of the tour are vague. I was drunk and high on weed most of the time. The weed that I had harvested from my small spot at Bhazabhaza's house kept my band mates and I going for a long time. It was good dagga.

Moving from township to township, from town to dorpie, we got to hook up with old musical friends such as Dalton Khanyile, who was with the Keynotes on and off. Some of these friends jammed with us whenever we hit their town. A good time was had by all. I think we were somewhere in the northern parts of the province when we got a report that Bhazabhaza's house had been attacked by angry neighbours determined to rid the township of the reputation it had gained, thanks to Bhazabhaza, as the centre of prostitution.

In the ensuing attack, it was said, Bhazabhaza had been seriously injured. It took the intervention of the police to save his life. We had no way of going back to the township to find out what had happened. Besides, we were scared that we would also be attacked for our association with Bhazabhaza. So we decided to prolong our tour. We were on the road for about two years. It had been agreed between the members of the band that we would soon be winding up the tour and would be heading back to Johannesburg. We hadn't heard from Bra Viv in a long time. But we hoped that he had forgiven us and would gladly use our expertise now that we were a fully-fledged and very famous band.

But then we had a fall-out. I was fired from the band. Remember, during my first encounter with you, Lettie, I told you how I was fired from my own band after I objected to the manner in which the manager of the hotel treated us? I went back to Chesterville where I found myself not far from Sis Jane's. I spent a few months there making a living by helping Sis Jane run her shebeen.

But a few months later, the Zeppelins called me back. I joined them in Estcourt and resumed my position at the helm of the band. We continued touring again.

The chemistry was no longer there. I had become temperamental. When the manager of the hotel we were staying at said we wouldn't be eating in the main dining room with their guests, who happened to be white, I lost it again. I started smashing plates against the wall. The white people, who had marvelled at our playing just a few hours earlier, were dismayed. The manager threatened to fire the band if they didn't distance themselves from me.

The rest, as you know, is history. I was kicked out of the band, got on the bus and that's where I met you, Lettie. My beautiful Lettie.

Twenty
Four

The Flight

Dear Zakes,

The day you took me to my aunt's house in Clermont I didn't know the history behind her husband, the history behind the Bhazabhaza you've just told me about. Anyway, the first week I stayed with them – my aunt and her wheelchair-bound husband – I remember feeling pity for him. Ag shame, poor man. Sitting all day long in the wheelchair, with nowhere to go. Now and then his friends would visit him. They would sit out on the porch, smoking dagga and drinking beer. His friends tried hard not to speak about the good old days when they used to go around robbing shebeens and banks, when Bhazabhaza was the biggest hustler around. They didn't want to speak to him about the bevy of women who had been at his command. But he was always the one to bring the pain upon himself.

'I see all these *laaities* who think they know what they are doing,' he would say when he got drunk. 'I used to drive the best, drink the best, and fuck the best ladies around. Ek was Bhazabhaza, man. The one and only. Everybody knew me; everybody worshipped at my feet.'

His friends would laugh nervously because they knew what usually followed these walks down memory lane. He would suddenly pull his gun out, and scream, 'I know you,' he would say, pointing the gun at the nearest man, 'I know you are fucking my wife now. Just because I am paralysed you think I can't do anything to her! You think I can't bone her. My boy, this is a passing phase. One of these days, I will stand up on my own feet. I'll go and fuck your wife in front of you – show you how to fuck a woman, bloody bitch!'

And then he would turn to my aunt, his wife: 'I know that you're wasting our profits from the sale of booze, paying this boy to fuck you. Shameless bitch! Pay a boy to fuck you! Sies, shameless bitch!'

Sometimes he would even start firing the gun in the air. Gradually, his friends stopped coming to the house. He was his miserable self again. Moaning that he never had true friends; that true friends do not forsake one of their own just because he has fallen on hard times.

It broke my heart to see him like that. Truly speaking, Bhazabhaza was a nice, warm-hearted person. He needed to be loved and protected. He needed somebody to help him forget his glorious past. To start all over again in life. There was a penetrating glint in his eyes. A spark of danger. A yearning for the person he used to be, I suppose. I truly liked Bhazabhaza. But then something happened between the two of us that changed my attitude towards him.

One day my aunt was away in town. I woke up early as usual and went about my chores, cleaning the house. Later in the day, I prepared him his lunch. He was sitting in his wheelchair, in his bedroom when I brought him the food in a tray.

'Put it there, sweetheart,' he said tenderly, pointing at a bedside table.

No sooner had I put the tray on the table, he had quickly shut the door. Startled by the noise, I looked up. There he was, smiling, a gun in his hand, pointed at me.

'One sound from you, you are dead,' he said coldly.

My lips trembled with fear as I suppressed a scream that was forming inside me.

'Now,' he continued, 'take off your clothes, and lie there on the bed.'

I took a deep breath as tears began to fall. Slowly, I slid off my *seshweshwe* dress. I stood there next to the bed with only my panties on.

'Hhhm, that looks lovely,' he said, unzipping his trousers with his free hand, and playing with his penis.

He continued: 'Take the panties off, and lie on the bed.'

I obeyed.

Swiftly, he rolled his wheelchair towards the bed, heaved himself out of it and he was on top of me.

I had been told that paralysed people couldn't get it up. In fact I was praying he couldn't get his manhood up. But I was more worried about his weight on my protruding tummy.

He forced his half-hard manhood into me. I was frozen with fear as the gun was sitting on the pillow, just next to my head. One slight mistake, and it could go off.

He was making groaning noises as he moved in between my legs. He was trying to probe deeper into me. I felt him tremble.

He pulled himself out of me, his seed staining the inside of my legs.

'Bitch,' he growled at me from between clenched teeth, 'why did you make me come so early?'

He slapped me hard across my face. He slapped me again and again until I felt a thread of warm blood coming out of my left nostril. I tried to move, but he reached for his gun. I froze. Still pinning me down with his body, he pushed his finger into my womanhood. He probed deeper, angrily.

I bit my lower lip in order to suppress the scream.

'This is what I do to bitches who think they know,' he said, pushing two fingers into me now, his long nails cutting me. He moved up, trying to force his tongue into my mouth. In the ensuing struggle, his gun fell to the floor. That's when I got the opportunity to run for it. I kicked the gun underneath the bed, grabbed my *seshweshwe* dress and bolted out of the room.

People shouted in shock and horror as they saw me running into the yard naked, frantically trying to cover my private parts with my dress.

Later, when I told the story to my aunt, she laughed harshly and said: 'Ag, that bloody gun does not work any more. Just like his dick.'

Even though she reassured me that I had nothing to fear, I decided to move out. I went back to Chesterville where I walked into Sis Jane's welcoming arms. By that time you, Zakes, had already left for Joburg. I heard you were running a shebeen in one of the townships up there. Sis Jane and I were soon going strong running our own shebeen. By that time, my child with my homeboy, Thabiso, had been born. Thabang, as I had named him, was a quiet child whose demeanour allowed me to put him to bed while I continued running the shebeen.

The shebeen soon developed into a busy place where men could come and pay for the company of young ladies.

Twenty
Five

Someday my Prince will Come

HER NAME WAS ROSE. She entered my life when my son Thabang was just over two years old. Lithe and fragile of body like a rose stem itself, she had a face that was open and inviting, lips tender and soft like the petals of a flower, lips pining for care and love. Our paths crossed when I was staying at Sis Jane's house, helping her run her brothel. It wasn't a brothel in the true sense of the word because we never allowed the girls to sleep with the tricks at the place. Many of the girls stayed with us for extended periods of time. To them, our house was home.

On their off days, they sat around, grooming themselves, drinking a bit, gossiping. You have to give your girls time to relax, otherwise they get sick. Business suffers. That's what male pimps don't understand. They drive the girls into early graves. Maybe it's the woman thing in us, the maternal instinct that tells us not to drive the bitches too hard.

But what we did do, like male pimps, we put the girls on the streets every evening, and drove around, making sure they worked hard.

Later, we would drive home, take the money from them and give them their share. Sometimes they found their own way home. That's another thing: male pimps never gave the girls any money whatsoever. They fed them, housed them, and clothed them. Period. They never went the extra mile to ensure that the girls' living standards were at least maintained, if not upgraded. It was our belief that a girl who felt good about herself, who felt taken care of, would go the extra mile in satisfying customers, making sure they came back for more tender loving care. Repeat business was the essence of a good hooker. And it was our role to make sure they maintained their standards and gave us a good name on the street.

Anyway, this particular Sunday morning I woke up, changed my boy and fed him. Then I gathered his toys before him and left him there enthralled by the colourful collection of what must have been the most beautiful things he had ever seen. This was a new collection of dolls and toy cars I had brought from town a few days earlier. Thabang was happy.

I was busy preparing a cocktail to remove the cobwebs of a hangover from my head when I heard a noise outside. Tap-tap. I paused. I thought that it had begun to rain outside. It had rained all night. However, when I had woken up it had stopped. As evidence of the night's rain, the leaves on the trees were still wearing glistening coats. The sky had cleared and the promise of a bright warm day glimmered on the horizon.

The noise came again. Tap-tap.

'Come in!' I called.

But no one came in. I was in the middle of tasting my cocktail of fresh lemon juice, Eno fruit salts and a dash of brandy when the timid knock sounded on the door again. A bit urgent this time: tap-tap-tap-tap.

'Stop fucking around,' I said irritably, 'you piece of...'

My heart almost stopped when my eyes fell on her. She could have been fourteen, fifteen, a tiny girl standing there at the door. She was trembling in her sodden dress. Her ribcage was visible through the flimsy rag stuck to her frame. Her eyes were terrified cockroaches darting about between the folds of swollen flesh on her face.

'Why, come in, baby. What happened to your face, who did this to you?' I had seen this girl in the neighbourhood before. But as a grown up you rarely pay attention to the brood of kids flowing through the streets. Now I took a close look at her. She must have been desperate to come to us, because we did not have children her age. She had never been to our house before.

The warmth in the kitchen overwhelmed her. She fainted. Quickly, I boiled water on the stove. I took her dress off. A few minutes later, I gently eased her into a bathtub of warm water mixed with bath salts to soothe the welts that criss-crossed her body. Her breasts were just jutting out of her tiny body. I slid the soapy face rag under her armpits, between her breasts and all over her body, making sure to be tender around the areas where the welts were visible and angry.

'Ow,' she cried out.

'Sorry, my dear, I'm very sorry,' I cooed to her.

Under her breath, she murmured: 'The bastard will rot in hell.'

I was scared of what I was about to hear. I didn't press her. I wanted her to tell the story at her own pace. I washed her hair and the back of her neck, moved slowly down her back, down to the crack between her buttocks. From there I moved to her thighs, then down to the tiny folds of flesh around her vagina. Her pubic hair was thick and soft as it should be in one in her early stages of puberty.

I could feel her relaxing as the warmth of the water enveloped her body, and the soothing effects of the bath salts took over.

Slowly, she told how she had come back home the previous evening to find her parents having an argument.

'Look at your little bitch,' her father had said as soon as his eyes landed on her. 'The little bitch is exactly like you, she comes and goes as she pleases.' Then he'd turned to Rose: 'Where have you been? Is this the right time for young girls like you to be moving around the streets, tempting the township's horny thugs?'

Her shoulders started vibrating with strong sobs. Teardrops plopped into the warm water in the bathtub. I let her cry it out, not saying a word.

Then she continued her story. From past experience, she knew to keep her mouth shut when her father got violent. Now he suddenly leapt at her, smacking her across the face. A thread of warm blood slid down a nostril. Her mother, who'd been busy chopping onions, turned around. Wielding her knife, she said: 'You touch her again, this knife will drink your blood. Coward of a man, attacking defenceless children!'

It seemed as if he was thinking of lunging at her, but the resoluteness in her eyes stopped him. He stormed out of the house.

Later, he came back home when mother and daughter had already put out the candles and were waiting fearfully in bed for his inevitable return. He barged through the door, burdening the dark air with a series of insults. He was drunker than he'd been earlier.

Fresh sobs shook her body violently for a long time. At long last she calmed herself enough to continue telling the story. Her father lit a candle in the kitchen and started walking towards the bedroom he shared with his wife. But she wasn't there. She was in her daughter's bed, the two of them hugging each other for warmth and protection. In one of her hands, the woman clutched her knife.

He kicked the door open: 'Okay, bitch, are you ready to stab me now? You'd better do it now, because I can't face the thought of you slaying me in my sleep. Let's get the shit spread thick and good on our slices of bread right now.'

'Rose's father, please go and sleep.' That's what she called him when she was sad or angry: Rose's father. Not sweetheart, not my lovely Ndlovu, not my strong Zulu bull. Just Rose's father. 'What are the neighbours going to say with you shouting obscenities like that? What are you teaching this child of yours?'

'What will the neighbours say, what will the neighbours say,' he mimicked her, twisting his face so that it looked like that of a bulldog in the dim candlelight. 'The neighbours will say a lot of things tomorrow. A lot of things I tell you. Now, come out of this room. We need to talk.'

Rose got up.

'And where do you think you're going, miss?' he asked.

'To the toilet, Daddy.'

'Shit in your pants if you like.'

'Let the child go to the toilet, for God's sake.'

Rose paused in the telling of the story. Her body remained calm, but I knew that deep inside her, she was experiencing the deepest pain thus far. She was wailing from the depths of her heart. It was a cry so deep and primordial it was taken up by the neighbourhood dogs outside. They started howling sorrowfully, the cry starting slowly, moving into a heart-wrenching crescendo.

Owwww! Owwww! Oooowwww-oooowwww! Oooowww-oooowwww-oooowwww! Like another dog had died. Owwww! Owwww!

She started again, quoting her mother: 'Let the child go to the toilet, for God's sake.'

Before she could finish the words, he started laughing. It was an emaciated laughter. Emaciated because it had no mirth, no happiness in it. It was such hollow laughter it didn't even have a germ of mockery in it. It was the kind of laughter that staggers crazily, weakly on its spindly legs, looking for shelter where it can hide its shameful face and die a quiet death. A laughter that, when it finally collapses on the ground, gives birth to maggots of furious, directionless anger. He started hitting mother and child with a sjambok. Her mother had not seen the sjambok as he'd been concealing it behind his back. For close to thirty minutes, he stung them with his sjambok, raising angry welts on their soft skin.

Rose's mother found an opening, surged towards him and plunged the knife in the area next to his heart. Stunned by her boldness and shocked by her accuracy with the knife, he said hesitatingly: 'Bitch, you... you... you're killing me? Now have a taste of this!'

There was a loud bang as he shot the woman smack in the middle of her forehead. He fired another shot, and missed. Then he collapsed. Rose's mother had been killed by the first bullet.

Her father was still breathing but it was clear he was fading away. Rose stole out of the house and ran around the yard like one in a trance, not knowing where to go. It was raining hard by then. Ultimately, she lost her strength and collapsed under a peach tree where she remained until the morning, enveloped in the smell of fresh rain and rotting peaches, mosquitoes swooping over her like fighter jets over Vietnam.

If any of the neighbours had heard the sound of the gunshots during the night, there was no indication that they were interested in finding out what had happened inside the house belonging to Ndlovu, who was a well-known watchmaker when he wasn't drinking and harassing his family.

Before sunrise the following morning, Rose had gone back into the house. Her father was still breathing. Possessed of an insane energy, the girl rushed outside. She gathered scoops of mud in her hands, small stones, rocks, and rushed back into the house to where her father lay breathing in long tortured gasps. She stuffed the dirt into his mouth. He gagged. She forced in more of the dirt. She stuffed some of it into his nostrils. He spluttered weakly. She pinched his nostrils shut and placed her tiny hand over his mouth. He spluttered weakly, shivered, and was still.

Later that day the police came to fetch the bodies.

Over the next few weeks, then, Rose became part of our family. Her house remained unoccupied until the council reclaimed it as she had no adult relatives to take it over. As part of our family she was assigned some chores – sweeping, washing pots and dishes after school. At weekends she played around with other children. Sis Jane proved to be a good foster parent who made sure the girl not only read her school books, but also went to church and attended catechism classes, which Rose enjoyed in any case.

On a warm Sunday afternoon, more than a year since Rose had moved in with us, Sis Jane and I were sitting out on the stoep enjoying a cold beer when a car stopped at our gate. Since we were not expecting any visitors, we paused to watch. In the driver's seat was a white man. There was always a fear that the authorities might come back and resuscitate the case of the death of Rose's father.

On the day the policemen came to collect the corpses, one of them had wanted to know who had stuffed the dirt into the man's mouth and nostrils. However, that line of questioning was never pursued. Nevertheless, I feared that the law might come back to haunt Rose, to haunt us.

But soon enough, we realised that the white man was dropping off Beatrice, one of our girls. It was the first time a white trick had dropped one of our girls in the township. As if of one mind, Sis

Jane and I got up and rushed towards the car. White tricks were generous. We needed to know how much he had paid her.

Sis Jane was the first one to lean into the driver's window, and spoke in honeyed tones: 'Did she give you a good time, sweetie?'

The white man looked puzzled.

'Sis Jane, Sis Lettie,' Beatrice spoke, 'he is not like that. He's not a trick.'

Shit! What game was she trying to pull? 'Okay,' said I, 'what is that supposed to mean?'

'No, man, he's my mother's boss. My mother works as a domestic for his family. Has been with them for as long as I remember.'

The white man was looking from Beatrice to Sis Jane to me, totally confused. 'Can someone tell me what's going on here? Why are you guys talking in codes?'

Rose, who'd stopped playing with her friends and was watching the scene with interest, started running towards the car. She was dressed in her play clothes – dirty white shorts, and a sleeveless shirt that also used to be white. No shoes. She edged Sis Jane out of the way, and stuck her head into the driver's window.

'Come, mister,' she said, 'the ladies are very rude and uncivilised. I'll show you how a gentleman should be treated.'

She tugged at his hand. A silly smile on his face, the white man opened the door, and got out of the car. All three of us women stood there, and watched Rose leading the white man into the house.

'What are you guys waiting for?' she said in her tiny voice. 'The gentleman has been driving, he must be dying of thirst.'

We burst out laughing as we pulled chairs onto the porch, sat down and opened two bottles of beer. The man had relaxed by then. He introduced himself as Dieter Schneider. Beatrice took over. She told us how the Schneiders were like her own family. How Schneider senior had come to South Africa after the Second World War to found a successful company that manufactured ball-bearings. As soon as he arrived in the country, he hired Beatrice's mother as a domestic. Over the years, she became a member of the Schneider family. Schneider and his wife paid school fees for all the members of Beatrice's family; those bright enough to go to university did not have to worry about funds as the Schneiders were always there to help.

Dieter turned out to be as effervescent and generous of spirit as his father had been in his lifetime. By the time he left, he was quite drunk. The following week he came back. And the following week. I sensed a strong chemistry between him and Sis Jane. Whenever he was around, Sis Jane would be dressed in her Sunday best. She would try to polish up her accent and diction, occasionally throwing German and French words into the conversation.

'The man says he wants us to leave for Swaziland,' she confided in me one day. Those days, because of the Immorality Act, which prevented sex or marriage between people of different races, mixed couples had to cross the border to Swaziland, a country with no apartheid, where they could get married and start families without having to worry about stupid laws.

In life, young prostitutes dream of fast cars, fancy clothes and jewellery, and good food – the fast life. An old woman like Sis Jane, a woman who'd lived dangerously and in sin all her life dreamt of a prince who would come to save her from the rigours of life. They would get married, get rich and live happily ever after. To start preparing for that kind of life, Sis Jane was spending a lot of time at Dieter's house in New Germany.

I envied her. But I felt shame caressing my face. How could I be jealous of a friend, an elder sister, one who'd taken me under her wing when times were tough, and was almost like a mother to me?

But such feelings of piety flew out of the window when Dieter came knocking on the door one day. For a moment I was puzzled by his arrival because only the previous night he had come to fetch Sis Jane.

'Did Sis Jane leave something behind here that you want to collect now?'

'No, nothing of the sort. Where's everybody?' he asked after noticing that the house was quiet.

'*Ag*, all the girls have gone to town.'

'Perfect. Because we need to talk.' He moved towards me, touched my hand and didn't let go even when I tried to pull it away.

'It's you that I've always wanted, Lettie. You. But I was disappointed that you already had somebody else's kid. After thinking hard, I don't think that matters now. After all, you've never seen the guy since giving birth. You are not keeping a place for him in your heart, from what I have seen. You are lonely, quiet, humble, thoughtful. Just the woman I want.'

'Go away, Dieter, you don't want to spoil what you already have. It's lust that's talking'

'Give me time, Lettie, and you will see it's genuine love. It's just that Jane came onto me too heavily, drove me into a corner. All the things that we've done are of her own doing, her own design. She is just such a powerful woman. She is driving the whole process. And I realise that I will live to regret what I am getting into.'

'Go away, man,' I tried to break away. But there was no determination in my movements. I wanted to be touched, to be held. There was a strange emptiness in my heart. For the first time in my life I understood the meaning of loneliness. It was a feeling I had never felt before; a strong feeling that had a mind all of its own, a feeling that was determined to influence how I reacted to Dieter's entreaties.

So we ended up doing it on Sis Jane's bed. Rose walked in on us. Perhaps she had been in the house all along for we never heard her coming home. We were busy on the bed, when we suddenly saw her standing at the foot of the bed, watching. There was a deep coldness in her eyes.

'Please, Rose,' I stammered. 'Don't tell Sis Jane. Please.'

Dieter said: 'Please my girl, keep your mouth shut and uncle Dieter will make you happy.' He fished out a handful of banknotes from his trouser pocket.

Rose accepted the bills, but continued standing there, eyes cold and penetrating. Then she spat out: 'How could you?' There was an adult, mature ferocity to her voice.

She walked away. As I gathered up my panties, I paused for a moment wondering: what was it that I had done with this man? There was anger in my heart because the whole thing hadn't been worth the trouble in the first place. One, two, three thrusts, and he was groaning like an injured bull. Then he collapsed. But what also collapsed was a relationship I had worked so hard at: my bond with Sis Jane.

Over the next few weeks, I waited anxiously for Sis Jane to confront me. She never did. She remained her own warm self, dreaming loudly about their imminent departure for Swaziland. I searched Rose's eyes for clues. There were none. I soon forgot about the whole sorry incident.

Then one weekend Rose disappeared.

On Monday, Sis Jane came home in tears. Dieter had called the wedding off. He was moving to Swaziland that very week – with Rose, who he was marrying. She was only 17 years old and he was in his mid- to late thirties.

Sis Jane fell headlong into drinking sprees. She started beating up our girls.

Dieter and Rose were married in a wedding that was covered by Pace and other society magazines. Over the following months Rose was on the covers of magazines, she had suddenly become a sought-after model. Her body, which had been all bones and protruding ribs not so long ago, had filled out, making her a lanky young woman who seemed destined for the pinnacle of the modelling world.

'God will avenge me,' Sis Jane never stopped chanting.

As if in answer to her incantation, God rolled his dice: Rose ran away from Swaziland. Gossip columnists had it that she had eloped with a young fashion designer, a coloured fellow who was a close friend of Dieter's and they had fled to South Africa.

The nights were many and long when I would lie awake at night, staring into the darkness, blaming myself for what had happened between Sis Jane and Dieter, and what was happening to Rose's life. Surely little Rose wouldn't have turned out the way she did had she not stumbled on Dieter and I that day. Our fling had planted ideas in her mind. She took advantage of Dieter's weakness for the female form, I suppose.

As I lay there thinking, what was killing me most was that I had just realised that I was pregnant once again. And this certainly the result of the fling with Dieter. How could I do this to Sis Jane, a loyal friend who had rescued me from the wintry frowns of city people to the summery warmth of her heart? For a moment I felt like running away, back to my home in Lesotho where the sun shines bright and true, soothing the most troubled soul. I longed for the warm breeze of the Lesotho highlands, which would be a balm to my wounded conscience. I longed for the endless fields of sunflower plants and butterf…. I stopped myself before I could even think of the butterflies.

Then out of the blue, Dieter phoned the house one weekend. Sis Jane, who'd picked up the phone, dropped it angrily upon hearing his voice. He phoned again. I picked it up, told him to fuck off, and put the phone down. He phoned almost the whole day, sounding agitated, a breathless urgency in his voice. At last, I decided to listen to him.

'Listen, you guys must come over to the house. I'm having a major party. Rose and Marc, that's her husband, are with me celebrating their honeymoon.' He paused, took a deep sigh as if in appreciation of the fact that someone was at last prepared to listen to him. He continued: 'We need to sit down and talk like the family that we've always been. Things are cool between me and Rose. Make sure Jane comes along. We really need to hook up and talk. For old time's sake.'

I relayed the message to Jane who cursed and cursed. But later in the evening, she decided we should go to the house after all. There was a menacing glint in her eyes. We dressed in our Sunday best. Earlier, I had seen Jane tucking her gun into her handbag. While she wasn't looking, I took it out and slid it into my own handbag. We drove away.

It was getting dark when we parked outside the house. There were two cars parked out on the street, a flashy Valiant Regal and a Toyota bakkie. I couldn't help noticing that there were bags of cement on the back of the bakkie. There were other tools – saws, hammers and stuff.

Wordlessly, we walked through the gate and were suddenly hit by loud music coming from the house. There were bright lights shining in all the windows. But other than that, there was no life.

We walked across the threshold and shouted hello above the din of the loud music. When the song came to an end, the silence was eerie. I shouted again. Still no answer. We walked from the kitchen, down the passage, into the lounge. And right in the middle of the floor, Dieter lay in a pool of his own blood. There was a gun next to his head, and a white piece of paper.

'Phone the cops!' I said.

Sis Jane fumbled through her handbag. With a knowing smile, I reassured her: 'Your gun is in my bag.' She scowled before dialling the local police station.

The police did not take long to arrive.

'How long ago did he phone you?' one of the three policemen asked.

'Between two to three hours ago,' I said, hugging Sis Jane who was sobbing like a baby.

'Hey,' the other cop who was crouched over the body, holding the piece of paper, 'this is a curious little suicide note: "Rose and Marc wanted to concretise their relationship in true matrimony, so I helped speed the process. Now they are as concrete as concrete can be, with a honeymoon awaiting them in heaven. Ha ha ha!" '

So he killed them, I thought. As if reading my thoughts, the senior policeman said: 'Their bodies must be somewhere in the house. Their car could be one of those parked outside.'

We sprang into action, searching under beds, inside cupboards, every nook and cranny. Apart from three empty whisky glasses, a half-full bottle of Johnny Walker Black, three dirty plates, a salad platter, and twelve empty beer bottles, the house was spotlessly clean. We ended up outside, checking the garage, the garden. Still nothing.

'What's this smell here?' one of the policemen said, shining a beam of torchlight around a huge drum.

A swarm of butterflies suddenly materialised, fluttering towards the drum. They settled on the drum. I almost jumped out of my skin.

Sis Jane noticed, and asked: 'What's wrong?'

'Ah, nothing.'

It seemed to me I was the only one who could see the swarm of butterflies. Some of them fluttered towards Sis Jane's face, landing there temporarily before moving on. They flowed brightly under the dim evening light. They fluttered into the policeman's face, and landed on his bare arm. He did nothing to show he was aware of their presence.

He peered inside the drum. We joined him. There was what looked like concrete inside it. The senior policeman probed it with a stick.

'Still wet,' he said, 'I wonder what he was doing mixing concrete and then killing himself?'

We lost interest and walked away to continue the search elsewhere. I remembered seeing bags of cement on the back of the bakkie parked outside the house.

'Fuck!' the senior policeman shouted suddenly. 'The concrete. He used the word concrete in his note!'

We rushed back to the drum. The men tipped it over. The thick concrete started sloshing out, and the torchlight guided us through lumps in the concrete, which the senior policeman probed to reveal a severed arm, and then what looked like a face.

Today, so many decades later, when I look at my half-white son Prince I see in him a two-headed ghost of Dieter and Rose. The Lord God knows how hard I've been trying not to cross paths with these ghosts in my mind.

It's hard, the Lord God knows it's hard.

Twenty
Six

Chasin' the Train

Dear Lettie,

I never got to hear about these tragedies crowding Sis Jane's life because, by that time, I was already in Johannesburg. Too far away.

You will never understand what my discovery that you were carrying Thabiso's baby did to me. It killed my heart that the person I loved the first time I laid my eyes on her belonged to somebody else. I felt that if I turned my back on Durban and its surrounds, the distance would help heal the emotional wounds.

You probably have heard of Laluki Molewa. He is one of those few people who are single-minded, focused and ruthless – refusing to let anyone stand between him and his goals. Back in the day, as they say, I remember this skinny little bum coming to me when I was at the height of my musical career with the Zeppelins. He said he could play the trumpet. We gave him a chance to prove himself. He turned out to be disaster. When I told him so, he cursed and cursed, saying we black people would never conquer whites because, instead of helping those darkies with some potential and determination, we run them down. We pull them down, and trample on them. He left our rehearsal room in tears of rage. But he kept coming back to take more doses of humiliation at the hands of my band members. After a few months of begging, cajoling, threatening, I gave him a semi-permanent position as a reserve trumpeter in my band. Some of the band members would turn up for performances as drunk as sailors, at which point I would call poor Laluki to join us on stage. With time, he blossomed into a good trumpeter. But his other interests – bootlegging booze into the township – eventually took precedence. He was to become the benefactor of the band, paying

223

our transport costs, buying us food and booze, before our final departure from Johannesburg down to Durban. He was rich, he loved music and felt he needed to help the struggling musicians.

Anyway, to cut a long story short, when I went back to Johannesburg to flee the emotional pain of losing you, Lettie, to the father of your unborn child, I took refuge at Laluki's place in Soweto. He had become quite a big businessman. Such a generous spirit he was. He never took issue with the fact that during my years of fame and relative fortune in Durban I never once invited him to come down and bask in my glory.

'You darkies will never learn,' he said, taking a swig from his whisky as we sat at a private booth inside his famous Blue Fountain nightclub. 'The minute a darkie thinks he's got it made, he forgets where he comes from, cuts all associations with his sorry past, and lifts his arrogant nose to the skies. But when the skies fall down on him, and he comes down crashing down to Mother Earth, he expects other poor darkies to sympathise with him, to pick him up, dust off his trousers, put him on a pedestal, so he can start all over again with his arrogance.'

Now Laluki's fame lay in the fact that he did favours for people. He appreciated it very much if those people returned the favour. If, however, people failed to do so, unfortunate things happened to them. For example, the police would suddenly discover that the person who had failed to return Laluki's favour was in Johannesburg illegally, that his papers were not in order.

Also, spouses of the people who failed to return Laluki's favours would suddenly discover that their dearly beloved was maintaining another wife and family elsewhere in the rural areas. But those who failed to return Laluki's big favours, tended to simply disappear off the face of the Earth. I think that's how Laluki got to be known as the Godfather of Soweto, after Don Corleone in the famous movie The Godfather. He was ruthless.

So, when I got to Johannesburg the second time around, Laluki accepted my humility and my preparedness to work for him. My duties included collecting booze in one of his many bakkies from some of his white connections. In turn these whiteys collected the booze from the breweries at a discounted price.

We made the necessary adjustments to the price, and distributed booze to satisfy the parched throats in the many illegal shebeens in the townships. I loyally helped Laluki to make his fortune, to continue buying new car after new car, to buy new house after new house.

But I was living large as well. I was at liberty to drive any of his cars – even in my leisure time. I entertained ladies, drove around with my old musical buddies. When it took his fancy, Laluki would hire one of the many halls in Soweto and throw a musical shindig. A hastily put together band would see me at the helm, enjoying myself. But by Monday, it would be business as usual, collecting booze from the whiteys, distributing it, collecting money and sending it back to Laluki.

Routine has never been my strong suit. I soon got bored. But this time, greed got the better of me. I wondered what would happen if I were to clinch private deals with the white middlemen, and become another version of Laluki myself.

I had developed bonds and trusting relationships with the white middlemen so that when I broached the subject with one of them, he merely shrugged and said: 'I actually don't care, just as long as I get my money.'

I set up three shebeens in quick succession. At the beginning, I would fulfil my obligations as expected by Laluki, and then work the extra hours collecting my own stock from the suppliers, to deliver to my own shebeens.

When I felt financially confident, I told Laluki that I had found my own place to live. I told him I was ready to start a family.

Soweto summers are full of cheer. The sky above the huge township is free of the dark, smelly, coal smoke belched from millions of chimneys in the winter months.

Schools close down for the long summer holidays at the end of November. Children can be seen moving in little groups. They might look aimless, but they've got their days planned down to a T.

Their main intention is to cause as much mayhem as possible. Except they don't call it mayhem; they call it 'having fun'. They use their slingshots to shoot birds perched on tall electric poles. Not all of them are good shots, of course. As a result, their stones veer towards the houses, breaking windows. Sometimes a passer-by gets his nose stung by a stray pebble from the slingshot. Finding the culprit is like searching for the proverbial needle in the haystack. And these kids can run fast too. And they all look the same and dress the same. You can't say: the culprit was dressed in such and such colours. You'd look really stupid because they all wear faded jeans and takkies and caps worn backwards.

Now and then an unfortunate mongrel falls victim to the stones from the slingshots. Brave boys jump fences into neighbours' yards to steal peaches while the owners are away at work. The scent of ripening peaches is thick in the air. It overpowers all the other smells: the smell of coal fires from last winter; the smell of dog shit in the streets; the smell of stale water trapped in sewers that line the streets; the smell of desperation and shattered dreams and suppressed anger... all these smelly things that are part of what we call life in this Soweto.

Braver boys venture out of the townships to play cowboys and Indians on the mine dumps that glimmer yellow on the periphery of Soweto. But playing on the dumps can be dangerous. Many of these dumps tend to cave in, the ever-hungry Earth swallowing a boy or two in one go.

By mid-December, the merrymaking has intensified. Factory workers – which means the bulk of the employed denizens of Soweto – receive their end-of-year bonuses around the twelfth of December. In the days that follow, they plunge themselves into a well-deserved break, a welcome respite from their 6-to-6 shifts, six days a week. The merrymaking is real thirsty business. Each person can easily drink 12 quarts of beer each day for the whole week. There is more drinking on Christmas and Boxing Day. People slaughter sheep, dozens of chickens. Some very rich ones do not hesitate to slaughter a strong ox – a metaphor for their virility and strength.

All of this merrymaking is, of course, good business for us shebeeners. But it is bad for the people who spend their money down to their last cent so that by the time they go back to work in early January they have to bow before the loan sharks for bus and train fare. But, hell, that is life. A bird feathers its nest with other birds' feathers, as we say in Zulu.

It was during this festive period that I found myself sitting on a chair in front of my house, watching people go about their business on our busy street. Laluki parked his car in front of my yard and got out, smiling broadly at me. We exchanged greetings, and started drinking, joking.

Later, when he was about to leave, not only did the man congratulate me on my business acumen, but he gave me an Electrolux paraffin fridge. As we sat in the lounge at my newly-acquired four-roomed house in Dobsonville, he said: 'You've worked hard for me. Perhaps it's time you started something for yourself. Maybe you need to start a little shebeen, which will be supplied by us,' he said smiling, 'That's the only way you can run a shebeen successfully without being harassed by the police. By being part of the Laluki Molewa organisation. If you try to buy directly from the white man, going behind my back like you've been doing over the past few months, you will only invite trouble to yourself. You will burn your fingers.'

He paused, took a swig from his beer. Then he continued: 'I love entrepreneurship. I admire innovation. But just don't try to challenge me here in Soweto. If you want, I can help you move out. Go establish yourself in the east somewhere – Daveyton, Springs, Tsakane, you name it. I can help you get started over there. Not here in Soweto.'

I decided to eat humble pie and took him up on his offer.

My shebeen was a roaring success right from the onset. Famous businessmen and musicians such as Peggy 'Belair' Senne and Dolly Rathebe became regular patrons. I was happy. But at the back of the mind, I still felt beholden to Laluki. For every bottle of beer I sold he was collecting money from me – for doing nothing.

For every bottle of beer, Laluki was taking a 30 per cent profit – for doing nothing.

Then an idea struck me, like bolt of lightning.

My neighbour was an old man called Ntate Chimeloane. He must have been in his 50s. But his love for the bottle had added 20 years to his age. He made his living cleaning people's yards and running errands. They rewarded him with food, drink and sometimes money. He was an *isimbamgodi* – a factotum.

Chimeloane lived alone in the four-roomed house. His wife had died some time before. His children were scattered all over town, having started their own families. They were too embarrassed to even visit their father who was always drunk, smelly and a nuisance to all humanity.

When I told Ntate Chimeloane about my idea, and how much money he could make from it, he was elated.

It came to pass, then, that I started using his house as a distillery and selling outlet for homemade beer. I couldn't dispense the cheap brew from my own premises. I thought this would offend my regular, high class customers who drank clear beer, whisky, brandy and all the other top notch white man's liquor. This type of black person did not take kindly breathing the same air as Ntate Chimeloane and his ilk. The Chimeloanes of this world were an embarrassment to the black community. It was true that the black man was oppressed; but he should endure the oppression with quiet dignity, the top class darkies reasoned. He shouldn't grovel and refuse to take a bath just because he was oppressed.

Anyway, I took to the business of brewing the illegal concoction with alacrity. I had learnt the skill of brewing *isqatha* – a lethal concoction of sorghum, bread crumbs, yeast and sugar – back in Durban. To speed up the fermentation process, I would add tartaric acid. Elsewhere in the township, other brewers used car battery acid to give the concoction an extra kick. *Isqatha, spapala lemazenke, umgodi* – it had many names, this concoction. It was popular with the lowest paid workers, or the unemployed and pensioners, because it was cheap. The overheads were low. Unlike beer, which sold briskly over the weekend, *umgodi* sold all day, every day, because its consumers were people like my neighbour. Even the so-called respectable people resorted to this cheap concoction when the days were lean, and the money scarce.

When Laluki heard that I was brewing and selling this concoction, he laughed long and hard. Then he said: 'You just don't give up. You're a real businessman. But one piece of advice: don't consume the poison you're brewing.' He laughed again.

My sorghum beer shebeen at Ntate Chimeloane's place became a roaring success. Some of Laluki's regulars, factory workers who could not afford clear beer until pay day, gravitated towards me when the days were dark and the cash flow hesitant. My brew was cheap and potent. Even younger men, who had just finished school but were still looking for work, or were scrounging for some money to register at university, sought solace in my brew.

I developed many friendships with some of these young men. They would come any time of day, any day of the week, with some books, newspapers, magazines and start reading or discussing what they'd read. The more I listened to them, the more I realised that their discussions were not just naïve and time-wasting talk about soccer and fashion. These young men were talking about heavy issues: the state of the nation. They spoke of an impending revolution. My own political theories had mellowed over the years; I was too busy making money to start making enemies with the government. But I never interrupted the young men in their animated discussions for in them I saw a younger version of myself. Ah, the idealism of youth.

But the camaraderie and friendship that had developed between the boys and I was not to last. On the winter morning of 16 June 1976, Soweto exploded. Students protesting against inferior education turned the township upside down. Beer halls, buildings, police stations and other municipal buildings were at the receiving end of the wrath of angry students who blamed their parents for sitting still and passing time with booze while the future of the next generation was being suffocated by the ruling racist government.

A week into the uprising, one of Laluki's shebeens was burnt down. The rumour was that he was a mole planted in the township by the System to delay the struggle of the people. It was also said that the many political activists who had been arrested, some of whom lost their lives in police detention, had been betrayed by my friend.

I did not wait to see what happened to my own enterprises. I packed my musical instruments, rushed to the train station in town and fled to Durban, which, although it had been singed by the fires of the revolution, remained relatively calm.

Once again, a new life awaited me in the city of my birth.

Twenty
Seven

The Test

Dear Zakes,

With Rose gone, life at Sis Jane's house became an endless dirge. Sis Jane and I were in endless mourning. One by one, the girls who worked the streets for us began to drift away. Finally, they disappeared altogether from our lives. We didn't mind. We were too engrossed in our mourning. We now concentrated on booze sales in order to put food on the table. There were my two boys to take care of as well, Thabang and Prince.

Sis Jane had become a shadow of herself: gaunt, dark in complexion, and generally badly groomed. She didn't seem to care about her looks anymore. Even the men who visited us to buy drinks on Fridays whispered about this transformation. She had become cantankerous and irritable, which is why fewer and fewer men frequented the place.

Also, she had started to have nightmares, almost every night; sometimes even during the day when she nodded off.

'I'm afraid of going to sleep, you know,' she told me as we sat drinking beer under a mango tree one hot Saturday afternoon, 'as soon as I fall asleep, I have all these vivid visions of Rose being chopped into pieces by that… that… Dieter. Then the blood-soaked pieces of her seem to have a life of their own, gradually moving together until they form a mound. Then the mound turns into Rose herself, except she doesn't have eyes. Just empty sockets. But her lips are trembling with anger. Her nails are long, almost as long as her fingers. Then she starts moving towards me with that face of hers contorted in anger. Then her nails start digging into my face, she tries to gouge my eyes, to cut my throat. I fight back, but she is much, much stronger than me. I have a feeling that one of these days

233

I will die in my sleep; you will find my blood-soaked body in my bed.'

'But Sis Jane, these are just dreams. Problem is you are blaming yourself for her death. That shouldn't be so. You did nothing to contribute to her death. It's all God's doing. Fate.'

'But had I not fallen for that ... that Dieter, things would have been different. Rose would still be alive had I not welcomed that... that Dieter into this house.'

'Don't be hard on yourself.'

'You don't understand what I am saying, Lettie. I drove the girl into the man's arms!'

'Don't be ridiculous,' I said. Images of me and Dieter in bed started flashing in my mind.

Sis Jane searched my face suspiciously, and said: 'You know how I drove her into Dieter's arms. You do know!'

'No, I don't know of such foolishness.'

She sighed. Tears started running down her cheeks, her lips trembled as she tried to arrest the sobs building inside her. Her shoulders trembled.

At long last, she calmed down. She said: 'You do have a beautiful child.' She was brushing Prince's thick hair as he played on the grass mat in front us.

I did not utter a word. I knew what was coming.

'I wish I could have one of my own, a chubby little thing like this,' she said, smiling sadly.

I swallowed hard, my heart pounding.

'But my time is over. I'm too old to have a child now. The gods have turned their backs on me.'

'Don't say such foolish things, Sis Jane. One is never too old to conceive. You just have to take your time. One day your own prince will come.'

She looked sadly at me.

'Lettie,' she said, taking a swig from her beer, 'you've been such a good friend to me, such a good sister.'

'You have been good to me too, rescuing me from the streets and all...'

'Don't talk for the sake of talking. Only open your mouth if you have something intelligent to say. Otherwise shut the fuck up and listen.'

Sparrows were making a racket in one of the trees. The smell of ripe mango rose to my nostrils.

'You've been a dear friend, but I've never taken you into my confidence. Of course you do know that somewhere in my family tree there's white blood; that I can rightfully be called a coloured woman. But that's not the end of the story. You see, my mother came from the Balobedi people, in the extreme northern part of the country, on the border with Rhodesia. That's where my mother's people come from. The Balobedi swear by Queen Modjadji, the rain queen that you must have heard about. She is not a figment of the imagination; she is very much alive. When she dies, her throne will be inherited by her favourite daughter, who, as we speak, is being taught the skills of talking to the gods above to ask for rain. But that's not where my story is going; I'm not interested in how, during the dry months, they pray to the gods above and the heavens suddenly burst forth with life-giving rain. No, the story I want to tell is about the queen herself. She doesn't keep a husband, but keeps a harem of wives. She sleeps with these women and treats each of them like a man would a woman: she is affectionate, spoils them with gifts and so forth. Whenever she wants these women to conceive, men are summoned to the palace to make love to these special women. The women's duty is to bear children who will keep the tribe going. But more importantly, one of these women will bear the next rain queen. Only on rare occasions does the reigning queen sleep with a man and conceive. More importantly, offspring from such a liaison has never been known to ascend the throne of the rain queen.

'But a girl who has been earmarked by the reigning queen as her successor is kept under a strict watch. When she reaches the age of 12, the most trusted elderly woman in the palace is assigned the duty of testing the girl. The testing entails inserting the woman's little finger into the girl's vagina. This is done to ensure her chastity has not been violated.'

Sis Jane suddenly threw her head back, laughing like one possessed. The children, who had fallen asleep in the torpid heat, were startled out of their slumber. They started crying. I gave them their bottles. They calmed down.

'For some reason, this practice, which was originally confined to the palace, spread over the years, during my great grandmother's time, to the houses of ordinary people. Women started testing their daughters. A daughter whose chastity had been violated was hastily married off to an old man of the village if she couldn't be made to confess who had violated her.

'It came to pass, then, that my grandmother got tested, and my mother after her, and my mother's sisters, and their cousins. It became an acceptable practice. Mothers took pride in the chastity of their children – even though the subject was never discussed openly. When I was around six, I occasionally chanced upon my aunt testing her daughters who were older then me. I couldn't wait to be tested myself. When I became of the right age, I took to the tests with alacrity. But as I grew older, I became more uncomfortable. As she inserted her finger, my mother would tell me fairytales in order to distract me.'

Fistos, a neighbour, disturbed Sis Jane's narrative when he suddenly appeared from behind the house. He wanted three bottles of beer, a take away. I got up to serve him. He went away.

'Then one day – I must have been about fourteen – my mother led me to the bedroom for the test. I positioned myself on the bed as usual. She inserted her finger; then stopped telling the fairytale she had just started telling. She inserted the finger again, and started shivering. 'Who did this to you? Who damaged you? Who broke your girlhood?' For a moment I lay back there, enjoying her shock, her sudden panic. She hurried to the door, made sure it was locked. 'My girl, which boy did this to you? Please tell me before your father finds out, before the whole village finds out.'

'I told her this was the work of my grandfather from my father's side, the very light complexioned man who was known in the village as 'the white man' even though it was well known he was of mixed breed. By that time, my father was working in the mines. Which is why his father thought it was his responsibility to check up on us.

'That evening, my mother took me to a local woman who was good with herbs. When we arrived at the herbalist, she and my mother conferred for a brief moment, talking in hushed tones so that I couldn't hear what was being said. Later, I was made to drink a herbal mixture that had a honey aftertaste. That night I couldn't sleep. There was a revolution in my stomach; I kept vomiting. I rushed to the toilet endlessly, until I thought my intestines and every organ inside me was going to come out of me. The following day I slept for the whole day. Three days later, my mother took me back to the herbalist. She kept telling me not to fear; no herbs would be administered to me that day. I cried and tried to run away, but three of my mother's friends – formidable women with big arms and big bottoms – caught me every time I tried to run away. Resigned to whatever lay ahead of me, I allowed myself to be dragged to the house of the herbalist.

'There was no waste of time. The women dragged me to the bedroom and flung me on a grass mat. My panties were duly removed. I was made to lie on my back, my legs wide open for the women to look at my private parts. My mother forced two spoons of a bitter-tasting liquid into my mouth. I began to nod off.

'The following day, I woke up on my own sleeping mat, disoriented and confused. I sat up. My mom was sitting on a chair in front of my mat, looking expectantly at me. I felt the urge to go to the toilet.

'Where are you going?' my mom wanted to know when I tried to brush past her.

'I want to go to the toilet.'

'You can't.'

'Why not?'

'Relieve yourself in that bucket,' she said, pointing at a green bucket in the corner. I looked at the bucket, then at her face. I squatted on top of the bucket and started urinating.

'A hot, sharp pain burned my privates and I screamed out loud. My mother jumped to help me from falling. In the process of screaming, I had toppled the bucket. Now urine was running down my legs. Because of the sudden, unexpected pain, my bowels had emptied themselves. Human waste shamed the floor. The pain continued to burn my private parts. I think I fell into unconsciousness.

'I spent so much time in bed, in deep pain, that I lost count of days. I felt disoriented. The pain continued to burn my genitalia whenever I tried to urinate; I tried to postpone my date with the smelly bucket as much as I could.

'It was much, much later that I discovered the lips of my vagina had been stitched shut, leaving a hole small enough to allow the passage of urine.'

By that time, darkness had fallen. My face was sodden with tears as Sis Jane said: 'Dear Lettie, that's how I have spent the rest of my life running away from that pain; but I just can't seem able to run away from myself. I've spent my womanhood trying to get men to free me from the shame visited upon me by my own mother; all in the name of culture. I'm crippled, Lettie. Men love my face and my charm – until they discover my handicap. I drive them into the arms of my friends.'

Over the following weeks, Sis Jane became an old hag wallowing in self-pity. During the day, she would sit under our mango tree, beer in hand, staring vacantly into the distance. She would stay like that until the beer in her hand got warm, or some insect drowned itself in it.

At night she would wake up screaming, in the throes of a nightmare. 'She was back again tonight,' she would speak out excitedly.

She told me the nightmares involving our little friend Rose were becoming more frequent, more violent.

'Look at what the bitch did to my face,' she told me one morning, showing me sheets covered in blood, her face full of scratches, 'she scratched my face, Lettie, see? She scratched my face.'

Indeed, her face was covered with fresh cuts. But there was also blood on her long fingernails: 'Sis Jane, these cuts on your face are self-inflicted. You injured yourself in your sleep. Your guilt is killing you. You are constantly blaming yourself for her death, and you try to compensate for that guilt.'

'No, you think I'm that stupid? You think I would injure myself?'

'No, you are doing this in your sleep, subconsciously. You are still blaming yourself for her death; you subconsciously believe you need to be punished for it. Walk away from this shit, Sis Jane. It's just not good for you.'

'No, she comes to me at night and scratches my face, using my own hands. I think you would say she hypnotises me so that I don't know what I'm doing to myself. She's a vicious bitch. She's a vicious spirit.'

Over the following weeks I decided to sleep in her bedroom, sharing her huge double bed with her. My system soon adjusted itself to the new sleeping arrangements and I would wake up just as her nightmare was beginning to rouse her from the weight of the demons in her subconscious. Miraculously, the nightmares seemed to stop.

But that signalled the beginning of something else.

Twenty
Eight

Drive

A NEW JAZZ BAND WAS ROCKING Durban around that time. It was called Drive. The Shange brothers played in it – I think one of them was Claude and the other Sandile. I could be wrong about the first names, but they were from the Shange family, one of the well-known families in Chesterville. Radio Zulu used to play their music a lot.

Then someone decided to host a huge music festival. I think it was called MilkAfrica Music Festival. The line-up was so colourful that Sis Jane and I decided to go the Kingsmead stadium where the music feast would be served.

'Hey,' I rushed into Sis Jane's room excitedly just days before festival. I was carrying the latest edition of Ilanga newspaper. 'They say in the paper that Zakes will be playing with Drive! Let's go to the festival, give him a pleasant surprise.'

'Damn!' Sis Jane whooped excitedly, looking at the picture of the band emblazoned on the page: 'I haven't seen that man in ages. Look at his face! He hasn't aged a day! We definitely need to go there and bask in his glorious presence.'

The day before the festival, we arranged with one of our neighbours, an elderly woman called MaSithole, to come over to the house and look after the kids. She agreed readily to help two young, excitable women who had been starved of a good time by the duties of running a shebeen and a house filled with the noise of two energetic children.

The day of the festival came. I rose early, intending to be the first in the bathroom. I wrapped my body in a towel and tiptoed towards the toilet. I tried the handle. It was locked. I didn't want to disturb whoever was inside. Maybe it was MaSithole, or Sis Jane. Seeing that it was still early, I decided to go back to bed and catch some more minutes of warmth and comfort.

I fell asleep for when I woke up the sun had already forced its fingers of warmth through my slightly parted curtains. I got up in a hurry. The toilet was still locked. I could hear MaSithole talking to the boys in the kitchen. I was now convinced it was Sis Jane in the bathroom.

'Please finish up, we are running late!'

No response.

'I don't know what's wrong with her,' MaSithole shouted from the other room. 'She's been in there for hours. The irritating thing is she is not responding. I was so pressed I had to go and squat behind the house. My bladder is not young anymore, ha ha ha!'

I banged some more on the door. Still no response. I began to panic.

'Maybe she's fallen asleep,' MaSithole said, 'I think she drank too much last night. Deep into the night I could hear her moving about the house, rattling glasses, opening cupboards. I think she's collapsed from the effects of too much alcohol in her system. Give her a few minutes.'

I wasn't going to give her any more minutes. I rushed out the house, round the back, and started knocking on the window to the toilet. No response. I picked up a rock, smashed the window pane. I propped a rubbish bin against the wall, climbed on it and opened the window. I could see her down there on the floor, sitting in a foetal position, her back against the wall. She was breathing loudly, with some difficulty.

'Somebody help, somebody help!' I screamed, rushing to the yard next door. Three young men were standing idly, smoking cigarettes.

'I need some help,' I said, grabbing the nearest boy, 'Sis Jane has hurt herself. She's locked there in the bathroom. I need you to squeeze yourself through that window, unlock the door from the inside, and let's see what's wrong with her.'

Sis Jane died on the way to King Edward VIII Hospital. Not only had she cut her left wrist, she had also driven a huge piece of wood that we used to stir our stiff porridge into her private parts, rupturing all the sensitive organs down there. I cried long tears at this loss. She had been my big sister, my anchor. But I knew that wherever she was, Sis Jane was smiling happily. She had triumphed over those who'd tried to own her sexuality. She had broken the sad tradition of having to pass on the madness of genital mutilation in the name of culture and preservation of women's chastity.

Yes, Zakes, that's why I didn't come to the music festival to see you play with Drive. That's why you didn't come to the funeral. You didn't know about it. But now you know what happened to Sis Jane.

Twenty
Nine

Something for Nothing

LETTIE,

I was a man on the run. Well, not really. But I had been uprooted from a life I had gotten used to in Soweto. In that huge township I had built a thriving business, had made a reputation for myself as an entrepreneur, a shebeen king of some repute, a hustler.

But now here in Durban, the city of my birth, I had nothing to my name. I did not even have permanent shelter, always moving from the house of one benefactor to the next.

I did not even want to think of what had become of my businesses in Soweto. I tried my best to avoid newspapers and television news about developments in Soweto. But Laluki Molewa had become so big it was difficult to avoid hearing his name. Now and then you would hear snatches of TV news about him sponsoring a huge marathon, or starting a bursary fund for disadvantaged black children, or opening a new hotel somewhere on the East Rand. Popular magazines even ran a series on him buying a casket for himself. He had also bought a plot of land where the Molewa family would be buried. They showed pictures of him inside the casket, smiling, a speech bubble saying: 'You'll never catch Laluki napping. He's ready for any eventuality.'

My friend was such a show-off, such an exhibitionist that he made me cringe.

Although I still had strong feelings for him as a friend who had helped me through some of the darkest years of my life, I now regarded him as part of the past I wanted to turn my back on.

I was resigned to the reality of having to start all over again in Durban. I knew I had the tenacity, the staying power to start another business down here. I wasn't exactly sure what. But in order to earn my right to a roof over my head and something for my stomach,

249

I jammed with a number of bands, playing hotels and private clubs. The cats around these parts still remembered me from those bygone days when me and my Zeppelins were happening around these parts.

I moved from one boarding house to the next hotel with various members of the band we'd decided to call Drive. By that time I had been back in Durban for about two years, give or take. The original Drive had collapsed, with some members dying in a car accident, others quitting music altogether in order to dedicate the last of their remaining years to their long-suffering families. Most of the original members were older than me.

Drive now existed in name only. Youngsters with some talent would stagger into the ranks of the band and hang out with us for a few months. When they thought they had imbibed the magic of Drive, they would stagger out of the band back to wherever they'd come from.

Zorro Sibisi, one of the few remaining old school philanthropists around Durban, took an interest in the band. Sibisi was one of those characters that grace this Earth with their presence once in forty, fifty years. When they do finally pass on, they leave in their wake numerous legends. So it was with Sibisi.

Sibisi was loved for his respect for the poor man, for his great regard for the downtrodden masses, for his sense of justice, for his help to those who remained loyal to him and for his decisive action and implacable punishment of those who crossed him.

I think there is a part of me that appeals to the sensibilities of influential people. I have inherent leadership skills, if I might say so myself. Whenever my path crosses that of a powerful man, he seems to warm to me. I thought about this, not for the first time of course, when Sibisi decided to put me in charge of the band. Not only that, but he provided me with lodgings of my own at the back of his huge house in Siyajabula, the shack settlement which Sibisi ran as his own personal fiefdom. By the time the authorities woke up and complained that Sibisi and his people had illegally occupied land belonging to the municipality of Durban, it was too late. The authorities knew well not to interfere at this late stage. Disputes over land always ended in bloodshed. With the political situation already fluid in the country, with supporters of the Inkatha Freedom Party and the African National Congress at each other's throats, battling over scarce resources, it would have been disastrous to try and forcefully remove Sibisi and his people from this piece of land. They were left alone.

Sibisi's house stood majestically on top of the shoulder of a hill, a huge mansion with six garages, countless bedrooms and lounges, a huge swimming pool at the back. This huge jewel of beauty lording over the huge expanse of land dotted with shacks made of plastic and pieces of zinc. In the dry season, the untarred roads boiled with dust; when the summer rains came, some of the roads were so muddy that they became impassable. But in the midst of this squalor, Sibisi had his own stretch of tarred road linking his house to the nearby township of KwaMashu. Sibisi graciously allowed taxi drivers and other car owners to use his stretch of road at their leisure, even though he had constructed the piece of road at his own great personal expense. But as a father to his people, he couldn't consider the indignity of making his 'children' pay for using his own private road. His children showed their gratitude for his leadership and his continued presence in their midst in other ways.

If a newly arrived person needed a plot of land on which to construct his own shelter, he had to seek Sibisi's approval. If one of the local schools wanted to hire a new teacher, the principal of the school had to notify Sibisi. If a woman was having problems with her abusive husband, a word with Sibisi would straighten the matter out. Because of his power and influence, Sibisi had a troop of personal minders, hulking giants of men with muddy eyes, scarred faces, hands always massaging huge guns, men who would, as it would happen later, lay down their lives for their boss.

A few months after he took me under his wing, he put me in charge of some of his businesses around the huge settlement.

It was said that before Sibisi came here, there was no settlement called Siyajabula. There was just this uninhabited piece of land on the outskirts of KwaMashu township. Sibisi had stumbled upon this piece of land after fleeing Pietermaritzburg, where he had been born and had grown up to become an influential politician. He had had to flee his place of birth after members of an opposing political party started a vicious campaign to kill members of the party to which Sibisi belonged.

Homeless, Sibisi had fled to KwaMashu where he squatted with some relatives while he sought permanent lodgings for himself. He had a gaggle of loyalists who had followed him from Pietermaritzburg looking to their leader to find a new home for his family and his followers.

It came to pass then that Sibisi's eye landed on a piece of uninhabited land outside KwaMashu, and he decided to set up a camp for himself and his followers. The camp was just a collection of shacks fashioned out of plastic and pieces of zinc. Sibisi's was the biggest. He lived there with his wife and six children.

No sooner had the settlement started, than Sibisi opened his first shop. He stocked bread, long-life milk, condensed milk, salt, flour, cooking oil, candles, tinned pilchards, paraffin, and other basic commodities for poor people.

The settlement expanded when young people who had outgrown their parents' houses in the townships and were ready to start their own families sought shelter at Sibisi's settlement. He readily allocated them pieces of land on which they pitched their own shacks. He used his own vans to help the people transport water from the township to their new homes. Next, he helped them dig a dirt road that linked their settlement to surrounding townships.

It was tough at the beginning, but the people were happy at finding respite in this new settlement untouched by political turbulence. Many of the new arrivals exhibited an entrepreneurial spirit right from the outset. They opened small shops, bottle stores and other small enterprises typical of a new community trying to rise from the ashes of a political inferno. Sibisi extracted tariffs from all the businesses. Soon, he opened his own bottle stores, butcheries and dry cleaning enterprises. The settlement had grown so big that each of the small businesses had enough clients. There was no need for rancour among the competitors.

The new arrivals were told in no uncertain terms that they couldn't affiliate themselves with any of the existing political formations. What Sibisi did next marked him as a genius of a man. Systematically, he went to the leaders of the established political parties up in arms against each other. Should you need soldiers to defend your turf, do not hesitate to speak to Sibisi, he told the leaders of the warring factions.

Soon, Siyajabula rose to prominence, was reported on in the newspapers as the politically neutral reservoir from which fighters – people who killed not out of hate, but out of a need to feed their families – were groomed. Siyajabula became the training ground for the best mercenaries in the country, thanks to Sibisi.

By the time I arrived Sibisi was already big. Siyajabula had become a semi-formal settlement with running water and sewage. There was electricity. The roads had been tarred. The settlement was now part of the Durban municipality, but Sibisi continued to extract whatever tariffs he deemed necessary from those who were running businesses there. He was the unofficial mayor, tax collector, counsellor, social worker, spiritual leader, provider of entertainment.

This was the man who had a sense of justice, a man who couldn't tolerate men who cheated on their wives, a man who had no truck with philandering youths who impregnated girls and tried to run for it. Sibisi appointed a group of men to protect his interests in the settlement. Men who were fighters. Whenever a political party needed 'muscle' Sibisi could count on these trusted lieutenants to get a group of fighters ready to be dispatched to wherever they were needed. These were men who spoke the language of money, and not ideology.

It was said, and no one ever challenged this assertion, that Sibisi had strong war medicine for his fighters. Before going to war, his men would each drink three mouthfuls of war medicine from a huge cauldron. It was said, and again no one challenged this assertion, that at the bottom of the cauldron was a human skull. After all the fighters had had their fill before going to fight, Sibisi himself would reach for the human skull at the bottom of the cauldron, and also drink his fill.

The final step in the preparation for war would see each warrior – gun or spear in hand – being made to jump over a huge fire, while at the same time stabbing the air with his weapon, and shouting: 'Ngadla! I have hit him!'

Another story is told of how a young man from Siyajabula suspected of trading information to one of the political parties was summoned to Sibisi's house. As it happened, Sibisi was sitting in his garden, eating lunch. Like many rich Durbanites he always had his meals outside in the summer; it was oppressively hot indoors. As usual, there were bodyguards hovering around the yard when the men who had caught the suspected spy entered the yard.

The young man was brought in front of Sibisi, and immediately started pleading for his life. It was so hot Sibisi had stripped down to his shorts, his big torso sweating steadily as he speared a piece of meat with his fork, sliced it with his knife and took a bite.

'I don't know anything about selling information to the enemy, baba,' the young man was crying his lungs out, tears streaming down his face, 'I would never betray the community. It is all lies.'

'Can't you feel it's hot enough without you spreading your spittle into my food?' Sibisi said, rising from his chair and stabbing the young man repeatedly in his left eye with his fork.

The young man collapsed on the ground.

Sibisi went back to his steak, spearing it carefully with the same fork, slicing it with the knife, and pushing it into his mouth.

It was a story that was to be repeated in many shebeens in the years to follow.

By the time I arrived, Sibisi had mellowed somewhat. At the height of the fighting, it was said, Sibisi did a roaring trade selling Mandrax tablets. It all started innocently enough. As part of a training regimen for war, his fighters were fed a steady diet of Mandrax tablets. By the time the fighting stopped, the fighters had become addicted to the pill. Sibisi continued to supply them – but at a price. His drug business extended beyond the borders of the settlement. He established partnerships with people who had been selling dagga before, traders who took readily to the new drug that was more profitable.

Unlike dagga which was voluminous and had to be carried in trucks from across the border with Lesotho, Mandrax was easy to handle and conceal. The retail price of each tablet was R50, a profit of R40. You couldn't make that amount of money on a handful of dagga. A dagga 'hand' retailed for R30 on the street. While it was true that the peasants who cultivated the plant charged you almost nothing, it was cumbersome to handle the herb. The future of any self-respecting and visionary drug lord lay in Mandrax.

Initially, Sibisi got his supplies from some white policemen with whom he shared the profits.

Then his white friends started disappearing. It was rumoured Sibisi was behind the killings as he wanted to control the drug business by himself, unhindered by the white policemen who he didn't trust anyway.

By the time the last policeman was found hanging from a tree outside his house, Sibisi had established direct links with Indian businessmen who brought the drugs from South America, using a complex network of cargo ships.

'I've been hearing a lot about your work with Laluki Molewa,' Sibisi said to me unexpectedly as we sat nearby his swimming pool one Sunday afternoon, drinking beer. We spoke at length about the work I'd been doing for Molewa. It later dawned on me that I had no business telling this man about the work I had done for Molewa. He had done his research thoroughly and knew about the personal tiffs that I'd had with The Godfather. He even knew about my rocky relationship with Bra Viv, the playwright.

We spoke at length about my work in Johannesburg. A few months later, Sibisi put me in charge of his nightclub Ziyasha Nite Club. As soon as I took control, I changed the rules. People younger than 18 were not allowed on the premises. The dress code also changed: no shorts, no takkies, no floppy hats. There was an outcry at the beginning. But youngsters, hot-headed as they can be, knew not to mess with Sibisi if they still wanted to live in the settlement.

Once a month, my band Drive would entertain, and I would be there on the stage making love to my trumpet. We had guest artists every now and then – big names and upstarts as well. This of course made me very popular with lovers of live music. It didn't hurt my chances with the ladies as well, young and old, of all shapes and sizes.

Despite the activity around me, there were times I would stare into the distance, thinking about you, Lettie, wondering if you'd let me into your heart. I kept wondering how old your son would be by now.

I felt sad every time I thought of you. I was afraid to go out looking for you in case you had married and settled down with the father of your child. Worse still, I feared you might have met someone else, had another baby, and gotten married. I was too scared to face disappointment. I decided to shut you out of my mind, and continued chasing other skirts.

But my escapades almost got me killed one night. A certain lady friend who lived in Umlazi asked me to drive her to her home after a sweaty session at the back of the club. Slightly tipsy, I decided to drive her myself instead of getting one of the drivers or bodyguards to do the job.

As I stood kissing her outside her home in Umlazi, we were accosted by three youngsters who wanted the keys to my car. I fought viciously, but one of them stabbed me in the right eye.

I spent the next two months in hospital recovering from the attack. Needless to say, my life was never to be the same again, cursed as I was to seeing the world through one eye.

But by that time Ziyasha had become the nightclub of choice for classy young people. They flocked from neighbouring townships to enjoy themselves there, driving in their fancy cars, dressed to the nines in the latest fashion. The Mandrax really took off within the confines of the club. Sibisi was unhappy with this arrangement initially.

'I don't want the pills to be traced back to me,' he told me one night as we sat drinking and smoking at the back of the club. 'We can't afford to sell from the premises.'

He was pleasantly surprised to learn that I had a comprehensive list of names of top cops who were on my payroll. I worked closely with one of his three sons, Sibusiso. He was a bright young man who was prepared to listen and learn. He treated the policemen on our payroll with great respect and courtesy. Whenever they stumbled into one of our establishments, he would be the first one to know and would facilitate money, or some other gift, to be offered to them. Our chances of being busted were remote.

Soon enough, as Sibisi's lieutenants and runners in the greater Durban area gained my confidence, and we expanded our drug business. We made Sibisi rich in the process. But individually, as the top lieutenants we were also doing well. Some of the lieutenants entered the lucrative taxi business. Whenever there were fights over routes between the various taxi associations, our coterie of fighters could always be counted upon to provide the necessary muscle.

I personally bought five kombi taxis which operated in Umlazi.

Everything was looking all peaceful and prosperous when Zorro Sibisi died suddenly. His death was to change the course of my life yet again. A bloody war for the control of Sibisi's empire was about to begin. In my forties now, I didn't want to run away from the fight. I had run away from too many fights in my life. I wasn't getting any younger. I needed stability in my life. But stability, that sense of equilibrium, always came at a price.

Thirty

Chronic Blues

ZAKES,

With Sis Jane gone, life at her house soon became one long nightmare, literally. One constant dream I had featured a group of people, with my late father, my grandmother and Sis Jane at the forefront. The other people in the crowd had faces that looked vaguely familiar. I think one of them looked like Rose's, except she looked much older than the Rose I'd known.

These people would appear soundlessly, without ceremony, and stand at the foot of my bed, to just stare at me. Butterflies would suddenly sprout out of my grandmother's eyes and float about.

Although they never made any threatening moves towards me, these people always had me screaming and sweating when I woke up. In the middle of the night, I would hear rustling sounds like the flapping of tiny wings. The first time I heard the sound, I knew exactly what I would see if I turned on the light. Indeed, when I did finally turn on the lights, I saw the butterflies, a swarm of them floating about in the bedroom.

I tried to close off the sadness of my heart by keeping myself busy. I worked hard at reviving the shebeen. Our old clientele that had turned its back on us gradually came back. I had bought a new music system to entertain them. I had over the years developed a good ear for music. I knew what sound was in, what was out. Because I wanted to attract a mature, respectable kind of client, I knew I had to play the likes of Stompie Mavi and Era. There was also Philip Tabane and Malombo in my collection. Sakhile was top of the charts on the radio and they were one of the popular requests from my clients. One of my favourite records was Paradise Road, by a girl band called Joy. Because I played the song so frequently people decided to call my place Paradise Road instead of the old Sis Jane's place or, now that Sis Jane had passed on, Sis Lettie's. Paradise Road was to be the name I would trade under throughout my life as a shebeen queen.

Although my life was kind of back on track, the void left by Sis Jane could not be filled by anyone. It was a void I was going to feel for the rest of my life. Sis Jane had entered my life at a crucial stage when I was a nobody, when my heart was a cold, empty, bare cupboard. And so when she passed on, the void she left in my soul was palpable. Not even the biggest material success in this world could fill that gap. I had not experienced as much difficulty closing my mind to the family I had left behind in Lesotho as I was experiencing trying to come to terms with the fact that Sis Jane was no longer with me. You do not know the importance and value of what you have in your possession until you lose it.

During the day, almost every day, I would see the butterflies swarming around the yard. My children would scream excitedly at the colourful display. Men sitting in the yard, drinking beer they'd bought from me, would wonder aloud what the children were getting excited about. Adult people didn't possess the power of children. The children's innocence and purity enabled them to see things that couldn't be seen by adults, whose souls had been corrupted by the world we live in.

I knew my granny was trying to tell me something by sending me this visitation of butterflies. Sometimes the swarm took the shape of her face. But sometimes the swarm took the shape of your face, Zakes. I could see you in those butterflies. Maybe I was imagining things. Maybe I was going crazy, but I thought I saw the swarm of butterflies taking the shape of your sad face.

I knew in my heart of hearts that wherever you were, you were sad. It hurt my heart that I couldn't get myself to go out looking for you, to tell you how much I missed you, how much I needed you, to ask you to love me, to humble myself in front of you for having failed to open my heart to you those many years ago.

It hurt me even more that while you were wherever you were, sharing your sad love with whoever you had encountered over the years, I was suffering and dying of loneliness.

I never got to understand the meaning of the butterflies that had become a part of my life. Maybe I was not prepared to probe the meaning behind their appearance. All I knew was that they almost always appeared when my life was taking a significant turn. I tended to associate them with my grandmother. I think they were meant to tell me that I could have the same powers as my grandmother, to see things that could not be seen by other ordinary people, that I had special gifts. But I think they were also telling me something else.

Thirty
One

You think you know me
(But you'll never know me)

I SURPRISED MYSELF WHEN I woke up early one Saturday morning and started packing my things as if preparing for a long journey. The baby was kicking violently in my tummy. The man who had impregnated me, MaSharps Hlongwa, had become a regular at my shebeen but had not been to see me in three weeks. He was good company to have, as a lover and a handyman. He had fixed Sis Jane's car, which had been standing in the yard unused for some time. He also taught me how to drive it. Thanks to MaSharps, I was now using Sis Jane's car to run the business, and take care of my personal needs.

I was, however, angry with MaSharps for abandoning me. I didn't want to see him again ever. I don't think he missed me much. The good-looking, well-heeled businessman that he was, he had too many women vying for his attention.

I think my fight with him started the day he proposed marriage to me. In fact it wasn't a proposal as normal people know it. It was a conditional offer of marriage. He said he would marry me only on condition I 'got rid' of my two sons. What did he mean 'get rid' of my sons, I wanted to know. He said he didn't care what happened to them, as long as they were not living with us once he'd taken me down the aisle. I could take my children to my parents or grandparents or whichever relatives were prepared to have them, as long as they were not living under the same roof as us, he said. As if he was doing me a favour by offering to marry me.

I had lost all energy to get angry. Anger can be a one-way avenue – many times it's the person who harbours this emotion that gets hurt by its potent poison. The person who sparks the anger in you

267

is rarely scathed by its poison, even when you try to show him how deep your anger is. I had learnt this lesson through years of emotional turbulence.

So, when MaSharps made his otherwise infuriating remark, I just smiled at him, shook my head, and told him to fuck off, I wasn't interested. I started whistling the popular tune: 'You think you know me (But you'll never know me)'.

It's rare for black women to turn down marriage proposals, especially if these come from a well-heeled 'catch' such as MaSharps. So when I told him to fuck off and continued with whatever I was doing, he thought I was joking. No matter how kind and soft-hearted you are, life in the cities hardens your resolve in whatever you do. You become suspicious of everyone. I had always been a strong-willed person, but the city only hardened me.

I told MaSharps I would keep our baby and raise it all by myself, without his interference, thank you very much. He still thought I was joking.

Anyway, thoughts of MaSharps were the least of my worries as I loaded my things into the car and prepared to turn my back on Sis Jane's haunted house.

Having loaded all the crucial possessions that I thought I would need into my car, I bundled my two boys in and drove off.

I didn't know exactly where I was going. I drove around the city for some time, looking absent-mindedly at shops, the people, the cars and all that could be seen in the city centre.

Thirty minutes later, I found myself knocking on the front door of my Aunt Lizbeth's place in Clermont.

When she appeared at the door, she was her usual cheerful self: 'Oh, my, Lettie! Look how big you've grown!' She hugged me passionately.

Then she stepped back and inspected my two boys who were looking from her to me as if to ask: 'And what's this performance in aid of?'

There were three little girls standing behind Aunt Lizbeth. They all had the striking features of their father Bhazabhaza.

Aunt Lizbeth invited me inside the house.

'You are by yourself today. Where are your friends Jane and that man, what's his name? Zakes! Where are they?'

'Ag, it's a long story,' I said as I sank into a leather sofa. Compared to the last time I had been there, the place was exquisitely furnished. There were wooden tiles on the floor and a huge glass-topped coffee table in the middle of the room. One of the corners was dominated by a huge sound system. The walls, painted an attractive peach, were dominated by a huge framed print of Bhazabhaza playing the saxophone.

'Where is he?' I asked, nodding towards the huge picture.

Without skipping a beat, Aunt Lizbeth said: 'Sad story that. The man couldn't live with the fact that he was going to be confined to a wheelchair for the rest of his life. I went to town the other day, only to come back to some hullabaloo at this very house here. Neighbours were wailing, pulling their hair. My lovely husband had shot himself dead. Just like that (she snapped her fingers). I don't know where he got the gun from. Remember his old gun, the one that he once pulled on you, was no longer working?'

I kept quiet, looking at the picture while sipping the Coke Aunt Lizbeth had poured for me.

'Have you got a driver waiting for you in the car? Why don't you call him in for a drink or are you in a hurry?' she asked at length.

'No, I am the driver.'

She looked at me in disbelief, her eyes widening: 'Don't fuck around with me girl! Since when did you start driving cars? You are still so fresh from the sticks that your feet still stink of cow dung!' She laughed good-humouredly. 'How did you learn how to drive a car?'

We walked to the car. I opened the door and she joined me inside. While she admired my driving skills as I drove down the road, I casually said to her: 'Auntie Lizbeth, I would like to stay with you for some time. I have nowhere else to go.'

'Ag,' she said, and from the corner of my eye I saw her shrugging, 'you might as well stay with me forever seeing that these men who keep pumping your stomach aren't showing any willingness to marry you. I see you're expecting number three. Who's the father?'

'Ag, another piece of shit from Chesterville.'

'Number two's father is probably white, judging by the boy's looks?'

'Yes, he was white.'

'So you have three children from three different fathers?' Her delivery was deadpan, not remonstrative or cruel. Just stating facts.

'Yes.'

'At least Bhazabhaza gave me three children before he passed on. Which makes the total number of my brood five – from two different fathers. Not bad considering the circumstances we live in. I don't blame you for being mother to a bunch of Choice Assorteds.'

We were still laughing when I parked the car outside the yard, and started unloading my things from the boot.

In addition to the house she was living in, Aunt Lizbeth was renting two extra rooms at the back from where she sold her booze to clients. Unlike the classy shebeen that I had been running back in Chesterville, Aunt Lizbeth's establishment was homey and very downmarket. No fancy whiskies and wines here; only quarts of beer and home-brewed beer. But the place was busy and clean. The music was surprisingly upmarket – Harold Melvin & The Blue Notes, The Commodores, Aretha Franklin, Jimmy Smith, Stanley Turrentine, Big John Patten, Lou Donaldson, the lot.

I did not waste time but got right onto the job, running the shebeen. This released Aunt Lizbeth to do what she liked most: to go and work for white people doing their washing and cleaning their houses. She found two women who each needed her services two days a week. Consequently, she worked Monday and Tuesday for Mrs A, took a break on Wednesday, and worked Thursday and Friday for Mrs. B.

The car helped us a lot because when we ran out of supplies before the brewery truck came through with our weekly ration, I could rush to town for replenishments.

'You've brought a spark of glamour to the place,' Aunt Lizbeth remarked one day as we were in the kitchen brewing our special home-made beer. 'Since your arrival here I've seen new faces, faces of young men who take good care of their appearances. Clearly they see in you somebody they can impress with their clothes and money. You don't seem to be paying much attention to them.'

'But I'm very pregnant. What are they looking at me for?'

'I think they have done their research and found out that you have no attachments to a man, that you could use a shoulder to cry on. The very fact that you're giving all of them the cold shoulder seems to be driving them to high levels of desperation. I've overheard them talking about you, wondering how a man could be so foolish to allow a woman like you to be by yourself all the time.'

'Auntie, let's keep them talking. I've got enough problems as it is now. I don't want to add a man problem to the shit that's already suffocating me.'

'Bhazabhaza wouldn't have loved the way you relate to men,' she said quietly. Aunt Lizbeth had built her life around Bhazabhaza. She used him, even long after his death, as a point of reference. Bhazabhaza wouldn't have loved to see two women laughing and carrying on in the company of so many men. Bhazabhaza wouldn't have taken kindly to a woman who sometimes drove a car by herself late at night.

Even though she had behaved so dismissively and brashly towards her husband when he was still alive and confined to a wheelchair, she'd loved and respected him. It was clear she missed him.

Aunt Lizbeth's hands were working deftly on a strainer, squeezing the thick, brown, nourishing brew into a bucket. She would occasionally pause to clear the strainer of the chaff from the brewing mixture, throwing this into a separate bucket. The room was redolent with the aroma of good umqombothi beer. Our brew was popular with men. On account of the fact both Aunt Lizbeth and I did not have men in our lives, and on account of the fact that we had sharp tongues, the men had decided to call us the Two Bitches. The shebeen was called Two Bitches' Den.

Our special brew came to be known as Bitches' Brew. Remember, our patrons were jazz fans many of whom thought highly of Miles Davis's number Bitches Brew, which he released in 1969. But some of them, jazz purists to the core, spoke derisively of the number. They therefore took pleasure in reviling our brew, which they thought was for low-class *moegoes* who couldn't afford brandy and other white man's liquor.

There were stories circulating in the township explaining the popularity of our brew with our clientele. It was said we used a litre of our urine as part of the ingredients. Who could resist the urine of such attractive ladies, the men said, laughing.

Others said we used our dirty panties to strain the beer with, which explained the pungent aroma and the bitter aftertaste of the brew. We allowed these funny rumours to fester unhindered, adding a sense of mystery to our brew.

Strange objects such as dead babies' arms or the skulls of dead people being used to stir home-made beer during the brewing process have always been shebeen lore. It was said using these objects brought the drinkers under the spell of the brewer so that they always came back for more. It was therefore entertaining, refreshing that the men decided to come up with innovative, if not sexy things to associate with the supposed spell we had over our customers.

Eight months after the birth of my third child, a girl whose given name was Nokuthula but whose nickname was Lovey, I found myself sitting outside the house, paging through one of the weekly newspapers.

A story caught my eye:

> *A security guard who says his wife bullies him has been told by police to bring her to the station so she can be charged.*
>
> *But Josiah Maluleke (33) said yesterday that to bring his 29 year-old wife Matlakala to Orlando Police Station in Soweto would be a daunting task.*
>
> *"When I come back from work, the minute I get out of the train*

I have to run home. If the train can be late, even if it is five minutes late, I fear to go home because I know what I will get," he said.

I started shaking with laughter, but I read on:

He said the beatings by his wife, who is much bigger than him, had been going on for some time, but he has been too embarrassed to tell anyone.

In desperation Maluleke turned to the police for help. The police laughed at him when he tried to lay an assault charge against his wife.

He said he was still in love with his wife, but the beatings were taking their toll on their marriage. They have a two-year-old son.

"All I want is for the police to stop her from beating me, otherwise our marriage is fine."

In a bold move yesterday, Maluleke, a security guard at a shopping centre, asked our reporters to accompany him to the police station to prove that he was being ridiculed when he asked for protection against his abusive wife…

I was laughing so much that a section of the paper fell onto the floor. I bent down to pick it up. It was the society section and it was emblazoned with a picture of you, Zakes, standing amidst a cheerful crowd of men and women, mostly women. The caption said you'd just been appointed senior manager of Sibisi Enterprises, a big company, which owned shops, bottle stores, nightclubs and a string of taxis in the larger Durban area.

Aunt Lizbeth must have noticed the look of shock on my face, for she rushed to have a look at the picture that had jolted me.

'I've been wondering what happened to your friend Zakes,' she said after reading caption, 'maybe it's time you guys hooked up again, if only for old times' sake.'

Thirty
Two

De Javu

HAVING LISTENED TO MY LIFE story so far, you might be forgiven for thinking I had not made clever plans for my future. But if you are too busy struggling to make a living, you find yourself lurching into the future blindly, without realising how much time has passed by while you were too busy trying to fight the storms of life.

When I first got to Durban my plan was to register with one of the night schools to finish my high school education. With some education under my belt, I could find a better job and earn a decent salary that would enable my children and me to live a decent life. I would then register with the University of South Africa and study part-time.

But all these dreams evaporated under the harsh gaze of reality. Before I knew it, I had three children to feed, clothe and send to school, and I had no reliable income. I didn't have enough education to guarantee me a well-paying job. But I still had a good head for numbers; I could run a small business. What I liked about people in Clermont was that they were all entrepreneurs. Even those who held down full-time jobs ran small business at home during their spare time – selling boiled eggs, or cooked pigs' trotters, or fried fish to the neighbourhood. Many of the people in the neighbourhood were single young people who came back from work late at night, too tired to cook. They could count on these small time pedlars of such delicacies as pigs' trotters and boiled eggs to supply them with supper. I soon plunged into the business of cooking and selling pigs' trotters.

My advantage over other pedlars of pigs' trotters was that I did not only sell take-aways, but my customers were welcome to sit down at a table, inside the drinking place or out in the yard and enjoy their meal, even if they were teetotallers. Soon, we added dumplings and salad to our bill of fare. The place became something of a restaurant, a place where families came for healthy helpings of soul food.

I was sitting at a table one day, going through my ledgers when an irrational thought hit me. I reached for the telephone book and started looking for Sibisi Enterprises.

I dialled the number. Somebody picked up on the third ring: 'Sibisi Enterprises, can I help you?'

My mind froze. I sat there holding the handset with the person on the other end saying: 'Hello? Are you there? Can we help you?'

I was sweating by the time I hung up. What had come over me? Deciding to make the call had been simple enough, but deciding what to say was rather complex. Would Zakes still remember me after all these years? If he did indeed remember me, would he still be interested in talking to me? After all that I had done to him? Yes, in my daydreaming I had spoken to him and laughed with him many times; in my mind I had written him thousands of letters, and he had responded warmly, reliving with me all the good times we had had. Now I was dealing with reality: I had allowed him to turn his back on me even though he'd been prepared to share his life with me and my first unborn child. Now I had three children, from three different men. What could a sensible man possibly want with such a woman? Zakes now a top-class businessman who, I reasoned, had a bevy of young, beautiful things at his beck and call. He appeared in popular magazines in the company of powerful businessmen and beauty queens. What could he possibly want with an unemployed, unemployable, uneducated piece of rural cow dung like me?

'You haven't been eating your food for the past two days,' Aunt Lizbeth said one night as we sat in front of a brazier. 'Is something bothering you? Sulking and not eating is not good for you. Remember, you are breastfeeding, and whatever emotional poison is eating away at your body will affect the baby. Pick yourself up, girl.' From her plate, she took a handful of pap, rolled it into a ball, dunked it into a bowl of tripe stew and threw the morsel of food into her mouth, chewing hungrily.

Thabiso and Prince were sitting on a grass mat close by, eating their food. Lovey was babbling in her cot, celebrating the warmth from the brazier. My own food remained untouched on the small table next to the brazier. The brazier burned brightly and warmly on the porch where we were sitting, watching the street teeming with people walking home from the nearby bus rank.

I picked at my food, had a glass of beer, fed little Lovey and took all three kids to bed.

The following morning, just an hour after Aunt Lizbeth had left for work I reached for the phone and dialled the number for Sibisi Enterprises.

Somebody picked up on the third ring. I introduced myself as Lettie Motaung, one of the suppliers for Sibisi Enterprises. The switchboard operator hesitated, pointing out that she had never dealt with a supplier by that name.

'Mr Zakes Ndaba said he wanted to hire a limo from us, and my boss at Bhazabhaza Enterprises said for me to phone so the two of them can discuss prices.'

'Awright, awright, I'll get Mr Ndaba on the line.'

There were a few clicking sounds before Zakes' voice, sounding hesitant and unsure, came from the other end: 'Hello, who's this?'

'Why haven't you phoned? Why haven't you been in touch with me all these years?' I don't know how I mustered the courage to say those words, or what exactly I meant by them.

'But Lettie it's all your fault,' Zakes said, all flustered and confused, 'you just disappeared off the face of the Earth.'

Taking advantage of the confusion and uncertainty I detected in his voice, I pressed ahead: 'What do you mean "disappeared off the face of the Earth"? Don't you remember that it was you who turned your back on me and went to Joburg? If you wanted to get in touch with me once you were tired of those bitches in Joburg you knew where to find me. I've always been with Sis Jane ever since you left. You should have known that!'

'But what happened to your... to the father of your baby... I thought you two had plans... didn't want to interfere with whatever you had planned...'

'That's bullshit, Zakes. It's bullshit and you know it. You work for Sibisi, one of the most powerful men in town, a man who has eyes and ears all over the townships and shacklands. If you were serious about finding me you would have used your people, your spies to track me down. Now you are bullshitting me as if your decision to go to Joburg when you could see I had feelings for you all those years ago wasn't enough!'

'Okay, okay, let's not fight now. Where are you? I'll come and get you.'

Men are strange. 'I'll come and get you.' Just like that. Why had I waited so long to phone him?

Thirty
Three

Rediscovery

LETTIE,

Your face, when I saw it the afternoon I came to pick you up from Bhazabhaza's place, wasn't a radical departure from the picture of you I had carried in my mind all these years.

You had gained a bit of weight, true, but your skin was still as smooth as ever, not a wrinkle in sight, not a blemish on your face. It was as if you had stayed indoors, away from the harsh Durban sun for all the years I hadn't seen you.

I kept stealing glances at you through the corner of my eye as we drove back to my house in Siyajabula. I knew you were also stealing glances at me. At one time I caught you looking at my dead eye. When I looked at you, you looked away.

Because we did not have a baby seat in the car, I allowed you to sit in the passenger seat next to me, with the little girl safely ensconced in your arms. The boys sat in the back, laughing, playing, marvelling at the lamp posts and trees whizzing past as we drove.

It was getting dark by the time we got home. I had supper prepared and we sat down to eat. While we were busy eating, Mr Sibisi came through to my room. His many eyes and ears had heard and seen that I had company in my room. He sat down at the dinner table. He drank beer while we ate. He spoke freely to you after I'd explained to him who you were, with all the honesty and frankness I could muster. I was like a son to him. Sometimes he would forget I was there and start talking about elaborate plans for the future, where he saw the businesses going – with my hard work and imagination. It wouldn't be very long after that encounter that Mr Sibisi passed away, his death tearing the family asunder. But let's not get there, yet.

After supper you asked to use the phone. You had a long conversation with your aunt. I caught snatches of the conversation. From the sound of your voice and the tenor of the conversation, your aunt wasn't overly worried. For all I care, she had been party to the plan for me to come fetch you from Clermont.

Later, I helped you wash the children and put them to bed. Then we sat in the lounge, listening to soft music, talking a little. It was clear we were both shy about broaching the subject of sleeping.

Ultimately, I went to the bathroom and ran you a warm, foamy bath.

'The water's nice and warm, you can go ahead and take a bath,' I said, showing you to the bathroom.

You looked at me, smiled, shook your head and went into the bathroom.

When you emerged, you had shed your clothes, and now a towel wrapped around your body. With your hair in curlers, your forehead looked pronounced; your high cheekbones were even more prominent. For a moment I just stood there, my eyes moving from your face, down to your exposed arms, and further down. It looked like you had huge grapefruits where you hips should be.

'Well,' you said, 'are you going to join me in the bath? You'd better hurry up because the water will soon get cold.'

Before I could answer you turned on your heel and went into the bathroom. When I joined you there, you had shed the towel. I looked at your innocence and started taking my clothes off.

The awkwardness of the two of us in the nude, sharing the same bath, soon went away. We spoke as we washed each others' bodies. We reread each other the mental letters that we'd never written to each other, reignited the conversations that we never had, took long mental walks down valleys and plains that we'd never visited, shared the music that we never had a chance to explore together.

When the water got cold, we emptied the tub, and refilled it with fresh water. Again, we soaked in the foamy bath and continued talking, massaging each other's bodies.

Later, we dried each other and padded to the bedroom. The two boys slept in a separate bedroom, while Lovey, the little girl, slept in a makeshift crib near our own bed.

As we snuggled under the covers, touching, laughing quietly, kissing, making love over and over again, it was like we'd known each other all our lives.

Why hadn't we started earlier?

Thirty
Four

Let the Good Times Roll

ZAKES,

You spent the first few months teaching me how to run the various businesses in the Sibisi empire, how to read ledgers, how to check stock, the days to go to the bank to make the deposits.

By this time, Sibisi's wife had passed on. He was now left with three sons who would inherit his riches. Of the three, only Sibusiso cared about the family businesses. The eldest son, Zimele, was a successful lawyer in his own right. He lived in Umlazi, had a law firm of his own in Durban. He visited the family businesses every now and then, not enthusiastically, nor with the intention of finding out who was eating his father's money. To him, visiting the family businesses was like performing an onerous task. He was friendly towards you, and it was clear he trusted you to run the businesses efficiently. I was to later learn that you had done huge financial favours for him so he could open his law practice. His father had refused to help him, telling the young man to stop worrying about starting a law firm – telling lies on behalf of murderers and other criminals as he called it – but to concentrate on the family businesses.

Sibisi's third son, Sifiso, was a drunk who was always demanding money from cashiers at the family businesses. He didn't hold down a job, nor did he make himself useful in any of the businesses. In fact his father had sent word to all the managers and cashiers at the different business outlets to keep an eye on Sifiso, to keep him as far away from the cash registers as possible.

He was entitled to a weekly ration of booze from the family bottle store. But he would decimate the ration within a matter of hours, and spend the rest of the week harassing family employees for more booze and money. He was no longer allowed to drive family cars as he never failed to render a car beyond repair whenever he found himself behind the steering wheel.

You and Sibusiso were therefore responsible for running the Sibisi businesses. A few months after I'd been staying with you, word started circulating around the Sibisi estate that I was beginning to behave like a madam. Who was I to start ordering around people who had served the family loyally for years?

I think your decision to host a huge engagement party for me was, in part, inspired by your anger at these people; you wanted to shut them up. Sibisi was happy that, at last, you had seen the light. He wanted a good wife for you, his son.

All along you'd been staying at a cottage behind Sibisi's main house. The cottage had three bedrooms, a lounge, kitchen and a bathroom. It was a huge house by the standards of one who'd spent so many years in the matchboxes of the township. But the cottage was a hovel compared to Sibisi's mansion.

When Sibisi heard of your intentions to marry, he moved you out of the cottage and built you a huge house a kilometre away from his own house, but still within the estate. I didn't know how big the estate was in hectares and acres, but what I can say is that it was so big it could swallow the whole of Chesterville township with all its five thousand four-roomed hovels.

People loved to come to the house to jam with you, listen to your records, or listen to you playing the piano or the saxophone. Almost everyday after work, people would start straggling towards the house. Sibisi would sometimes complain that you were becoming too friendly with 'the help'.

'You are a grown-up boy now, son,' he would say, 'you need more privacy with your woman. These people should be going to our nightclub instead of coming here.'

One of the people who liked coming to the house was Jennifer, a cashier at the main supermarket, Bhovungana Supermarket. I knew that many girls working at the various businesses had eyes for you, Zakes. But Jennifer was the most brazen. She liked teasing you in front of me, making faces at you. She would spank your bum and make you chase her around the shop. She looked at me like I was some piece of shit, you know, dismissively. Sometimes she would tickle you, and turn to look at me as if to say: 'What are you gonna do about it?'

You didn't seem prepared to fend her off, even after I'd told you many times how your games with her irritated me.

One day you slapped her hard when no one but me was looking. My jealousy, an emotion I had never thought could grow inside my heart, subsided.

One night you had a braai at the house. A couple of friends came through. Jennifer was there as well. She was with a man. That made me relax. There was music going. Booze was flowing. Couples were necking out there in the shadows. As the party got hotter, I was busy moving around to make sure every body had a drink or snack. When I was satisfied that everybody had been taken care of, I went back to the crowd meaning to rejoin you.

'Where's Zakes?' I asked. People looked away in what looked like embarrassment. I confronted one of the girls and asked her. She waved her hand in the general direction of our garage. I started walking towards the garage. Inside the garage, I found you struggling with Jennifer.

'What's happening here?' I shouted.

'Uh, nothing, sweetie, nothing,' you said, standing straight like a schoolboy caught with his hand in a cookie jar.

'What do you mean nothing's happening when I can see you are all over this bitch here?'

'She, uh, uh...'

The woman walked away angrily.

Your asthma condition, which had stopped when you were still a child, had resurfaced and worsened since you'd started smoking too much dagga.

Now you reached for your asthma pump and squeezed it into your mouth, inhaling greedily.

Then I went for you. I tripped you to the ground. I was soon all over you, kissing you violently, rolling you on the floor until you moaned. We made love right there on the floor until we collapsed in exhaustion.

'Do you love that bitch?'

'No, I don't.'

I knew you meant it, but I still wanted to hear you say the words yourself. We walked back to rejoin the party.

Thirty
Five

Disappearing Acts

NOW AND THEN I COULD SENSE some tension between you and Sibusiso. But this would soon dissipate. You knew how to handle him. Whenever there'd been a verbal exchange between the two of you, you would book him and one of his girls a long weekend at one of the lodges. He would come back two, three weeks later, all cheerful and mellow. Out of the blue, you'd hire him one of those sleek BMWs and he'd sing your praises for a long time.

Life was so good on the estate I sometimes forgot that many parts of the country were on fire. The two major political parties were killing each other off as they battled for political control of the various townships. But soon I noticed a different kind of activity on the premises of the estate. Ziyasha Nightclub, which you'd renamed Paradise Road in honour of my favourite song, started being frequented by a different kind of clientele. I saw policemen coming in and out of the nightclub. They were never in uniform. But the township had trained me to smell a cop from a mile away. Some of the cops would sit around, drink with you, listen to the music. Others were businesslike. They'd come in, disappear to the back of the club with you, emerge a few minutes later and promptly drive away.

One night I stumbled upon a package of pills. I had been reading a lot of newspaper reports about Mandrax tablets, which were being called the new scourge of the townships. I put two and two together and realised that the nightclub was being used as a distribution outlet for Mandrax.

When I confronted you about it, you got very angry. I had never seen you so angry. I warned you that the Mandrax trade would ruin us all.

You slapped me so hard I fell to the floor.

You seemed shocked yourself. You bent down and picked me up from the floor, where I sat stunned, my nose bleeding.

You rushed me to the car, drove home where you cleaned me up and put me to bed. We made passionate love. That sorry incident at the club was never to be mentioned again.

As the political infighting intensified in the township, there were newspaper reports that said the fighting was being fuelled by highly trained, well-paid mercenaries who were prepared to back either side of the conflict as long as they got paid for it. When the violence was at its lowest, it was reported, the mercenaries would launch their own attacks on either of the opposing sides. I noticed that you'd begun to take a huge interest in local politics, especially the confusing political violence.

I asked you about your sudden interest in this. You said any sane businessman had to follow political developments closely because politicians wielded a lot of influence on where and when one's products and services could be delivered. You had to know what each of the political parties expected of you as a businessman to ensure the safe passage of your trucks, vans, personnel, goods and services.

I noticed that when Sibisi died, the fighting intensified. You increased the number of bodyguards in your employ and improved security around the estate and at all the businesses. A couple of people employed by the company died, victims of the intensified fighting. The number of policemen visiting the estate, sometimes staying over, increased. You explained to me that we needed the extra security. I noticed that the Mandrax trade had not stopped at the nightclub. But I said nothing.

I had made peace with the fact that I couldn't stop you from selling the drug. You confided in me that the tablets were bringing in a lot of money, that they were more profitable than all the other legit businesses combined. You backed up these claims by buying new flashy cars, new jewellery for me, new works of art for the house, new electrical appliances. But I was still worried that something might go wrong.

But the presence of the cops on the estate, cops who obviously were party to the expanding trade in the drug, reassured me of our safety.

I had to stop worrying, as long you, my husband-to-be and my children were safe, I was happy. Besides, I had created a respectable safe nest for us and the children in case things went wrong. I couldn't vouch for the loyalty of those cops, but I think you knew what you were doing. I didn't think you would do anything nasty to me. But, hey, you never know.

I had been staying with you for just over two years by then. Just a week before I had discovered I was four weeks pregnant. When I told you the news you were ecstatic. You said you would speed up the preparations for our wedding.

Just like that.

Thirty
Six

Jingle Bells, Jingle Bells

THE HALL HAD BEEN BOOKED, the wedding dress bought, a limo hired, all the preparations made for our wedding. In just over a month, we would become Mr and Mrs Ndaba. I'd never been so happy and so anxious in my life.

One night you and your guards were happy, celebrating the death of some businessman from Umlazi whom you considered your rival. He had died in a car accident, the radio had said. But you celebrated, drinking and playing music.

Later that night, you invited Sibusiso to our house as well as your senior bodyguard Nonkonyana and two others. You asked me to join you for dinner. We ate, and you drank noisily. I recall that sometime after midnight I heard what sounded like an angry verbal exchange. I couldn't make out the words, but I could hear that the exchange was between you and Sibusiso. I sat up in bed and continued to listen, worried that you might hurt each other. The noise later died down. I heard the crunching sound of your feet as you walked across the gravel in the parking lot outside.

I saw you standing in the parking lot. Sibusiso was walking with some difficulty; it looked like his hands had been bound behind his back. He was shoved into the boot of the car. The car then drove off. He was never to be heard of again. A week later, we read in the papers that he had been found shot dead somewhere in the Transkei.

You expressed shock at the news, and held an expensive funeral for him. It was then that I decided it was time for me to go. I didn't want to know anything more about your business as it was becoming more and more dangerous. One day, when you were out of town on business, I loaded my things into Sis Jane's old jalopy and left.

Thirty
Seven

More Disappearing Acts

Lettie,

Your disappearance caused me great discomfort. I worried that you might have crumbled under pressure from the police – not the ones who were on our payroll, but other hostile forces who were investigating the death of Sibisi's son. I knew they'd been talking to a number of my employees.

One of the guards who had been at the dinner when Sibusiso was last seen in my company, was picked up by the police one morning. They intercepted him while he was driving from our headquarters on his way to town. They found fault with his driver's licence. My moles within the police force told me that the cops who had actually done the arrest were not even traffic officers, but detectives from the Criminal Investigations Department. It was clear that they wanted to get to me through the boy. I had to move fast. I had Mokoena bailed out by one of the girls at our bottle store. The girl would go there under false pretences, saying that she was his girlfriend.

By late that afternoon, Mokoena was safely home. That night, I took Themba Nonkonyana's car, which had Transkei registration plates, and drove to Mokoena's house.

He opened the door on the third knock as if he'd been expecting someone.

'Looks like you are going out,' I addressed him cheerfully.

'I guess,' he said hesitantly, 'I thought I was gonna go for a drink.'

'Yeah, I guess you can use a drink after your experience at police headquarters. Let's go.'

We got into the car and drove off.

'I'm sure those arseholes at the prison quarters were not kind to you,' I spoke casually.

'Ag, the whole thing was no big deal. All traffic related shit, my boss. First, my learners' licence had expired, secondly, I have not been paying my traffic fines as conscientiously as I should be.'

I knew he was lying. But we drove on. When we were in the middle of a dark stretch of road, I stopped the car.

'Now, I've got a delivery to make before we go for a drink. A couple of AK–47s in the boot and some other hardware.'

He looked at me in the darkness.

'But the tricky part is I don't trust the bastard. I want to catch him off guard, spring a surprise on him,' I said, getting out of the car. 'Come, let me show you what I've got in the boot.'

I opened the boot, flicked on a torch and allowed him to look at the machinery tucked away there. He didn't say anything.

I ducked into the boot of the car and emerged with an AK–47 which I duly gave to Mokoena.

'Now, listen very carefully. Take this AK–47, go and hide in the boot, among the other hardware…'

'But why?'

'Because I want to spring a surprise on the bastard.'

'So you want me to shoot him as soon as you open the boot?'

'Something like that.'

'But why go to the trouble of hiding me in the boot? Why not just waste the bastard as soon as he walks towards our car?'

'Do as I say, soldier. The boss has got a plan.'

Mokoena shrugged, squeezed himself into the boot, among the tools of death.

I drove off. I drove around in the darkness, taking arbitrary turns in a deliberate attempt to confuse and unsettle the man in the boot. After an hour of driving, I stopped the car, took out my Beretta, checked the ammunition and got out of the car.

When I opened the boot, Mokoena poked his head out, whispering desperately, 'Where's the target? The magazine is empty. I need some ammunition.'

'Just relax, buddy, relax,' said I, 'what did you tell the police?'

'Nothing, boss. Nothing. We spoke about the traffic related stuff as I told you earlier.'

'You wouldn't lie to me, would you?'

'Boss?'. His voice was a strangled plea. Then I squeezed the trigger of my Beretta.

I drove off to KwaMashu township where I parked the car in front of the popular OK Shopping Centre. Themba Nonkonyana was waiting for me in one of my cars. Nonkonyana was with Thato Sefularo, a new recruit to my security detail. Nonkonyana was a trained killer, having worked as member of the Special Branch that hunted down ANC freedom fighters in the great war between apartheid forces and freedom fighters. Sefularo was also a trained killer. But, more importantly, he had been a double agent operating in the ANC underground machinery, while at the same time selling information about his comrades to the apartheid government.

In fact he had earlier offered to kill Mokoena himself. I'd declined his offer as I felt the primordial instinct to kill. I wanted Mokoena's blood on my hands. Don't ask me why. I just felt that way. Again, don't ask me why I chose such a melodramatic way of getting rid of him. Over the years I had begun to experience a thrill, a morbid satisfaction from the prolonged suffering of others. I guess fate had kicked me in the teeth so often that I wanted to pass that hurt on to others. The urge to hurt visited me every now and then.

Anyway, when Nonkonyana saw my car, he started the engine, and we drove off in convoy. Two hours out of the township we found a deserted strip of dusty road where we parked. We doused the car I'd been driving with petrol, set it on fire, and pushed it down the steep slope on the side of the road. The ball of flame hurtled down the steep incline, and made a thunderous noise as it exploded further down. The three of us drove off into the night.

A few minutes into our drive, Nonkonyana turned to me and said, 'You know what, boss?'

'What?'

'You are fucked-up. Totally fucked-up.'

'I suppose that's a compliment, coming from you.'

Thirty
Eight

Picking up the Pieces

AFTER LEAVING YOU, ZAKES, my first instinct was to go and stay with Aunt Lizbeth at her place in Clermont. But then common sense told me that Clermont would be the first place you would go to if finding the kids and I was your intention. So, I moved to an obscure little township called KwaNdengezi. I found myself lodgings with an old couple. To the couple I was Minky Letsoalo. The old couple were kind enough not to pester me with questions about where I got the money to survive since I was unemployed. I had taken enough money from the business to sustain me for a long time. I enrolled the children at a nearby nursery school. To keep boredom at bay, I bought myself a small paraffin fridge and stocked with soft drinks, which I sold to neighbours. Entrepreneurship was now in my blood. My eyes were always on the look-out for business opportunities.

When the old man of the house died, his wife asked me to find her an opening at the Umlazi Home for the Aged, which I gladly did. Because the old couple had no relatives, the house automatically reverted to me by an agreement I had made with the old lady after I had softened her up with a couple of hundred rands.

With the whole house to myself, I immediately went about turning my small soft drink business into a shebeen. I called Aunt Lizbeth to come and live with me. It was soon like old times as we had clients eating out of the palms of our hands. We sold both clear beer and our old concoction, Bitches' Brew.

Our brood of children buzzed about the big house, and did not want for material things. Behind the façade of happiness, however, our lives were incomplete. We had cut ourselves from our past — with no parents, uncles, sisters and other relatives to turn to in times of emotional crises. We had a long parade of men walking in and out of our lives.

311

'There's something I don't understand about you,' Aunt Lizbeth said to me one night as we sat drinking beer.

'And what is that?'

'You and your men. I mean, you are a beautiful young lady, financially successful and all, but you can't seem to keep your men. What's wrong?'

'Why do you think I need a man to make my life whole and complete? I use men as one would use chewing gum. I chew them, suck them of their juicy flavours, and then spit them out.'

Aunt Lizbeth stared at me, shaking her head sadly: 'If lying to yourself makes you feel better, well then, go ahead and lie to yourself. You know as I know that you need somebody, a man to share your success with.'

'That's so old fashioned and boring. Have you seen what all these men that I've tried my luck with have done to me? They come to me with their preconceived ideas of how a woman should behave, and when they find out that I want to accept them into my life on my own terms, they pick up their pants and run as fast as their legs can carry them. Yet every time I see a new man I keep feeding my heart with hope that he will not be the same as the others, that he will understand what I'm all about, how I want to be treated.'

'Don't tar them with the same brush. They might all have balls and dicks dangling from between their thighs, but they are different; they are from different wombs. All you need to do is open your eyes, open your heart. Think very carefully about the men who've walked in and out of your life. Claw back your past, and grab some of the missed opportunities by their ears and bring them to the present. I think one of the biggest fuck-ups you made was with that musician guy, Zakes Ndaba. I can't for the life of me understand why you ran away from him.'

'Don't speak to me about that criminal, about that murderer...'

After I'd told Aunt Lizbeth about all that I knew or suspected about you, Zakes, she sat there looking at me sadly. Then she said: 'You missed out on the greatest challenge of your life, girl. That man needed you as much as you needed him. I wonder what he is up to now, but you certainly missed out on an opportunity to wean him off his obsession with crime…'

'Look who's talking now! You lived with that criminal of yours, Bhazabhaza, until he died. Now you come here telling me I should go back to Zakes and take him out of the life of crime. Who do you think I am? Houdini? God?'

'By the time Bhazabhaza died, girl, he was a clean living man. Through the power of the ever merciful God, I managed to wean Bhazabhaza off the life of crime.'

'You talking shit, Aunt Liz! You talking rubbish. You never weaned him off crime. When he was paralysed, his usefulness in the criminal world plummeted. The hand of fate weaned him off crime, not you and your ever merciful God…'

'That's where you are wrong. Bhazabhaza became even more lethal and powerful after he'd been paralysed. He ordered the killings of his enemies – perceived or real – from the comfort of his wheelchair. Confined to his wheelchair, he had more time, anger, bitterness and solitude to mastermind his criminal schemes. Think carefully about these things. The main guy doesn't have to be there at the scene, pulling the trigger and all that. He has to come up with ideas. By the time you left Zakes, he was a successful businessman. With your help, he could have extricated himself from the life of crime…'

'Why do we women always have to be the ones suffering on behalf of our men, trying to help men who don't necessarily want to be helped?'

'You never bothered to look deeper into Zakes' heart. He was a man in need of love and attention. He used the violence as an outlet for his frustration. He was crying out for help, but you did not hear his cry. When he started getting involved with the woman you've told me about, he was trying to draw your attention to the emptiness in his heart. But all you did was concentrate on the running of the businesses, at the expense of fanning the flames of love.'

For a moment, we just sat there in the lounge, staring blankly at the peach tree in front of the house.

'I suppose you don't know that your grandmother died three weeks ago.'

I shook my head no.

Thinking back, I realised that the butterflies that had buzzed freely three weeks previously at my new place had been a message from my grandmother, saying something to me. But over all these years I had been too preoccupied with my private anguish that I never came to fully understand granny's language, and the messages she sent to me. But she hadn't given up on me up to her last day, it seemed. Maybe if I'd opened my heart towards granny, I would have inherited her gifts to 'see' things. But then, maybe, I wasn't called to be a seer. In my culture, a herbalist, a seer, a diviner doesn't choose to be what she is. She is called by bigger powers to divine on behalf of God's creatures. She is given the powers to foretell things, to see that which can't be seen with the naked eye by ordinary people. Maybe mine was to be a life of trial and error, a life of learning from my mistakes instead of having knowledge of the bad things that lay ahead of me. Maybe I had been doomed to a life of eternal darkness and suffering, where there was no hope of redemption.

In the years that followed, me, Aunt Lizbeth and our families moved from pillar to post. Zakes, I could sense your energy in the air. I could feel your eyes piercing my skin. My heart was crying out for you Zakes, but I feared the disappointment I would experience once we saw each other again. It was healthier, safer to hold you in my mind, in my dreams, than to touch your flesh, to smell your breath.

now
(decisions)

Thirty
Nine

Bye, Bye Blackbird
(South Africa, 2006)

THIS VALLEY HAS NO NAME. However, those who like to name things but lack the imagination to conjure up a fitting sobriquet have decided to call it Big Man's Valley. Indeed, a famous man lives here whose name is The Big Man. Maybe that's not even his real name. But that's what they call him, far and wide. No, he doesn't own the valley. Nobody does. It's God's gift to man. But man, in his complicated and infinite stupidity and greed, has attached a monetary value to land. As a result, pieces of land such as this valley have been classified 'prime property' for the enjoyment of the moneyed classes of society.

The valley is on the cusp of the rolling hills of the Kwazulu-Natal midlands.

Now and then, the observer can see swallows, *amatitihoye*, *amaphothwe*, swooping down to the valley to drink of the pleasures of life. When they emerge, their plumage has a sheen of good health about it. And they are smiling their unique bird smile. And the bees emerge from there humming like a swarm of sailors who've just been to a place of pleasurable sin.

To get to all this lushness, however, is a challenge. The valley is bounded by a range of mountains on three sides, the fourth side escaping into the shimmering waters of the Umgeni River. There is a dock on the riverbank. Then there's a tiny strip of road starting from the water's edge. The road then crawls to the cluster of dwellings – a huge villa and some outbuildings – at the centre of the valley. In other words, in order to leave or enter the valley, you have to take a ferry across the river. There is even a special freighter for cars that need to be ferried across. The village is a veritable fort. Even on

317

foot, the intruder has to negotiate the treacherous mountains in order to gain access.

The centrepiece of the valley, the Tuscan style villa that I've just mentioned, is surrounded by a tall brick and mortar wall fringed with electric fencing. Armed guards stand sentry at the main gate. Others move about the premises, occasionally pausing to scour the mountains with their binoculars, hoping to spot unwanted intruders. So boring is their life here that they actually pray for an intruder. Pray for some action.

A ferry has just docked at the pier, disgorging four men and a woman. The men, who range in age from their mid-thirties to late sixties, are all dressed in black suits. The woman resplendent in a flowing Nigerian-style robe, powder blue in colour. She is in her late fifties, a light-complexioned African woman. From her earlobes dangle huge, wooden earrings shaped like the map of Africa.

The new arrivals have a stretch limo waiting for them. The driver of the limo greets them formally, helps them into the car, and drives towards the villa on the tiny dirt road.

Back at the dock, luggage belonging to the newly arrived people is off-loaded from the ferry and packed into a Mercedes Benz which had been brought to the dock for that purpose.

The serene visitors are dropped off at the entrance to the mansion, and ushered to where their host is waiting for them.

He is a great man, a politician, a businessman of note and, some say, a present day African mafioso, if there could ever be such a thing.

Peace Ndaba, for that was the Big Man's given name, lay dying in his huge bed. Even on his deathbed, Zakes, couldn't dampen his desire for wine. A half full bottle of burgundy wine sat on a tray on the bedside table. There was a variety of fresh fruit and hunks of different exotic cheeses as well.

'I lived in style, so I might as well exit in style,' he croaked to his audience.

They sniggered uneasily.

'I lived fast, drank fast, loved fast, hoping to die young and leave behind a good-looking corpse,' he sighed, 'but alas, I lived too long. Too bloody long. The Lord spared me. And now I am not going to leave behind a good-looking corpse, dammit.' He tried to laugh at his own joke, but his body was wracked by a series of coughs.

At one level, he was not telling the truth, but at another, he was. He was not telling the truth because the Lord had nothing to do with his long life; it was his goons, his coterie of hired killers, who had protected him from many who wanted him dead. He and his goons had killed viciously to protect themselves and the many businesses that they ran. They had run brothels, cocaine-manufacturing enterprises, hired their services out to the political parties.

But at another level, Peace 'Zakes' Ndaba was telling the truth when he said he wasn't going to leave a good-looking corpse. He was in his sixties now. His face was a mess. He was missing an eye, the result of a knife fight when he was still a young hoodlum. His face was a map of scars; testimony to a life lived hard on the mean streets of Durban and Johannesburg; the tough cities of South Africa.

Now that he was dying, he had decided to summon his trusted lieutenants and his one-time girlfriend and mother of his only child, to his deathbed so he could instruct them on what to do with his estate. Although he knew he had a son somewhere, he had never seen him since his birth 35 years ago. So preoccupied with his businesses that he had not been in touch with the woman for a long time.

The woman's name was Lettie. The young man with her was the lawyer who would henceforth take charge of the estate of Peace Ndaba when his day finally came, which wasn't too far off by the look of things. The other men in the room were all trusted lieutenants.

Mokone Mokone was a top businessman and a powerful figure in the body that controlled South African football. He also had his fingers in drug-manufacturing plants although no law enforcement agent had been able to pin this on him. He operated in Johannesburg. When the authorities pounced on one of his factories, he merely moved to the next town and opened shop there. He was elusive.

The other men were Themba Nonkonyana, who ran his operations in the Eastern Cape, and Lungile Williams, based in the Western Cape. Absent from the meeting were Jake Hlungwani, from Limpopo province, and Speedy Mogale, from the North-West province. The two gentlemen had excused themselves from the meeting as there were wars between the various taxi associations in their areas. They had to stay at home to protect their businesses and families. They had sent word to the big boss in Kwazulu-Natal that they would abide by whatever decision he took on their behalf. After all, they had him to thank for the wealth they enjoyed. He had made them.

Mokone, Nonkonyana and Williams were perturbed by the presence of the young lawyer at this meeting. Further, they didn't trust this woman who hadn't been there for their boss all these years. The gold-digging bitch!

One of the big man's minders came in and eased him into a wheelchair. He then wheeled him towards the dining room, while the rest of the entourage followed.

They sat at a huge glass-topped table where the food had been placed, platters of cold meats and jugs of freshly squeezed fruit juices.

'I know how you gentlemen feel about the presence of this lady here and her lawyer,' Peace 'Zakes' Ndaba said, as if reading the minds of his lieutenants. 'But I want her to be here with me when I die. Her lawyer will record everything that we discuss here. What's the lawyer's name, by the way?'

'Du Tau,' said the young man, spearing with his fork a thick slice of ham, baptising it with generous drops of chutney, 'like you, sir, I also have a nickname. My friends call me Kokoroshe.'

Zakes laughed weakly: 'Kokoroshe! Cockroach, ha ha ha, cockroaches are sly little creatures. But do be warned. Being sly with me can be a life-limiting move, Kokoroshe.' He was seized by a spasm of coughing, before he continued: 'I see. As I was saying, gentlemen, there is unfinished business between the lady and I. There is a lifetime that we have to relive together before I die. Now I must say bye bye, darling.'

Painfully, he bent to the floor and reached for his trumpet. He fingered it lovingly, and raised it to his lips.

'Boss,' Mokone cautioned nervously, 'boss, you don't have enough strength. You need to rest.'

Peace nodded his head slowly, smiling. He said, addressing the trumpet in his hands: 'Damn, the mother knows I could blow her. I could blow cats out of the water with this mother.'

He settled back in his chair. He whistled a few bars of Miles Davis's take on 'Bye, Bye Blackbird'.

'Boys,' he spoke earnestly, taking a generous swig from his wine glass. He wasn't eating much. 'I am about to embark on my last journey. I want you to promise me that when I am gone, you will not give up the fight. You will fight against that great fool at the Asset Forfeiture Unit who has tried to ruin the last years of my life. Will you deal with the dog, my boys?'

He handed them a newspaper clipping which read:

Alleged drug lord's assets seized in Johannesburg

The Asset Forfeiture Unit on Thursday seized a suspected drug dealer's assets that were worth more than R20m, including an R8m property at Ballito Beach, north of Durban.

In the early 1990s Peace Ndaba was a shebeen owner, taxi owner and organiser of beauty pageants, but within a few years he became a multi-millionaire.

His lifestyle quickly attracted the attention of the police who suspect that he is a drug lord. Ndaba and a number of accomplices have been arrested.

Ndaba was, however, released as there was no evidence directly linking him to drug manufacturing equipment found in one of his properties. Besides, said police, he is chronically sick and is on his deathbed living in squalor with relatives in KwaZulu-Natal.

On Thursday, the AFU seized more of his assets in KwaZulu-Natal, including a BMW X5 four-wheel-drive vehicle.

'This is the kind of shit I had to deal with in my life. I implore you to continue where I left off. Deal with these pieces of shit effectively once I am gone,' he said. 'I will show you in due course how to deal with the head of the Asset Forfeiture Unit. After all that I've done for him, the bloody power hungry bastard does this to me. Rattle the cage, boys, more politicians will fall.'

'Consider it done, boss,' said Williams using a bread roll to wipe his plate clean, 'left to his devices, the fool will ruin us all. Decisive action needs to be taken against him once and for all. He must learn never to fuck with Zakes' squad.'

In years gone by, Thato Sefularo had worked for Zakes' criminal empire as one of his sharpshooters. Now that Sefularo had been appointed head of the Asset Forfeiture Unit, he had set his men on his former boss. Peace 'Zakes' Ndaba wasn't prepared to go down without a fight. But now in poor health, he hoped his lieutenants would pick up where he had left off and deal with his former employee.

'Zakes's Zeppelins will zap him,' said Peace, laughing.

Mokone and Nonkonyana murmured in agreement, nodding their heads vehemently as they took sips from their glasses of orange juice.

The big man spoke again, 'But let's not get carried away now. We'll tackle the issue of the Asset Forfeiture Unit when we get to it. As I used to say to you, we will burn the next bridges when we get to them. For now, I would like to concentrate on this other grave matter before us. What to do with the business once I'm gone. Boys, I need you to listen carefully now as I speak to my woman here, for there's a lot to be learnt in what I have to say. There's a lot I wish to share with her, a lot I wish to leave behind with her. I can die with a clear conscience knowing that she knows all about me. I can die with a clear conscience knowing that I am leaving her a part of me that she deserves to have, a part of me I should have given to her a long time ago, were I not consumed by selfishness.'

He paused, took a deep breath. He wanted to say more, but no words could capture the sense of regret that was gnawing at his soul. While some men dedicated their lives to the struggle of finding God, to finding the truth about life, he had dedicated his life to the seemingly worthless cause of chasing after love. Other men had spent their lives trying to hear God's voice, to bask in his eternal glory. He, on the other hand, had spent his life chasing after happiness. A thankless, futile exercise.

Now he opened his mouth again, 'Boys, I know that this lady here has a lot to say to me about missed opportunities we were meant to share, but never had time to share. I want to give her what I owe her. As you will remember, she worked with me at Siyajabula, but our relationship fell apart, and she ran away from me. She had every reason to be scared and run away. But I cannot die without showing my gratitude to her, and the son she bore me. Her lawyer is here to ensure that this aspect of the business is taken care of, that mother and son get their due. That's why I had my security people track her down, and summoned her to this place, so she can take what belongs to her, and present my son to me.'

Kokoroshe the lawyer butted in: 'Sir, it's such a pity your son couldn't make it to this meeting. In fact, I, as the family lawyer, was not briefed properly as to what would be required of us.'

Lettie looked at him, eyes widening. That wasn't lost on the other men in the room who followed the body language between the lawyer and the woman carefully, asking themselves: 'What's going on here?'

The lawyer continued: 'Your son is in prison, serving a lengthy sentence, but we have a letter from him inviting you to do as you please with his share of his inheritance, if any. This is a letter from him. I also have a picture of him. Pity it's an old picture taken when he was much younger.'

The picture was that of a young man, possibly in mid-teens. Although it was so amateurishly shot and out of focus, it showed a young man with a brooding face, staring into the vacant space beyond the camera lens, looking longingly into the emptiness beyond.

The old man looked stared at the picture. His good eye was partially blinded by the mist of old age combined with the tears of regret, yearning to turn back the hands of time.

'My son in jail. What has he done to deserve that? What have I done to deserve that?' He was speaking to himself, not expecting anyone in the room to have the answers to his questions.

The woman started crying. The lawyer asked for a short break. He took the woman outside, so she could regain her composure.

Outside, the woman hissed at him: 'What are you trying to do? Are you crazy? I thought the whole objective of our coming out here was for you to introduce yourself to your father before he dies.'

'I know. I thought it would be easy for me to reconcile myself to the fact that I have such an arsehole for a father. A criminal, a vulture who preys on other people!'

'But he has changed…'

'No he hasn't! He's still talking about revenge. Look, I don't want to inherit anything from his dirty belongings. I don't need his money; I will make my own money.'

'It's not about money. It's not about inheritance. It's a question of blood. I realise you weren't going to hit it off while he is on his deathbed; but he will be happy to know that, at last, he is in the presence of his own blood.'

'Where was he when his blood was looking for a father, for inspiration and direction? You tell me that.'

'He's going to die a sad man.'

'So let it be. That's the price he has to pay, I suppose. Let's go home. I can't stand his pathetic face. I can't stand the fact that he is still bitter with his former partners in crime; that he is still planning to get people killed. It was you who told me that if you plant a clump of thorns you can't expect to reap a handful of carnations.'

'Mduduzi,' she said using his given name, 'please don't do this to your mother. Please, my child. Keep the promise you made to me before we got here.'

'But the man you call my father has supped with the devil.'

'Who hasn't?'

'In fact he's sold his soul to the devil. He worked with Sefularo, whom we all know was a functionary of the old regime.'

'But life is a struggle between good and evil, between darkness and light. One cannot be appreciated without the other.'

'But this man should stop associating himself with Biko. He is defiling the memory of Biko by continuing to say his God is Biko.'

'He who has no sin must cast the first stone.'

'I don't buy that cliché…'

'But life is a cliché. It's just how you pick up the cliché, polish it up and give new meaning to it.'

Impulsively, and in an act not typical of Kokoroshe, he lost himself in his mother's embrace. Their tears were long and warm.

Later, much later, he recovered enough to pose this question to his mother: 'We can go back to the house and tell him the truth, the whole truth, if you promise me one thing.'

Her face brightened. She said hopefully: 'Name a price.'

'When we finally get home,' he said, a wide smile on his face, 'will you make me a barrel of Bitches' Brew that made you and your generation such social fuck-ups?'

'Yeah,' she said, throwing her head back and laughing, 'the same brew that paid your university fees and made you such a stuck-up arsehole of a son who thinks life and all mankind owes him a favour. Come on, let's go back in there and spill the beans to your father. Let's just make it clear to him that our mission is not to get at his money. Our mission is to tell the truth and see what he wants to do with it. I will keep my promise. When we get home, I will get down on my knees and prepare you a gallon of Bitches' Brew.'

Mother and son walked hand-in-hand back into the house where the men sat waiting. A swarm of butterflies exploded into view, lighting up the room with a profusion of colour.

'What the fuck?' the men shouted, getting up from their seats, swatting at the cloud of insects.

Zakes and Lettie smiled at each other knowingly. They started laughing out loud as the butterflies touched their faces with their colourful wings.

Zakes was thinking: I'm so glad she's giving her heart back to me.

But Lettie was thinking: damn, after all this, I still don't know if it's the size or the feel of a man's penis that matters most to a woman.

THE
END

Other Fiction Titles by Jacana

Rules

The European Union Literary Award is presented annually by Jacana Media and the European Union to a first, unpublished novel by a South African. Submissions must be received by 30 September. The winner of the EU Literary Award will be announced at a ceremony in Johannesburg the following March. The winner will receive R25 000 and will have his or her novel published by Jacana Media. This award is open to South African writers resident in South Africa.

What to submit:
A first, unpublished work of fiction in English (translations into English from other languages are permitted only if the work has never been published in any language).
A manuscript of between 60 000 and 100 000 words in length.
Two securely bound, typed A4 copies (1.5 space, 12 point font).
A separate one-page summary of the manuscript.
A separate one-page biography of the author with all contact details including telephone numbers and email address.
The author's name should not appear anywhere on the manuscript.

What not to submit:
Memoirs, Short stories, History, Geography or other non-fiction books will not be considered. No drafts will be considered. Entrants are strongly advised to ensure that manuscripts are submitted in their final, publishable form. Published novelists may not enter this competition, even under pseudonyms. However, published authors of short stories, plays or poetry may enter their first novels.

Send to:
Jacana Media
EU Literary Award
PO Box 2004
Houghton
2041

No late manuscripts will be accepted.
No emailed entries will be accepted.
Manuscripts will not be returned.

The jury's decision will be final. No correspondence will be entered into.

For further information
Visit www.jacana.co.za or email euaward@jacana.co.za